Murder at the PTA Luncheon

Murder at the PTA Luncheon

Valerie Wolzien

ST. MARTIN'S PRESS
New York

All characters and events in this work are fictitious. The author knows that
the PTA and similar organizations are doing invaluable work in our schools
and that no work of fiction can in any way discredit them or their members.

MURDER AT THE PTA LUNCHEON. Copyright © 1988 by Valerie Wolzien.
All rights reserved. Printed in the United States of America. No part of this
book may be used or reproduced in any manner whatsoever without written
permission except in the case of brief quotations embodied in critical articles
or reviews. For information, address St. Martin's Press, 175 Fifth Avenue,
New York, N.Y. 10010.

Library of Congress Cataloging-in-Publication Data
Wolzien, Valerie.
　　Murder at the PTA luncheon.
　　"A Thomas Dunne book."
　　I. Title.
PS3573.0574M87　1988　　813'.54　　　　　87-28675
ISBN 0-312-01480-5

First Edition
10　9　8　7　6　5　4　3　2　1

To Tom

Murder at
the PTA
Luncheon

One

—◆◆—

Nothing is worse than having a nice sex fantasy interrupted by the memory of a murder.

Well, she just wouldn't let it happen again.

Stretching out her stiff back, she felt the skin tighten between her shoulder blades. Time to turn over. No need to get a sunburn; her nervous breakdown would be trouble enough. And that's what would happen if she didn't start sleeping through the night or begin relaxing during the day. But, lying on her back and squinting into the glare of the sun, another memory pushed aside her most delicious fantasy, and instead of Robert Redford's neck, instead of Paul Newman's eyes, instead of Harrison Ford's shoulders, she saw a woman's hands. They were well-manicured and were clutching at a strand of matched pearls circling an unlined neck, wiping away the spittle of saliva drooling from crimson lips. . . .

"Enough. I've got to stop thinking about it." In her anger and confusion she had spoken aloud.

"Sue? Did you say something? Are the kids okay?"

Susan recognized the sleepy voice coming from the chaise behind her. It was Paula Porter, her friend and the mother of her son's buddy. Paula had four children and a husband who was a very popular and thus a very busy pediatrician. She frequently dozed off at the pool. Susan knew a detailed answer wouldn't be necessary.

1

"The kids are fine. I think the older ones are still playing poker in the cabana. I was going to get some iced tea. Want some?"

"No, thanks. I've got mine over here. I just haven't had the energy to touch it yet.

"God, I'm tired today," Paula continued. "I'm still losing sleep over Jan's death. I can't stop thinking about it. You know, Sue, she must have taken the last canapé from the tray before she died. Does that seem odd to you?"

"I don't know," Susan answered, sighing. "I think about it too." But she really didn't want to talk about it anymore. "I'll check on the kids while I'm up," she offered, scrounging around under her lounge chair for the chintz beach robe that was just long enough to cover her thighs without, she hoped, being matronly.

"Don't worry about the kids. If they think we're checking up on them, they may decide to come over and pester us. Leave well enough alone."

"Agreed." Flipping a tasseled belt around her waist, Susan left the pool area and headed down the scorching cement to the clubhouse. The shade from the blue-and-white awnings around the building felt good, and once in the bar, she decided to sit at a table and enjoy her drink without the background noise of children splashing in the pool. The lunch rush was over and the large room deserted, except for a few kids who had wheedled permission from their mothers for an early snack and half a dozen teenage girls whispering and giggling in one corner. A calm, typical August afternoon had settled over the Club.

She leaned back and closed her eyes, willing away the repeating images of death. She was sick of seeing Jan lying dead, her hands clutched at her throat. She tried to remember her alive.

Susan had met Jan the way she did most of her friends these days: they were involved in the local Parent-Teacher Association. Susan had been active in the PTA for six years,

2

since her older child had entered kindergarten. Each year her involvement had increased. First she had been class mother, then a member of one or two minor committees. Later came chairmanship of a committee and, finally, a place on the governing board of the organization. For Hancock wasn't a town where apathy was the norm. This small suburb of New York City was active. Volunteers were numerous and, although unpaid, very professional. Most of the mothers were dedicated to seeing their children get the best education possible and were willing to put in the time, money, and energy to run an organization to carry out their goals. These women were not content to sit home and bake cupcakes for class parties. Their housekeepers would fill needs of that sort. These were women who ran things. They had been class- and student-council presidents in high school. They had run their sororities in college or the local branch of SDS if they were of a more liberal bent. They had organized offices, manned nurses' stations, and had had careers before becoming mothers. One day they might do all that again. Right now they were running their homes, their families, and the local PTA.

Jan's children were younger than Susan's, but she had risen more quickly in the organization. She was very organized, very capable, definitely destined to lead the group someday if she chose to do so.

The last time Susan had seen Jan was at the annual PTA spring luncheon: the time when the women stopped raising money, buying computers, judging curriculum, seeing which teachers were to be offered tenure by the Board of Education (an organization itself filled with graduates of the PTA), and they had a party. Jan had died at that party. She had taken the wrong canapé from a silver platter—the one filled with cyanide.

"Late lunch?"

Startled, Susan choked on the ice cube she had been munching.

3

"Susan! My God, are you all right? Bend over . . . let me . . ."

"I'm fine. I just swallowed some ice the wrong way," Susan gasped, waving off the other woman's attempts at lifesaving. After a few coughs and sputters, she mopped her streaming eyes with her sleeve and flopped her forehead down on the table exhausted.

"My God, Susan! Help! Somebody help!" the frightened voice shrieked to the room. The teenagers in the corner no longer feigned indifference. They rushed over to see what was going on. The waitress from behind the bar dashed over, whether from Samaritan motives or curiosity no one had a chance to find out. There were others streaming in through the open French doors as Susan regained control of herself.

"I was only choking on an ice cube. Why are you making such a fuss?" she asked.

"Oh." The other woman stopped her excited screaming and dropped into another chair. "I thought you were dead," she whispered. "I thought the same thing had happened to you that happened to Jan. Poisoned," she mumbled, almost too quietly for Susan to hear.

"I was choking on some ice," Susan repeated, this time to the crowd that had gathered.

"She just choked on some ice," the waitress repeated more loudly for the edification of people still coming into the room. "Happens all the time. Though not so often in the middle of the day as in the evening, if you know what I mean," she added in a confidential tone to everyone in the crowd.

"I was drinking iced tea," Susan protested. "You know that. You got it for me."

Seeing that there was no answer to that, the waitress returned to her station, mumbling about not knowing what certain people might or might not put into their iced tea. She couldn't be expected to watch *everything* that went on in the place.

4

"Susan, are you okay?" A man's voice rang out, singular in this weekday environment full of women and children.

She looked up and smiled at the man who had entered the room: Dan Hallard, her obstetrician. "Sure, Dan, I just choked on some ice." She had said it so many times that now she was beginning to feel that it must not be the truth, that somehow she was protesting too much. "I don't know why everyone was making such a fuss," she added.

"Because the last time I saw someone choking, she died. Remember?"

"I remember," Susan replied grimly. "I was thinking about Jan's death when you came over, Fanny."

"You women brood too much about that," Dan Hallard insisted. "It's all my wife can talk about these days. She should forget it and so should you. It happened. It's over.

"Oh, there goes my foursome," he added, looking out the door. "I'd better catch up with them before they decide to tee off without me. Glad you're okay, Susan. Can't have one of my prize patients dying on me. Just remember everything's fine."

Both women watched him weave his large body around the haphazardly arranged tables and chairs and leave the room.

"Did he deliver both your kids?" asked the woman Susan had called Fanny.

"Just Chad. How about yours?"

"All of them. I hated the way he always said everything was going to be all right every single time something worried me during those long months before the babies came. I always wondered if he said that about everything. Doctors!" Fanny added sarcastically. Her husband was an orthopedist with an impressive Fifth Avenue practice. She watched until the man was out of sight and then turned to Susan. "You were thinking about Jan's death?"

"I was thinking about Jan's murder," Susan corrected. "I can't forget it. Not that I wouldn't like to."

"No one seems to be able to forget that day. And you're right. It was murder. If she'd just died, we would have adjusted by now.

"I understand the police are asking questions again," she added. "Guess that's one of the penalties of living in the suburbs. If this had happened in the city, the police would have gone on to their next murder case by now. Here in Hancock, there just isn't going to be another one for them to sink their teeth into. I guess they'll be asking and re-asking the same questions for the next few years or maybe decades or until they all retire or something. Do you mind?" She picked up the remains of her friend's tea and drained the glass without waiting for an answer.

"You don't think they're going to find out who did it?"

"No way. They never found Jerry's ten-speed. Or the jewelry that Connie and Ed had stolen last year. Did they ever tell you the identity of your peeping Tom? How can they be expected to solve the first murder this town has had since Colonial days?"

"Colonial days?"

"There was supposed to have been a grocer killed here back in seventeen hundred-something. During the Revolutionary War. Ask one of your kids about it. They study the whole thing in fourth-grade Connecticut history."

"Can't a different police department help out?" Susan asked, interested in more immediate problems.

"Susan, there's no Scotland Yard in this country. Maybe the state police can do something, but how much would they know about murder? I don't know . . ." She looked out through the open door. "It's upsetting to think that we may never know why Jan died." Her voice trailed off and her last question was almost a whisper. "Do you think about it a lot?"

"All the time."

"Me too."

"You know what I was thinking when you surprised me? I

6

was thinking that the murderer couldn't have known that Jan was going to eat that sandwich. So how do we know that it wasn't meant for someone else?"

"'It'?"

"The poison. If it was placed in a sandwich and the sandwich placed on the tray, how could the murderer know that Jan was going to be the one to eat it?"

"And who put that sandwich on the tray and who put the tray on the table and who arranged the tables and in what order did everyone serve themselves from the buffet, et cetera, et cetera," was Fanny's reply. "The police have asked us all that so many times. We could use some female cops in this town. I keep thinking that any woman would understand how lunches like that happen, how they're organized or disorganized at the last minute."

"You're telling me," Susan answered. "I remember when I ran the luncheon two years ago. First I made lists of all the PTA members to be invited, then all the teachers and administrators that we sent invitations to. Then I made lists of food and called everyone and told them what to bring. Then—it was going to be held on Connie Buckley's patio, remember?—but her husband had some sort of business in Paris that Connie had to attend with him—"

"Why doesn't Jim ever have business like that? The last place I was needed to go was the wedding of the daughter of the Chief of Surgery. You would think a doctor's daughter would know how to avoid pregnancy until after the honeymoon. You should have seen her, she—"

"So then"—Susan raised her voice to drown out Fanny's complaints—"I had to find another place to have the party, since we couldn't do it at my house. You remember how the whole backyard was dug up for the new lawn we were putting in that year? And after asking everyone I could think of, Jan volunteered her yard."

"You think that has something to do with her murder?"

"How could it? That was two years ago." Susan tried to keep the exasperation out of her voice. "The point I'm trying to make is that I worked and worked and I had lists of volunteers to set up the tables and chairs and others to arrange the food—"

"And no one showed up?"

"Different people showed up than I had on my list," she corrected. "Kids get sick, husbands' plans change, no one knows exactly what they're going to be doing. But you know our group—they're responsible. Everything got done but I wasn't entirely sure by whom. It makes it difficult to write thank-yous afterwards. But the lunches are always a success. Of course, I still don't know who brought that good French wine we all loved. It really was awfully expensive for a PTA lunch. I've always wondered."

A shrill scream interrupted their conversation.

"Just one of the Pritchet twins pushing the other into the pool. Those kids are having a rough time this summer," Susan said, identifying the sound.

"No kids have an easy time of their parents' divorce," Fanny insisted. "Some just hide their feelings better than others. Poor kids. I can't believe Harold just up and left them. He always seemed like such a good and caring father."

Susan didn't reply. She had heard that said before. All the fathers who left their families in the suburbs and went off with secretaries, nurses, fellow executives, or whomever were always described as good, caring, and responsible. To her it only proved that being good, caring, and responsible didn't arm a man against the needs of his midlife crisis or, she admitted grudgingly, against really and truly falling in love.

"Susan?"

"Sorry. I seem to be having a hard time concentrating these days."

"I understand. You're thinking about the murder again?"

"I was wondering. . ."

8

This time the scream didn't come from a child, overtired and fed up with too much roughhousing. This time the scream was that of a woman, a woman unable to suppress her horror at finding her friend lying dead on the ground. A scream unchecked by even the presence of her own children and those of the dead woman.

Two

Children have to be fed.

You can braise beef with herbs, and serve a green, a yellow, and a starch. You can pop TV dinners into the microwave. In a pinch, you can pack them all into the car and stand in line with the other tired mothers at Burger King. There are options, but no escape.

Tonight it was a blessing.

She had pulled ground round from the freezer that morning, and it was sitting on the kitchen counter, a trail of blood leaking from the freezer paper and dripping down onto the floor. She grabbed a sponge and mopped it up, dumping the squishy mess into a ceramic bowl.

"No one is to sit down in front of the TV until the swimsuits are off and hanging on the line. Understand?" she called to her two children, who were rushing upstairs to their respective rooms. She could hear the argument going on about whose turn it was to pick the show to watch.

"There's a National Geographic special on," she offered, knowing it would keep down the arguing. They'd shut up when they realized that if they couldn't make a decision peacefully, she would step in and insist on something educational.

As she expected, complete silence greeted her suggestion. She shrugged and ripped the paper off the beef, returning it to the bowl before rinsing her hands and going to look in the refrigerator. Good. There were buns and fixings. That and the corn she had picked up at the farm stand on the way home from the Club would make an adequate supper. She hoped her husband hadn't had a hamburger for lunch. Oh well, not her problem. She had long ago given up trying to balance her dinner against his lunch. One day he'd come home starving after missing lunch, the next he would have had a steak at "21" and really need very little dinner. The problem was that they always seemed to be out of sync: on his hungry nights, she would be on her way to a meeting and offer him Lean Cuisine; on the business-lunch nights, she would have, in a burst of culinary enthusiasm, spent all afternoon and $45 on a rack of lamb, accompanied by a special bottle of wine. He usually appreciated the wine.

But tonight she wasn't hungry and the kids would love hamburgers and corn on the cob in front of the TV. She poured herself a large glass of wine from the jug that sat on the shelf in the pantry and started slapping lumps of meat between her hands, turning them into patties. She had only made two when the phone, hung on the wall close to the sink, rang.

Apprehensive, she reached for a towel to clean off her hands before picking up the receiver. But she knew she was going to have to face this sometime and it might as well be now.

"Hello?" Years of experience in the kitchen had taught her to cup the receiver in the crook of her shoulder and get on with her cooking while talking.

"Just making dinner. How are you?" First salt the frying pan. Start the water heating for the corn. Everything would happen automatically now. She listened to the voice at the other end of the line and thought out her choices. She could either tell all about it now or hope that someone else would do the dirty work. If there were people who enjoyed repeating over and over the details of finding the second murder victim in two months, she wasn't one of them.

11

When she realized who the caller was, she relaxed. Tell the town gossip something and let her pass around the news—she'd love every minute of it.

"Angie, good to hear from you . . . just cooking hamburgers for the kids . . . what are you doing?" Despite her decision to talk about this most recent tragedy, she was hesitant to be the first to mention it.

The voice on the other end of the line showed no such hesitation. "I thought you were at the Club this afternoon. That is, Marsha said she thought you were there."

"I was."

"Well, what happened?"

"Paula was murdered."

"That I know. Did you see her? Do you know what happened?"

Susan cringed at the lack of sensitivity, then consoled herself with the thought that if Angie were a nicer person, she wouldn't do a good job of spreading the story. She hadn't realized before that there probably was no such creature as a sensitive gossip. Gossip was using the problems of others for your own enjoyment.

"Susan? Were you there? Was it too horrible to talk about?" The tone of the question was hopeful.

"It was horrible," Susan confirmed. She took a deep breath before continuing, "Paula was poisoned too."

"Something she ate? Like Jan?"

"In some iced tea that someone brought her. At least, that's what I heard a policeman saying. There was a half-full glass—you know the kind the Club uses for pool service—on the ground by her side."

"You saw her?"

"Everyone saw her. Well, not everyone. You know Kevin Dobbs, that nice boy who's working at the Club this summer? Well, he must have seen what was going on right away because he herded all the kids away from the pool and onto the tennis courts. So I don't think many of the kids saw, but pretty much everyone else did."

12

"I had been lying on one of the chaises near the pool and Paula was on one of the ones near an umbrella on the grass—just behind me, in fact. She was still in the chair when I saw her. Her hands were . . ." Damn, another set of hands. "Her arms were dangling off the sides of the chaise. The glass was on the ground—"

"You said that."

"She was dead." Susan started to shudder.

"You said that someone gave her poison in her tea? How did you know that she didn't get it herself?"

"She wouldn't put poison in it herself, would she? Besides, she was napping. In fact, I was talking to her and—"

"What was she talking about before she died?"

Enough was enough. Susan pulled herself together and finished. "Someone put poison in her tea and she drank it and she's dead. The police were very nice. They let everyone collect their things and their kids and go home. After getting everyone's name and phone number, of course. They said they would question us later. I thought it was sensitive of them. We don't need the kids involved in this." She'd had it. There was nothing else to say, and if Angie didn't believe that, she could call through the membership list and ask everyone on it the same goddamn insensitive questions. "I've got to feed the kids," she insisted. "I'll call back later. Bye."

She hung up without waiting for another question or protest. Actually, the dinner was ready. She popped the meat into the buns, placed the corn on each plate and called the kids.

"You guys can eat in front of the set—if you can agree on a show and if you fix your own burgers and carry everything to the den." She pulled two glasses from the Praittzi cupboard and filled them with milk from the refrigerator. The kitchen had been remodeled two years before and she still felt a little foolish cooking everyday family meals in it. Its chic, smooth Italian lines and hand-painted tiles seemed to insist on something more gourmet.

"I'll carry the milk. You guys take everything else."

13

"We can take the milk too, Mom," offered Chrissy, her twelve-year-old daughter. "Just leave it on the table."

"I can't . . ."

"Yes, you can, Chad." Chrissy stopped his protest. "You take your plate and I'll come back for the rest."

Susan noticed the stern look that passed from older sister to younger brother. She knew it meant that they were watching something they didn't want her to censor. She was too tired to care. She had long ago decided that being a perfect mother meant always giving 100 percent and she had accepted that that was impossible.

"Wonderful. Try to keep the food from getting all over everything. There are some cookies in the jar for dessert—three apiece."

"I'm going to go out back and check out the roses that your father planted." She smiled at the kids, waited until they had left the room, then grabbed her wineglass from where she had left it behind the little kitchen TV, poured herself another glassful, and headed out the back door.

Jed, her husband, was the suburban version of a workaholic. Very successful in advertising (financial side), he worked hard all week in the city. To relax on weekends, he worked hard in the suburbs. To him tennis was a game to be worked at and won; a car was a machine to be washed and polished until it glowed; and his property, his home, was a place to be improved. Recently, he had laid out a bluestone patio, matching the colors with care, and selected an elegant and expensive set of Victorian garden furniture reproductions. Susan had given up wondering why the kitchen was sleek and modern and the garden was becoming more rustic every year. It seemed to be the same with all her friends. Tonight she was just grateful for a comfortable place to sit. Or, at least, a place. The Victorians hadn't been noted for their lounging positions and their furniture designs reflected that.

She shifted her weight to a more comfortable position and

14

took what must, she had to admit it herself, be called a gulp of her wine. What was going on? Why had two of her friends been killed—murdered—in the last two months?

"Mommy! There's a man at the door!" Her son's yell came through the open kitchen window.

She put her glass down on the patio near the leg of her seat and hurried into the house. Who would be calling at this time of night?

She rushed through her kitchen, out into the airy center hall of her home, and to the black-enameled front door, not even stopping for her customary glance into the hall mirror or to straighten her hair. Putting a fixed "for strangers" smile on her face, she approached the still-open entrance.

The man standing there made her all too aware that she was still wearing her swimsuit and cover-up, was without makeup, and couldn't remember the last time she had combed her hair.

He was young . . . well, not old. Probably about thirty-five, Susan thought. He was tall and blond and blue-eyed, but he didn't resemble a youthful Paul Newman, nor Robert Redford. In fact, she thought both actors would look pretty pale beside him. He was gorgeous.

So don't salivate, stupid, she told herself. He might be a mass murderer, for all you know. But then he smiled and she knew that was impossible.

"I'm looking for Susan Henshaw."

"I'm Susan Henshaw." That's all you can say? Is that going to make the impression you know you're dying to make? she asked herself.

"I'm Brett Fortesque."

Brett. Fine. But Fortesque?

"From the state police."

Susan looked at the photo ID he held out to her. Of course, he photographed well. And there was that name again. Fortesque?

"I'm here to ask you some questions."

"Of course. Please come in." She opened the door wider and moved back for him to enter, then was suddenly aware of being alone with her kids in this house. "May I see your ID again?"

"Sure." He passed it to her and waited patiently while she examined it carefully. But did she really know what an official Connecticut State Police identification card looked like? Could this be forged? Did people forge things like this?

"You and the kids alone?" he asked, seeming to know what she was thinking.

"My husband should be home soon" was her response.

"So why don't we sit out on your front lawn and talk," he suggested.

Susan was so grateful for the suggestion that she forgot that people in the suburbs sit behind, not before, their houses. But he had understood her hesitation about being alone with him and the kids and that made her trust him.

"There are chairs around back. Why don't we go there?" she offered.

"Good suggestion."

My God, he was even more good-looking when he smiled!

He followed her around the side of her house and down the three steps to the patio. She hoped he wasn't looking at her thighs.

"You're here about . . ." A horrible thought struck her. "Nothing's happened to my husband, has it?"

"Your husband? Why should something have happened to him?" He waited for her to sit down first.

"I thought . . . well, you're a policeman. I thought maybe a crash of the commuter train or something . . ."

"No, nothing like that." He moved his legs and kicked over her left-behind glass of wine. "Oh, I seem to have spilled something." He stood up, saw the problem, and righted the glass.

Lots of people have a glass or two of wine after five on a hard day, so why did she suddenly feel like a secret alcoholic?

16

"I was just having a drink when you called. I don't usually . . ." Why was she babbling like this? She took a deep breath and regrouped. "Would you like a drink?" Now why did she say that? He was on duty. He wouldn't drink . . .

"I'd love one . . . oh, I know. In books and on TV, cops don't drink when they're on duty. But that's not real life, and it's been a long day," he added, seeing her look of surprise. "Why don't you get yourself another glass of wine to replace the one I spilled and join me?"

Another smile.

"What would you like?" She stood up and accepted the glass he was holding out to her.

"Scotch. On the rocks, with just a little water."

"I'll be right back."

Too bad he wasn't royalty and she couldn't back into the house. He wasn't going to be able to miss her thighs if she kept leaving him like this.

She stopped on her way to the kitchen to peek into the den. Chad was stretched out on the couch asleep, his mouth open and his damp hair plastered against a needlepoint pillow she had spent two months making. Her daughter was sitting on the floor, watching a disco show and sipping a forbidden diet soda.

"Hi, Mom." A furtive attempt to hide the soda stopped when she saw her mother's smile. "Chad fell asleep," she added, stating the obvious.

"Fine. Just let him sleep. Your father can take him upstairs when he gets home. I'm going to be out back with Officer Fortesque. Call me there if you need me."

"Sure, Mom." Already she was back concentrating on the endless gyrations of the dancers on the screen.

Susan detoured to the liquor cabinet in the living room before returning to the kitchen. This called for the good stuff kept there. She grabbed a bottle of Chivas and headed for the kitchen. Five minutes later she returned to the patio, a full tray in her hands.

"Hey, great. How did you do all this so quickly?" was the appreciative comment when the officer saw the bottles, glasses, ice in a crystal bowl, and assortment of hors d'oeuvres laid out on hand-carved wooden servers.

"Just stuff we had in the house." She tried not to remember the state of her emergency shelf in the cupboard after this raid. Even a mouse would have a hard time finding something to eat there now. But it was worth it, she thought, watching this man dig into the smoked oysters, pâté, and other delicacies that she kept around for emergencies.

He ate for a few minutes and then suddenly seemed to remember where he was and, she hoped, what he had come for.

"It's been a long day," he started half-apologetically.

"You were hungry," she replied, looking at the devastation on the tray before him.

He took a long drink from his glass before answering. "That was the first meal I've had today, besides some lousy coffee and dry Danish that I had in the car coming down here from Hartford. But I should be used to that," he added, waving off the sympathetic comment she was about to make. "It's part of the job—rotten food, lousy hours, idiot local cops—"

"Idiot local cops?" she interrupted before she could stop herself.

"Do you know what those fools did? Of course you do. You were there."

Bewildered, Susan took a sip of her wine. Why—why was he here?

"You have no idea what I'm talking about, do you? Well, there's no reason you should. Listen to me; I've been around these Mickey Mouse cops so long, I'm beginning to sound like them.

"Look"—those blue eyes again—"I'm sitting here confusing you and making very unprofessional comments about

18

my colleagues because it's been a long day and I'm tired and hungry and frustrated. And you've had two murders happen in front of you and you're patiently feeding me and waiting for me to make my point. Who says women aren't the saner sex?"

Oh, how I love this man, Susan thrilled to herself.

"Susaaan! Hey, kids! Anyone home?"

It was Jed, home from work. Susan jumped up, startled, spilling yet another glass of wine onto the stones of the patio. This time the glass fell also, breaking into about six million pieces around her naked feet.

"Don't move. You'll cut yourself," Officer Fortesque ordered. He knelt down and began picking up the tiny shards of crystal, placing them on one of the heavy cotton napkins she had brought out. "We're back here," he called in the direction of the house.

"We?" Jed Henshaw appeared at the back door of his home, a perplexed frown on his face. "Susan? What's going on?"

Susan had just time enough to realize what a strange picture Jed must be seeing—his wife standing on the quickly darkening patio, a strange man kneeling at her feet; and then to smile at the picture of her husband, standing in the door, his Brooks Brothers suit rumpled from the long train ride home, his hair tousled, and his tired, slightly homely face appearing very dear to her—before she fainted.

19

Three

——◆◆◆——

There were hands again. This time, floating above her—reaching out. No, not up in the air, but coming down closer. Closer to her. Actually coming at her!

They were reaching for her!

Susan heard herself screaming and recognized the hands simultaneously. They belonged to her husband, and he was covering her with the afghan her own mother had crocheted for her one Christmas.

She sat up.

"My God, Susan, shut up or that detective will think I'm murdering you."

"Jed, I must have fainted."

"Or passed out," he said.

"Passed out?" She was silent until she realized what he was talking about. "You think I'm drunk. I'm not drunk." She swung herself up and her legs to the floor.

"I'm not drunk," she repeated, but she did feel a little woozy and she leaned forward, supporting herself with her arms. "I did have a drink or two, but you know I wouldn't get drunk here alone with the kids."

"You weren't alone."

"I was mostly. Anyway, how could you think—"

"Susan, I don't know what to think." He looked genuinely perplexed and concerned. She reached out to ruffle his hair. He was worried about her! How lucky she was to be married for fourteen years to a man who still loved and worried about her.

"I come home and you're swooning into the arms of a very attractive young man—broken glasses and wine all over the place . . ."

"Jed! Not all over the place. There wasn't that much wine. I just poured two glasses and I didn't get to finish either of them. And I was so upset about Paula and Jan and everything. And I haven't eaten all day. And now you think I'm drunk and—"

He reached over and pulled his wife against his chest.

"I'm sorry, Sue. Of course you're feeling rotten. The detective told me about Paula. I'm overreacting too. You lie down again and rest for a while. I'll tell Detective Fortesque that you'll have to see him in the morning."

She jerked her head up so fast she clunked him in the chin.

"He's still here?"

Jed felt his lower incisors to see if they were still there before answering. "Downstairs watching baseball with Chrissy the last time I looked."

"He must think I'm horrible. Did you get him something to eat?" She extracted herself from her husband's arms, stood up, and walked over to the dresser for her hairbrush. The poor man was not only hungry, he probably thought she didn't even own a hairbrush.

"When would I have had time to feed him? I was busy getting you up here and looking after you, although you won't remember that. No one has been served around here tonight that I know of."

"Oh, Jed, you haven't eaten either. I'm sorry." She put down her brush and started for the closed bedroom door.

"Wait a sec, Sue. I can live awhile longer without food and I'm sure the detective can after all the goodies you stuffed into him. We have some talking to do."

"Talking?"

"Talking," he replied firmly. "Did you notice anything unusual about your friend's ID?"

"He's not my friend and—" She stopped and turned back to her husband. "It's a fake." Her voice rose an octave. "I knew there was something fishy about that name . . ."

"Don't get so excited. I think it's real enough. Now please close that door and stop yelling down the stairs. We need to spend some time comparing notes."

She did what he asked, but didn't leave her position with her hand on the knob.

"You're listening?"

"I'm listening, damn it."

"Okay. The man sitting downstairs with our daughter is not just any state policeman. He's a detective with the Connecticut State Police. Has it occurred to you to ask yourself just why he decided to drop into your home? Besides the fact that we serve great drinks and noshes."

"I did not . . ."

"I'm sorry. I don't want to start an argument. I just think that he's here for a very serious reason and we better find out what that reason is before any more time passes."

"Of course, he . . ." She didn't know what to say. Why was he down there? Just what was going on? She flung open the door and started down the long elegant stairway before her husband could say anything else.

"Damn it, Susan." He was cursing, but he was right behind her.

The double doors to the den were open and Susan walked in without announcing herself.

"Chrissy, it's been a long day and you'd better get to bed. You have that swim meet tomorrow, remember." She didn't need to take a second look at her daughter to see what was going on. Chrissy had perched herself in a decidedly uncomfortable position at the end of the sofa on which her brother was still sleeping. The detective was sitting on a nearby chair, one eye on the Mets game and one on the girl. Chrissy had been chattering excitedly, brushing her bangs back from her forehead and swinging one leg, obviously keyed up from insufficient sleep and too little sophistication to deal with a man who looked as though he belonged on the TV screen rather than in front of it.

"Chrissy. Bedtime," Susan stated.

"I know the time," was the haughty reply. Susan thought she detected a smothered grin on the detective's face.

"I was just about to go upstairs," Chrissy said. An embarrassed look flashed from under her too-long bangs, but it disappeared as she turned back to her companion. "Good night, Detective Fortesque. I hope your team wins." She flashed another and more annoyed look at her parents, now standing together in the doorway, as she strutted past them. "You might think about putting your son into bed."

Her footsteps were heard going up the stairs, then overhead, then a door slammed in the distance.

"She's right about Chad. If you'll just hand him to me, I'll carry him up," Susan suggested to her husband. He scooped up their son from the couch and passed the small limp body to her. Smiling brightly and for no reason at the policeman, she carried her child from the room.

"Would you like a drink, Detective Fortesque?" she heard her husband ask. Since the only thing handy was Chad, he didn't get anything thrown at him. But how like a husband: after implying that she had done something wrong, he goes and does the same thing. She was going to have some conversation with him when this policeman finally left. She shoved her son up higher on her shoulder and opened the door to his room. Pew. The windows had been closed all day and there was no mistaking that gerbils lived here too. She gently placed her child down on his bed and opened the windows as far as possible. The fresh air was a relief. She returned to the bed and removed Chad's shoes and socks. She guiltily looked at his very dirty hands and face and shoved away any thoughts about his teeth. The kid needed his sleep.

23

She threw a light cotton blanket over him, thanked the gods for giving her a child who could sleep through anything, and left.

She heard rock music coming from underneath her daughter's door, but decided not to check on her. Chrissy was probably drowning her adolescent insecurities in an orgy of heavy metal. The last thing her daughter would want was wise words from a parent.

She sighed and headed downstairs, looking forward to finding out at last just why the police were so interested in her, but when she returned to the den, there was no one there. She followed the sound of voices to the kitchen.

". . . we had the same damn thing happen. Guess those guys will never learn . . ." The detective stopped talking when she entered the room, but she didn't have to hear the conversation to know that the two men had been comparing notes on some sort of common experience. "Male bonding," the magazines called it. She thought it was irritating. Just when was her husband going to get around to finding out the answers to his questions?

"You haven't told us why you're here, Brett."

My God, Jed could read her mind! Not exactly every wife's dream, but it served its purpose in this situation. He was also, it appeared, comfortable calling this man by his first name. So they probably liked each other. That was a relief.

"I'm here to find out everything your wife knows about the two murders in the last two months."

"You think they might be connected?" Susan leapt into the conversation.

"Actually, I don't know very much about them." He turned from her husband's side by the stove and, with a quick "Do you mind?" began rummaging around in the refrigerator. "I've read the reports that were filed in June about the death of Mrs. Jan Ick, and I spoke to your local chief of police briefly this afternoon about Mrs. Paula Porter, but my information is very sketchy. I'd like you to fill me in." Turning from the refrigerator and handing Susan a bottle of catsup and a jar of pickles, he asked, "Any mustard in here?"

"Let me," Susan offered, and moving around him, reached into the still-open refrigerator door.

It didn't take long to get the meal on the table, and no one spoke while it was being consumed. Jed had made a pile of hamburgers and boiled up the rest of the corn. That and a six-pack made a very satisfactory meal, and both men declined her offer of dessert.

"It's a hot night and I'd like to go back to the hotel and go to bed, but I still have a job to do. Could we go back to the first murder?"

"Sure," Susan agreed, dumping the corncobs into the garbage and the last dishes into the dishwasher.

"It was June the second, in the afternoon? After school?" he prompted.

"Tuesday, I know. I would have to go back and check my calendar for the exact date. But it wasn't late in the afternoon. The kids had a half-day of school that day, and so all the teachers were free from about twelve-fifteen on. And they all came to the lunch and . . ." She stopped, thinking that she was probably adding to any confusion. "Shall I begin at the beginning?" she asked.

"Please."

She sat back down. "Each year our PTA gives a lunch for the teachers . . . you know all this?"

"Assume I don't know anything."

"Okay. Each year we give the teachers a lunch. Everyone comes."

"Everyone?"

"All the members of the PTA executive board—the elected officers—and all the committee heads. There are about fifteen of us, maybe more. You must have a list of everyone who attended. I know the police got one." She continued after his affirmative reply, "Then you know that all the teachers and the principal and the school secretary, even the custodians attend.

"Anyway, it's held on a day that is a half-day for the kids. There are five or six of them each year. The kids get out at noon, so the teachers are free for the afternoon. Certain committees of the PTA spend the morning setting up the event: the food committee gets volunteers to bring food; the decorating committee sets up the tables and chairs and brings baskets of flowers for the buffet tables; the corresponding secretary sends out invitations . . . it's all done pretty much the way we do everything.

"By noon everything is set up, and the teachers come and we all serve ourselves and eat and talk and have a good time for three hours or so. Or that is what we would have done, if Jan hadn't died. She was killed by poison in a sandwich. At least that's what the autopsy showed.

"Do you want to know about that?" When he didn't reply, she assumed the answer was yes and continued. "We had all had our lunch. It was hot that day, though. Really very hot for early June, and so a lot of us were getting up from the tables to refill our glasses. Because this is held outside of school, we practically always have wine. And of course that just makes you more thirsty, so we were all pretty thirsty. Jan and I hadn't been sitting together. I was with Mrs. Silber— Connie—she's the librarian—most the afternoon. We were planning a day when the volunteer mothers would help her inventory the books. And, well, there must have been about eight or ten people at my table, but that isn't important. I don't know where Jan was sitting. Maybe on the other side of the patio near Dr. Tyrrell, the principal, and Julia Ames and Charline Voos. They were co-presidents of the PTA last year, but that isn't important either." She started to get nervous as she always did when talking about the death. "Anyway, Jan and I met at the buffet table. I wanted some crab salad, she was looking for some sandwiches. At least I assume that's what she got up for. Anyway, that's what she got. We stood there talking for a while and she took a bite of one of the sandwiches on her plate and . . . and she died. Is that what you want to know?"

"Not really. What I want to know is what really happened."

"What?" That was Jed. Susan was too surprised to say anything. "Are you implying that my wife is lying to you?" Jed stood up as he spoke.

"No, I'm not suggesting anything of the sort. Please don't misunderstand. Susan did a nice clear job of explaining the relevant facts, but that's not what I'm here for. I can read everything she said in the police reports—your local police are equal to that job, if not much else. What I want is details, personalities, perceptions—the real story. That's why I'm here." He waved his hand to ward off any interruption. "I've read the police reports and the transcripts of their interviews after the murder. If you remember, they did a pretty thorough job of interviewing and re-interviewing everyone who was at the luncheon. And throughout all that material, your name kept popping up, Susan . . ."

"Of course. I was next to Jan when she died, but . . ." Her voice trailed off. She was mystified. What was he saying about her?

"That's not what I'm talking about. You don't understand and it's my fault. Now I'm not explaining very well.

"I've been involved in investigations of groups before. Not just in murder, but in cases of fraud, kidnapping, blackmail, lots of horrible things, and in all those cases there are certain commonalities about the groups. And one of those things is that most groups are divided into three subgroups: the doers, the followers, and the observers. And I think that you, Susan, are an observer."

"I do a lot—"

"I know that you're very active in the PTA and that you've held office, et cetera, et cetera. But when I read the reports, your name came up often—not just as the person closest to

Jan when she died, but as someone who knew things about the organization's members. Once or twice you were referred to as the person to check on details involving how a committee worked or who really wanted to do what. You seem to be regarded by many of your peers as an observer. And observers usually see things other people miss. So, what I want you to do is tell the story all over again, only tell it your way. Tell me what you know about the people in the group."

"You think that I see things others might not." Susan needed some clarification.

"I hope so" was his answer. "Could you start at the beginning again? I'm looking for the people behind the names, the personality structure of the organization. I'll interrupt with questions. Okay?"

"Fine," she answered, but she wasn't sure where to begin or if she really understood what he was looking for.

"Maybe you could describe the people sitting at your table. You said the librarian. . . ?" he encouraged.

"Connie Silber. I know her well because I've been working as a volunteer in the library since Chrissy was in kindergarten. In fact, I ran the committee for a few years. But you're not interested in that."

"That is exactly what I'm interested in. Go on. The library committee is an important one in the PTA?"

It must have been the sympathy in those beautiful blue eyes that caused Susan to answer so honestly. "Not at all. I mean, it is important, but no one thinks it is." She knew she wasn't making much sense and tried to explain further. "You see, the work of the PTA is done by its committees—like the fund-raising committee, for example. The people on that committee run the two big fund-raising events of the year. This year they had a fall carnival and a spring social. It's a lot of work being on that committee, but everyone sees it and says, 'Wonderful, wonderful. Boy, you sure do work hard.' And, of course, the money earned goes into the treasury and everyone sees that. The money is used to buy things for the schools. Our PTA funded the first complete computer curriculum in the state with the money we've earned. *The New York Times* came out and gave it a first-page second-section write-up. That was eight years ago, but we always do things like that. We really are important to the school. I guess that's what I'm trying to tell you."

"I'm sure you are," agreed the detective. "But you were talking about the library," he gently prodded. "That's very important work too?"

"It is, but no one thinks it is." Susan answered quickly. "I don't know . . ." Anything she might add would seem petty, she thought, but the man was unwilling to let her stop there.

"You mean the teachers don't appreciate the mothers being in the library," he pushed.

"No. They do appreciate our work," Susan corrected. "It's the PTA that doesn't think . . . no, that's not right. Let me try again to begin this at the beginning." She took a breath and tried to sort everything out in her head. How was she to explain the political levels of the PTA and not end up sounding like a petty bitch with a gripe?

"There are two levels of work in the PTA," she began again, hoping this time she would make more sense, but she immediately began to stumble. "Not levels, really, but two different kinds of work. One kind everyone sees, so they appreciate it. Like the fund-raising committee. The other sort no one sees, but it's just as important, and it has to be done. In fact, in some ways it's more important."

She glanced at the man to see if what she said was making any sense and was relieved to see the look of understanding on his face. "The library committee keeps the library running in some ways. We have mothers in the library constantly and they check out the books, and shelve them, do repairs on materials, search for information for teachers . . . well, I could go on and on. We keep the books moving and leave the librarian free to expose the kids to reading and to teach a

29

very sophisticated library-use curriculum. Well, for an elementary school it's sophisticated."

"Sounds impressive to me."

Susan smiled at this encouragement and glanced over at her husband in the corner. He was half asleep, head resting on the palm of his hand. Well, to be fair, he had heard all this before, but she couldn't help but compare his interest level with that of the man sitting across from her.

"And you've been involved on this committee for years?" he was asking.

"Yes."

"And how many women do the library work? How is it divided up? Each person works one day a month. . . ?"

"No, each mother works half a day each week. It's really a major time commitment . . ."

"More time than the other committees?"

"Yes. More than most. But the real difference is that no one sees it."

"Surely the teachers, the principal. . . ?"

"But not the other members of the PTA. They don't see it and so no one gets any credit. If a mother runs a fund-raising fair, everyone knows about it. It's printed up in the PTA newsletter. The principal mentions it at assemblies. And . . . well, what I'm trying to say is that you get credit for it."

"And no credit is given to the library volunteers?"

"Not the same kind. The teachers appreciate it, the librarian appreciates it, but it's just drudge work to the rest of the PTA. In fact, some people who want to get into positions of power in the PTA avoid the library as a dead-end job."

There. She had said it, but had she gone too far?

"So you know the librarian well?" was the only response, much to her relief.

"Yes, Connie Silber. She's young. Around my age." She realized that probably didn't sound young to him. Just how old was he? "That is, she's young for a teacher in our school," she amended. "And she's wonderful. She has lots of enthusiasm for her job and the books and the kids. She's been working at Hancock Elementary for as long as I've been around there. And it's great to help her out."

"You're personal friends then?"

"Not really. I mean, we're good friends inside the school. We talk about our lives outside of school and everything. But, well, we don't really socialize outside the building." When he didn't ask any more questions on that subject she was relieved. She had never been sure how to account for the fact that teachers and parents rarely became personal friends. Could it be that in this very affluent community the people entrusted with the education of the children were simply not of the same social class as the parents?

"And who else was sitting at your table?"

"Let me think." Actually, she had gone over the day so often in her mind that she could remember things quite clearly. "I was the only mother; then there was Mrs. Nunn, my son's first-grade teacher; Miss McGovern and Mrs. Clancy, the two third-grade teachers; and Mr. Johnson, the gym teacher. Oh yes, and Mr. Daviette. He's the new fifth-grade teacher. That is, he's new this year. I always seem to forget him. Because he's new, probably," she added, to explain to him. And because he's so wimpy, she added to herself, using one of the words she was always telling her children to avoid.

"It's getting late." He looked at her now snoring husband. "And I know I've taken up a lot of your time today. If you could just give me brief character sketches of those few people?"

"Sure. Miss McGovern and Mrs. Clancy were sitting right across from me. They do a lot of team teaching—that is, combining of classes and regrouping according to the kids' needs—so they tend to be thought of together. Miss McGovern is the more elderly of the two. Gray hair, sensible shoes, and that sort of thing. You would never know to look

31

at her that she belongs to the Mountain Club in Colorado. That is, she's climbed all the peaks in the state over fourteen thousand feet. She goes all over the world to climb, in fact. She's a super lady."

"And Mrs. Clancy?"

"She's fine, too, although less dramatic. She's younger than Miss McGovern. And she's married, of course, although her kids are all grown up and have left home. She's very domestic. She knits the most wonderful sweaters and she always donates homemade bread to any event where the teachers bring food. She's really a lovely old-fashioned teacher. The kids love her.

"And then there's Mrs. Nunn," she went on quickly. She wasn't ready to go on about Mrs. Clancy, the only teacher either of her children had had that she didn't like. And she never knew why, really. She just had never felt comfortable around her the year that Chrissy had been in her class. It really wasn't relevant to this conversation. "Mrs. Nunn had my son Chad in her class this past year. She also taught Chrissy. But she's not the type of teacher to expect children to be the same just because they come from the same family." Detective Fortesque smiled as though he knew what she was talking about. Surely he didn't have children of his own! "She's been at Hancock Elementary for a long time and she's a great teacher, too. She's very involved in the outdoors and conservation and nature. Her kids come out of her class in June knowing how to read and things like where to find monarch butterfly cocoons."

"And the two men?"

"Mr. Johnson. I really don't know him very well. He's the gym teacher. Chrissy had him and now, of course, Chad does. He's always struck me as exactly what he is—an elementary-school gym teacher. But I don't know him very well at all. Chrissy wasn't involved in sports much and Chad is too young, I guess."

"And Mr. Daviette?"

"I can't help you there much either. He's new this year. And I haven't heard anything bad about him. You know how mothers talk about their kids' teachers," she added, wondering if he did. "I really can't tell you anything about him. Except that he grew up on the beach in Santa Barbara, California."

"How do—"

"It's what he was telling Mr. Johnson about at the luncheon. I overheard their conversation. But that's really all I know, I'm afraid."

"You've been wonderful. And you've helped a lot. But I'm going to need a lot more information. Could we talk again tomorrow? First thing in the morning, if it isn't imposing?" He stood up and stretched.

"Of course. Would you like to come for breakfast?" she said, wishing she could take the offer back before it was out of her mouth. She needed company early tomorrow morning like a hole in the head. Another one.

"No thanks, but could we start early—around nine? A few more hours and I should have a pretty good impression of what your group is like. You're really a very good witness, you know." He started toward the door, and she jumped up to see him out.

"Jed should . . ."

"Let him sleep till I'm gone. Nothing worse than waking up and finding out that a stranger has been around while you slept."

Susan thought that was very perceptive and knew that her husband would appreciate being awakened after this man had left, and so she alone showed him the way out. Walking to the door, she realized just how tired she was, and was relieved that he didn't feel he had to hang around making small talk. As he left she noticed the state patrol car parked out front. Was she going to get a lot of calls about that in the morning!

He was halfway down the walk when he turned around.

"Where do you find monarch cocoons?" he called out, loud enough for her to hear but quiet enough not to awaken the neighbors.

"On milkweed," she answered in the same tone of voice. "It's their food," she explained. "It's all they eat."

"Really? Well, good night." He walked around the front of the car and got into the driver's seat. Susan didn't think it necessary to stay around, so she waved her hand and went back into her house. What an interesting man, she thought, and went to get her husband to bed.

Four

———◆◆———

Brett Fortesque glanced across the small table at the woman sitting with him. Her gleaming blond hair was coiled into a twist at the back of her neck. The effect was both efficient and glamorous. Her shirt was tailored and silk, but opened one button lower than was absolutely necessary for comfort. And her long legs, currently tucked under the coffee-shop bar, were, he knew, toned from a strenuous running program and shapely enough for a movie star.

He wondered if she subscribed to the notion of not mixing work and pleasure and how long he should wait before finding out.

"I'd like to meet this Susan Henshaw, but if you don't mind, I'll wait until I've finished going through the files in town," Officer Kathleen Somerville was saying.

"Good idea," he concurred, thinking that he could probably get more out of these middle-aged housewives without her around. He didn't mean to be chauvinistic, but he needed all the information he could get, and he needed it fast. It seemed there was a killer in the midst of the Hancock Elementary School PTA.

"I cannot believe the incompetence of the police in this town," Kathleen (who had explained at their first meeting that she didn't plan to be a Kathy, or Kate, or any other diminution of her given name) said, looking carefully at the plate of whole wheat toast and fruit that the waitress had put before her.

"I thought I had heard of everything that could be done wrong in the last few years, but letting all those witnesses go home without being interviewed at the Field Club yesterday . . ." Her voice trailed off in frustration. "What were they thinking of? By the time we get to those women they will have talked to each other on the phone and in backyards and they won't know what they've seen or what someone else told them they'd seen. It's all going to be a garbled mess!" She spread a tiny sliver of butter on a slice of toast.

"There are always the employees of the Club. They remained at the Club until they made statements. Right?" Brett dug into his platter of twin fried eggs surrounded by bacon and white spongy toast.

"They sure were. And they were thrilled about it when I went out there with the sergeant from downtown." Her voice had a sarcastic edge she didn't try to hide. "Letting those club members, who had been near the dead woman, go home and then detaining the employees, who were busy inside and on back tennis courts and playing fields, smacks of discrimination to me. God knows what they thought. They were very polite, I'll say that for them."

"They wouldn't have those jobs unless they were always very polite," Brett suggested. "And I'll bet that they're considered plum jobs for people in that economic group," he added. "You check. I'll bet you find out that most of them are from a class that's usually employed as cleaning ladies and handymen. The Club may be the first time in their lives that they've had benefits like health insurance offered along with employment. They may not feel the same way you do about it. How you view a situation often depends on where you come from." He looked away from the task of getting grape jelly out of the infinitesimal tin container and onto his toast to see how she was taking his last statement, whether she was offended at his mild lecture, but she seemed to be paying no attention at all.

36

"They're certainly a racist group, though—the club members, I mean," she said, writing something down in a leather-covered notebook as she spoke. "A club full of white members with black and Spanish people working in all the menial jobs—I thought this type of thing had vanished in the sixties."

"No. And don't be mistaken. I've been around clubs like this before. Connecticut is full of them. A lot of the members are people who marched for the rights of blacks in the sixties . . ."

"And they've gotten so senile that they've forgotten what they believe?" she interrupted angrily.

Brett was somewhat surprised at her hostility, but he answered calmly. "I've wondered about that myself," he admitted. "Sure, some of them probably were just going along with the crowd back then and really didn't have any personal beliefs, but there must be an awful lot of sincere people whose beliefs have changed dramatically, or else they've learned to ignore a lot." Privately, he believed the latter. There were days, bad ones, he admitted, when he thought that getting old was the painful process of learning to ignore things that bothered you when you were young.

"Well, anyway, I didn't learn very much from any of the help. The waitress who works in the bar was the closest and also the most outspoken. First she mumbled about how she had nothing to do with the poisoning, et cetera, et cetera. When I had convinced her that no one suspected her of having anything to do with the death, she made some comments about how people drink all day and make her job hard. But nothing we can use . . ."

"And we're sure the iced tea didn't come from the bar poisoned?" he asked.

"It's doubtful. The tea is squirted into glasses from a big stainless-steel container. It was easy to check to see if poison was present there, and it wasn't. Besides, nobody else who drank the tea died. According to the preliminary lab tests, the tea left in Mrs. Porter's glass—and it was over half full—contained enough cyanide to kill a dozen other people."

"I wonder why she didn't taste it."

"There was so much artificial sweetener in that drink that she probably couldn't taste anything. There were four empty packets of the stuff on the ground."

"And we know that she used all of them in the one drink?"

"No, we don't know anything, but right now we're assuming so. We will know—approximately—how many she used when we get the results of the autopsy and the complete analysis of the tea left in the glass."

"We were lucky she didn't spill the glass when she fell," Brett suggested, mopping up the last of his eggs with a piece of toast.

"We deserve some luck in this case. Do you think the murderer is the same person in both deaths? Do you think we'll find him?'

"Or her?" Brett just couldn't resist adding.

She looked up sharply, a strawberry posed on a fork near her lips. Oh, oh, he thought to himself, a woman with no sense of humor. But he dismissed that conclusion when he saw her starting to smile.

"You're right; it probably is a woman," she said. "Just the law of averages. There weren't many men at the PTA lunch—just the principal and one or two male teachers. And the same goes for the Field Club—a few golfers and the groundsmen and the tennis and golf pro, but most of the people involved here are women. But which woman or women did it?"

"We won't find out sitting here. Are you finished? Do you want some more coffee or—you're drinking tea?" Brett asked, himself anxious to get on with it.

"I can have more of either down at the police station. I'll keep going through the files there and wait for our reports to come in. We should hear from the tech team and the coroner's office in the next few hours. I put a rush on our request for information. She stood up, smoothing out her skirt, and Brett hastily reached for the check. But there was no need. There were two checks, stacked one on top of the other. She extended a hand for hers.

"I thought it would be easier if we kept everything separate." She smiled.

If that's her way of telling me that she keeps her social life and her professional life apart, I've got the message, Brett thought, seemingly examining his own bill. "I'll call you at the station if I need you. Okay?"

"Sure. I'll be waiting," she answered. "You've been in charge of many murder cases?" she added, almost as an afterthought.

"A few," he answered, not adding that the total number could be counted on one hand.

Susan Henshaw wasn't smiling. How could she have told Detective Fortesque that she would meet him this morning without thinking of what she was doing? Her husband was upstairs, still asleep. They hadn't really had a chance to talk since he came home and found her on the patio last night. He had gone to bed and quickly to sleep while she had stayed up and watched an old David Niven film on TV. Her children were eating breakfast in front of Saturday-morning cartoons. She was going to feel really guilty about that if she let herself, so she wouldn't. How much could two meals in a row eaten without benefit of table manners harm two children? So stop thinking about it.

She glanced up at a clock. Did she have time to run to the bakery for some Danish? Should she offer a police detective Danish? And did this man think she was running a restaurant? Now wait, she had to be fair. He had never asked for anything, she was the one who kept running around like the mad hostess. Oh, damn. The coffee was running out of the

Melitta and onto the stove. She grabbed for a sponge from the top of the sink and reached for the glass pot with her other hand.

The coffeepot hit the ground within five seconds of the shrill buzz of the front-door bell.

"Mommy, that man is here again." She really was going to have to speak to Chad about his manners. But later. She pulled the whole roll of paper towels off its color-coordinated under-the-cabinet holder and started to mop up the steaming, glassy mess.

"I'll be there in a minute, honey. Would you or Chrissy show Detective Fortesque the way to the living room?" Susan heard her daughter pound up the stairs to her bedroom; she undoubtedly thought that her sloppy Saturday clothes were inappropriate in front of the detective. She was going to have to speak to her about this crush. But there wasn't time to worry about that. Right now she just hoped the child had the good sense to wake up her father before getting involved in going through her wardrobe for the perfect outfit.

"There's no reason for me to wait in the living room . . . Let me help you," Detective Fortesque offered as he entered the kitchen.

"Don't cut yourself," Susan cried out, wishing he had stayed where her son had put him. "There's glass and the coffee is hot and . . . oh, shit." The blood oozing out of her palm mixed quickly with the brown liquid on the floor.

"Don't move. Is the glass still under your skin?" He grabbed her hand at the wrist and kept it still. "Don't step in the breakage. Careful. Come on over here. Watch that glass by your right foot."

Holding her arm so that she couldn't twist it, he guided her over to the sink and very carefully, very gently wiped away the blood surrounding the wound. "Looks like the glass is still in there. We may need tweezers . . ." Susan couldn't help herself. She looked away. The blood was still coming out of the wound, a jagged one about an inch long, running right across her palm. How could she be so stupid? She felt a twinge of pain.

"I was right. It was still in there, but it's out now. A nice long piece, but I think I got it all. No sign that anything broke off. Do you have any bandages?"

"In the bathroom—that door over there." She motioned with her head. "I can get them . . ."

He grabbed a dishcloth off the counter and pressed it hard against her hand before answering. "I'll get it. You stay here and try to stop that blood from flowing. I think we should get you to a hospital for some stitches . . ."

"Hospital? What's going on here?"

Sure, now he gets up. Not when he was needed to go to the bakery, but now.

"Susan, you're bleeding. What's happened?" Her husband looked around the room, at the mess on the floor and the blood-spattered sink and countertop. "Are you okay?"

"Don't walk across the floor."

"Jed! Don't!" Susan screamed to her husband at the same time the detective spoke.

"Susan! I'm not going to step on any glass. And I'm not exactly barefoot."

She looked down at his top-of-the-line running shoes and decided that he would be fine. He could walk safely over a bed of nails with the insulation on the bottom of those shoes.

"Mooooommmmm. It's almost time for the swim meet. And we have to pick up Charlie and Stuart. Remember?"

Susan closed her eyes and sighed.

"Your mother's busy bleeding all over the place. Call Charlie and—uh—the other boy and tell them we're going to be a bit late. I'll drive you," Jed called to his son.

"But . . ." came the wail from the den.

"Just *do* it, Chad," his father insisted. Miraculously, the

41

boy didn't object. And Susan didn't have the time to worry about the differences in a child's response to the mother and to the father. Brett Fortesque was back with the large bandages she had bought the day her son had taken the training wheels off his first two-wheeler, and when the dishtowel was removed from her hand, the bleeding seemed to have stopped.

"It doesn't look so bad," Jed commented, leaning over the counter for a look.

"Stitches wouldn't hurt," insisted the policeman.

Her son burst into the room and would have walked right across the glass if all three of them hadn't yelled simultaneously.

"I just came in to tell you that Dr. Hallard is on his way over. I wasn't going to walk on that stuff. How dumb do you think I am?" He looked earnestly offended.

"Dr. Hallard?" Jed asked, frowning.

"Charlie's dad," his son explained. "He answered the phone and I told him that we were going to be late picking up Charlie because my mother was bleeding all over the place, and he said he would be right over. That's probably him now." He turned and left the room, pausing just long enough to give them a look suggesting just how dumb he thought they were acting.

Susan leaned back on the counter and began to giggle. "Just what we need now. An ob-gyn man."

"Susan, your son said . . ." Dan Hallard burst through the kitchen door, stopping just in time to avoid walking on the broken glass, although Susan noticed that he wore running shoes identical to her husband's.

"I'm fine, Dan. Although I would appreciate it if you would give your opinion about whether I should have stitches. But let's all get out of here first."

"Mother! What have you done?" Her daughter arrived on the scene wearing her best knit dress.

"Chrissy, your mother has had an accident. I am going

to drive your brother to a swim meet and Dr. Hallard and Detective Fortesque are going to take care of her cut hand. We don't know if it will need stitches or not. You would be a big help if you would clean up this mess," Jed suggested.

The adults left the room before she had a chance to respond.

Poor kid, all dressed up and no one noticed, Susan thought, sitting on the couch in the living room and watching Dan Hallard's face for any sign of a decision. She really didn't want to spend the morning getting stitches.

"It's messy, but not deep. I think we can put some butterfly bandages across the cut and it will hold all right. I have some at my house. I'll just run home and get them."

"Dan, you really don't have to do all that. I can go over there," Susan protested.

"Martha's still asleep. I'll be right back," he insisted and left the room.

"Martha's his wife?" Brett asked.

"Yes; they live next door," Jed answered for his wife. "I'm going to drag your son from the TV set and take the kids to the swim meet," he said to Susan. "That is, if you don't need me here, Brett."

"No. I just need your wife for about an hour or so, but I'll see that this hand is taken care of first."

"Then I'll be off. I assume I should stay for the meet?" he checked with his wife.

"Yes. Be sure all the kids have their beach towels and—"

"I can manage, Sue. Chad, let's go!" he called out, as he reached over to kiss his wife. "Take care of that hand, okay?"

Dan Hallard had come and bandaged her hand and was gone; Chrissy had informed them—from the hall—that the kitchen was cleaned up and she was going over to Janie's house; and Susan had once again asked Brett if he was hun-

43

gry and he had again refused before they finally got around to what he'd come for.

"I told you yesterday, I'd like to know more about the PTA. Can you give me some sort of rundown of the whole organization and the main people who are involved in it?"

Susan sat back and thought for a minute, then got up and went to her desk. "I have the information sheet we put out in the fall. It gives all the officers, their names, and also all the committees and their chairmen and co-chairmen. It's in here somewhere. There. I knew I could find it." She handed it to him and sat back while he looked it over.

"The PTA list is on the first page. The rest is about the faculty and the calendar of the PTA-sponsored events." She watched him thumb through the pages. Just how old was he? Certainly younger than she, but maybe not by that mu——

"You know all these people?" She nodded. He handed the list back to her. "Can you mark off the people who were at the luncheon where Mrs. Ick was killed?"

She spent a few minutes doing just that and then returned the paper to him.

"Fantastic. Now can we go through the list? Can you tell me about these people that you've checked off? Let's see, there are eleven of them. I think . . . let me recount . . . yes, eleven.

"Let's start with Julia Ames and Charline Voos. The co-presidents this past year."

Oh, great. Begin with something easy, she thought, but she kept it to herself and smiled when she answered. "They were co-presidents last year, like you said, and they're going to be in the same positions this coming year too. They've been involved in the PTA for fewer years than I have. They've always worked together on whatever they've done: fund raising for a few years, and they were co-vice-presidents for two years . . ." She faded off, not sure what he was looking for.

44

"They're very much alike then?" he prodded.

"Not at all. Well, a little," she contradicted herself. "They're both very good-looking, very New York City—as opposed to the pink-and-green preppie style that you see a lot of around here. Julia designs a lot of her own clothes. I think she may have designed professionally before she got married. Her husband is involved in some sort of exotic import/export business. He travels all over the world and she goes with him a fair amount. Their kids stay home with the housekeeper. They have two of them. Kids, not housekeepers.

"Charline is also chic. She really could be a model," she added, knowing that he would think that for himself when he met her. "She's also the perfect corporate wife. She's taken all the cooking courses, all the art classes. She also does volunteer work for the Metropolitan Museum in the City on weekends. She's working her way up the board of the New York City Ballet, I hear . . ." She stopped. Did she sound bitchy?

"Someone always has to run things," he offered.

"Yes, I guess so."

"You're vice-president?"

"Yes. And I run the library, too. So the next on the list is Patsy Webber. She's secretary—"

"But she wasn't at the luncheon. At least you haven't checked her."

"That's right. I'm sorry. Her father was having bypass surgery that week, I think. The only other officer there was Fanny Berman."

"Treasurer."

"That's right. She's great friends with Charline. She's pretty new to the PTA. Her oldest child is Chad's age and going into second grade. And she's an accountant. Our books have never looked so good. She's also a great cook. She teaches down at the gourmet shop in town. I understand that she's working on a book of recipes. I was talking to her at the pool when Paula died. That is, when we heard the

45

scream and went out and found that she had died. But I don't really know Fanny very well."

"Just keep going. I don't expect you to be the final authority on everyone here."

"Well, the committees are in alphabetical order. The first is class mothers; the chairman is Nancy Dobbs. She's been running the class mothers for years now. Found her niche, I guess, and wants to stick to it. She also can do a lot of the work from her home. Mostly the committee is organizing all the class mothers and calling them up when they have to call their classes. Does that make any sense?" she asked, thinking that it didn't.

"I understand. She gets information and then disperses it to the mothers assigned to each class, and they, in turn, call the other mothers in the class."

"Yes. You explained that well." And how did he know about this? He must be married, even though he wasn't wearing a ring. "Anyway, she likes to be involved, but she's Catholic and—well—she has a lot of kids. Five of her own and three more that are her husband's from his first marriage. His first wife died. Leukemia, I think. Anyway, with this committee she can take care of her preschoolers and still be involved."

"Her husband?"

"He's a doctor. An eye surgeon, I believe. He's much older than she is and very conservative. They live in a huge home on the best street in town, but his kids always have jobs. Paper routes and traditional things like that. It must work. They're all great kids. His oldest daughter, Cindy, has been our baby-sitter for years.

"Next thing." She looked at the list. "Oh, fund raising, that's . . ." She stopped and looked up at him. "You know, I never realized it."

"What?"

"Paula Porter and Jan Ick."

"The woman who died at the pool yesterday and the one who died at the teacher's lunch . . . yes?"

"They were co-chairmen of the fund-raising committee last year. It's probably just coincidence . . ." She looked at him for confirmation, but was disappointed. He had no particular expression on his face.

"Why don't you wait and we'll go back to them later. What's next?"

"Hospitality. That's one of my specialties. I did that for years. Now Martha Hallard is running it."

"That's the doctor's wife asleep next door?"

"That's right. Although I can't imagine that she's still asleep. Martha's a mover and a shaker. She runs her own real estate agency, is very active in her church, has unlimited energy. She's usually up and out of the house jogging when my alarm rings. Maybe she's not feeling well."

"She was at the pool yesterday?" When she nodded yes, he offered an explanation. "These deaths may have shaken her up?"

"Possibly. She and Paula were good friends. Maybe Dan gave her something to help her sleep."

"Probably. So she's usually an energetic person?"

"Very. She runs everything she's in. She'll be PTA president one of these years and she'll juggle that along with everything else. I don't know how she does it."

"But isn't being so involved in the schools and her church group good for her business?"

"Of course. We all go to Marty when we have to move or know of people looking for homes in the area. But that's because she's good at her job. Really it is."

"I'm not arguing with you. I was just suggesting that one part of her life enhances the other. How long has she lived next door to you?"

"We moved here after she did. About seven years ago. We left the city when Chrissy was ready for her last year of kindergarten. We bought this house from Martha when she was with another agency."

"You knew her before you came up here?"

"No. We had been looking all over Connecticut in towns

47

with good school systems and we walked into a realtor's office here one Sunday late in the evening. We had just finished viewing everything we could afford in Darien—which wasn't much in those days—and Marty was manning the office. Anyway, she worked with us for a few months and, in fact, found this house for us. I remember Jed used to say that the house must be good since the agent who sold it to us was living right next door. It was his idea of as good a guarantee as we were likely to get.

"Anyway, Marty's been moving up ever since then. She started her own agency about four years ago. She's also our PTA representative on the Hancock Town Council. Keeps each group informed about the activities of the other. Actually, come to think of it, she may not want to be PTA president. She might be happier running for a position on the Town Council."

"She would win?"

"Probably. She's very well known in town. And she's in with the establishment here. She's probably going to run the two-hundred fiftieth town birthday party. At least that's what I heard recently. It's a very big deal in a place like this."

"It's soon?"

"No. In two years. But the planning will have to start soon. I guess the mayor will announce a committee or something. I really don't know very much about town politics, to be honest. You should talk to someone else, if you're interested."

"Like Mrs. Hallard?"

"Like Mrs. Hallard. Next on the list is library committee. That's me." She was embarrassed.

"I think we can skip to the school-store committee."

"That's run by Carol Mann. She's a good friend. She has kids in both Chad's and Chrissy's classes. And they've always been friends with each other. In fact, Chrissy said she was going to the Manns' this morning. Their daughter is the Janie that she mentioned on her way out. Carol was my first

4 8

friend in town. I met her in a play group for kids Chrissy's age. And we went through our second pregnancies together." She stopped, wondering if a man could have any understanding of what a bond that could bring. "She works in a children's clothing shop downtown. It's owned by another friend. Anyway, even though she likes to be involved in the PTA, she needs something less time-consuming. The school store is only open four times a year. It carries school supplies, T-shirts and sweatshirts, and small items that the kids can buy with their allowances. It doesn't take a whole lot of work to run and so it's perfect for Carol."

"Is she the only one of the women who works like that? I mean, besides Mrs. Hallard and her agency?"

"Well." She paused and thought (how could she say this without sounding crass?). "She is the only woman in our group who has to work. Because her family needs the money, I mean. I told you about Fanny Berman and her cookbook. A lot of women have done things like that—in fact, quite a few do some sort of free-lance writing. Magazines and the local paper and stuff. And Paula Porter used to work in her own husband's office—he's a pediatrician."

"The difference is that the Mann family needs the money, I gather?"

"Well, yes." There was only one way to say it. "Her husband is a police sergeant in town and this is a very expensive place to live and, well . . ."

"Believe me, I understand." He chuckled at her hesitation. "I do understand," he repeated. "So what about the rest of this list?"

"The three representatives to outside organizations. That is, two of them are. There's the Town Council representative. That's Martha Hallard and we've already talked about that."

"And the two others?"

"Board of Education and legislative." She took the latter first. "Angie Leachman is our legislative representative. She keeps track of any state or federal legislation that might make

49

a difference to the schools or our kids and then she reports on them to the PTA. A lot of her information comes from the national PTA offices. They have quite a lobbying group, you know. Or you may not know. But we do try to add to the effort locally when necessary. Angie is very good at her job. Very thorough and concerned. She's a member of the League of Women Voters as well. She has one child in the school. In fact, she only has one child, and he is in the fifth grade. We're going to miss her next year. I don't know who is going to take her place. It's an important position, but not really appreciated. We all know we should be more involved in government, but I think it's one of those things that just doesn't get done in the process of day-to-day living. I know Angie sometimes feels like she's hitting her head on a stone wall. For instance, she tried to get members out to a march for some bill or other in Hartford and she and her husband were the only residents of Hancock who showed up. It was Labor Day weekend and there were parties, and people closing up their summer homes, and things like that. We were busy ourselves that weekend . . ."

"Everyone has things to do. We can't all do everything," he soothed, but she still felt a pinch of guilt.

"The last position is Board of Education representative. That's Ellen Cooper." She stopped, not knowing what to say. Well, onward. "Ellen's a good friend too and she does lots of work for the PTA. She's a very dedicated volunteer. The Board of Education representative goes to all the Board of Ed meetings—and there are a lot of them—and then she reports back to the group. We're a wealthy town and we have a good-sized school budget, but there still is only so much to go around to all the schools. The Junior and Senior High are always looking out for their share. And things aren't what they used to be. Elementary schools are closing all around us. The baby boom is over and town populations are getting older and there's always a push for funds. Ellen works very hard." She didn't know what else to say.

"Would you say that her position isn't appreciated? Like the library representative or the legislative representative?"

He really was a good listener! "Not really. I thought everyone appreciated the work Ellen was doing, but recently . . ." She paused. "I don't know. Maybe others don't see her the way I do."

To her surprise, he was willing to leave it at that.

"Could we go back to the two women who were killed now?" His voice was gentle.

Five

"Paula and Jan. I don't know where to start."

"Why don't you begin by telling me about the fund-raising committee? It's an important one, I gather. How much money is raised by the PTA each year?"

"Usually about six thousand dollars, I believe. But there are years when we earn a lot more than that. We sometimes have extra fund drives for special projects. Like when we bought twenty computers for the school, for example."

"But usually?"

"Usually, we have two big fund-raisers each year. And they're events rather than raffles or selling something door-to-door like some organizations do. We have a big fall book sale. The books come from a great children's bookstore in Darien and we get thirty percent of the profits. It's not too much work. The store does the inventory and we provide the space, a theme, publicity, and volunteers to lay out the books, help the kids, and collect money. Usually the profits from that go straight to the school library and not into the general fund, so I suppose it's not included in the PTA budget for the year.

"Anyway, our big event is in the spring. And that varies. We've had dinners, art fairs, science fairs, fashion shows, whatever the person running it dreams up—with the school principal's permission, of course. That event has been known to raise between four and five thousand dollars on its own."

"And this year? The year that Mrs. Ick and Mrs. Porter were doing the work?"

"It was great. It really was," she enthused. "The best since I've been involved in the PTA. Its theme was 'Bubble Magic and Other Flying Things.' It was part art, part games, and part science. The kids and the parents loved it."

"Tell me more."

"Well, it was held on a Saturday in the middle of May. The sixteenth, if I remember correctly. A man from San Francisco was the feature. He's a bubble artist and he gave three shows that day: one at ten when the fair opened, one at noon, and one at two in the afternoon. The fair ended at three. He did fabulous things. Made bubbles inside bubbles, blew gigantic bubbles—almost as big as a room—and when they floated into the sky it was amazing . . ."

"And the kids?"

"They made paper airplanes and cardboard Frisbees. They created animals out of balloons, they had relay races where they sat on balloons. They tried—each grade competing against the other—to see who could make a rocket that would fly the farthest without using any sort of flammable fuel. And there was lots of food, donated by the parents and then sold to the people who came. It was very, very successful. I don't remember how much money was made, but I know it was more than usual."

"And it was run by Mrs. Porter and Mrs. Ick?"

"Yes. You want to know more about them, don't you?"

"Yes."

"Well, I knew Paula the best, I guess. She had four kids and her husband is a pediatrician, but you know that, don't you? Well, she was a real hard worker, but not very creative. The inspiration for Bubble Day must have come from Jan, but I'm sure a lot of the work was done by Paula. Jan was different. She was an art student when she met her husband. He's some sort of headhunter, but he almost doesn't count, if you know what I mean. I mean," she tried to explain, "that when you meet the two of them, it's Jan who you remember. Their house is full of abstract and Pop and all kinds of art and I think everyone knows more about her years in the past as an art student than about what her husband does now. She was very dramatic and very flashy and . . ." She stopped talking, embarrassed.

"One of the biggest problems we have in a murder case, Mrs. Henshaw, is that no one likes to say anything bad about the deceased, and what we don't know about the deceased can keep us from finding the motive in the killing," he said, ignoring the times that he had walked into a room containing both a dead body and the killer and had immediately heard more than enough from the killer about the personality and attributes of the one he had murdered.

"I understand. It's not just that they're dead. I'm afraid I don't like to say bad things about anyone. I suppose it's the way I was brought up or something." She wondered briefly if she was raising her own children in the same way, but decided that if she was, it wasn't working. They seemed to have no trouble condemning others, especially each other.

"Mrs. Henshaw?"

"I'm sorry. I was just thinking of something else. Well," she continued, "we kidded around when Jan died that Paula had done it. Because, if I'm going to be honest, it's more than likely that Jan had all the ideas for the fair—wonderful, creative ideas, of course—and then Paula did all the work carrying them out. Jan could be very hard to work with. Mainly, I think, because she really didn't work with anybody. She expected people to work *for* her. Not that we ever heard Paula complaining. And, of course, Paula would never kill anybody."

"But you thought that she might resent doing all the leg work for the more creative half of the pair?"

The doorbell's ring gave her an excuse not to answer that question. "I'll just get that," she murmured and went into the hall. But the person who had rung was already inside and talking.

54

"It's a tragedy. Another tragedy. Poor little children left motherless. Another husband grieving. I don't know what to do. Of course, I made a coffee cake and took it over to the Porter house this morning. Jack was devastated. He looked like he hadn't slept for weeks. I didn't see Eric or Brad or Heather, but Samantha looked okay—a little dazed, but okay. A two-year-old can't possibly understand what's going on. I offered to take the kids, but Paula's mother and father are flying in from Phoenix and Jack thought all four kids should be at the airport to greet them. I'll make a big pot of chicken salad this afternoon and take it over to them. And, of course, everyone will help out. Could you?"

"I'll bake some cookies or a cake or something and get it over as soon as possible," Susan interrupted. "I should have thought of it before. Everyone's upset, but the boys at least will be hungry."

"I'll call Nancy Dobbs and some others. We'll see that the family is taken care of for the next few weeks. Jack said the funeral is probably going to be Tuesday or Wednesday. It depends on when the coroner releases the body."

"I'm pretty sure that the . . . uh . . . that your friend's family will be able to go ahead with their plans for an early funeral. The autopsy should be completed now and the coroner's office will probably be informing the family later this morning so that they can claim the body."

Susan was surprised that Brett had followed her into the hall. Ellen Cooper took his presence in her stride.

"Oh, I hope they let Jack know soon. It's so horrible that this happened to Paula; I'm sure the questions about her death are going to make it doubly hard on Jack and the kids," Ellen continued. "You're the police officer from Hartford, aren't you? Are you investigating Paula's death?"

"Yes . . ."

"Do you know when you're going to have some answers? And you're looking into Jan's death too, aren't you? You think the murders are related?"

"How did you know that?" Brett asked.

Susan smiled. He wouldn't be asking those questions if he knew how efficient Ellen was.

"I called one of my friends about helping out the Porters—her name is Carol Mann."

"Ah yes, the one who has to work," Brett mumbled.

"What?" Ellen gave him an inquisitive look before continuing. "Well, her husband is the Hancock police sergeant and he told her last night that detectives from Hartford had been checking into the files on the PTA luncheon and Jan's death."

Susan made quick introductions and Brett started the conversation. "I've been talking about that time with Mrs. Henshaw, too. If you're not too busy, maybe I could ask you some questions?"

"Of course, anything. Anything I can do to help find out who did this horrible thing, officer."

Susan looked at Ellen, a small woman with a clear complexion, brown eyes that were usually fixed in the same earnest expression they were in now, hair pulled back in a headband in a style that had probably been popular her freshman year of college, and wondered what Brett Fortesque thought of her.

"How many people were at the PTA luncheon and the Field Club yesterday?" was Ellen's next question. And Susan knew that the policeman, if he had been dismissing Ellen as merely another upset woman, would change that opinion. Leave it to Ellen to get to the heart of the situation immediately. If one person was responsible for both deaths, then that person must have been in both places. Why hadn't she thought of that?

"Maybe, if you'll help us, we can figure that out, Mrs. Cooper."

"Let's go into the den," Susan suggested quickly, as she saw Ellen heading in that direction.

"We'll need some paper and pencils, Susan. But this shouldn't be hard to figure out. We know who was at the

56

luncheon and we'll have to find a way to discover who was at the Club yesterday. Maybe we could look at the bar tabs? Can you get access to that?" She was talking to Brett, and Susan wondered just what he thought about her.

"I have someone looking into that, but I'd like your impressions, Mrs. Cooper. Yours and Mrs. Henshaw's," he added with a quick glance at Susan.

Susan smiled at him and assured herself that there was no reason to be jealous. She was acting like a child!

"Actually, we've been making a rather complete list of the members of the PTA who were at the luncheon," Brett continued. "I understand that officers, committee chairpeople, and representatives were the ones who attended."

"Yes. It's the same every year. Where is the paper in this desk, Susan?" Ellen was busily rummaging through Jed's antique partner's desk drawers.

"Let me." Susan gently displaced the other woman and went quickly to the place where supplies were kept. She knew how Jed would hate to think of others going through his things. "Here are the pencils, too." She handed them out, but when everything was sorted and distributed, she found herself sitting on the couch, while Brett and Ellen were sharing the large mahogany surface, papers and pens spread efficiently between them.

To put it bluntly, she felt left out.

In her search, Ellen had even found a duplicate copy of the PTA's information sheet and, ignoring her, the two others reviewed the list Susan had thought she and Brett had finished.

"Let's see," Ellen began, "Julia Ames and Charline Voos, and Susan, of course. Susan always shows up where she's supposed to be."

Susan knew that, coming from someone who held Ellen's values, that was a compliment, so why did it sound so very, very dull?

". . . and Patsy Webber . . ."

57

"But she wasn't there," Susan interrupted.

"Of course, her father's surgery. I'd forgotten. Well, I think everyone else was. Fanny Berman, Nancy Dobbs, Paula Porter and Jan Ick—do you think being on the same committee was something more than a coincidence, Detective Fortesque?—and Martha Hallard, Susan again, Carol Mann, myself, Angie Leachman, and"—she paused—". . . of course, we said Martha before. That's eleven people. Do we know who was at the pool yesterday afternoon, besides Paula and Susan and myself, that is?"

"I didn't see you," Susan cried.

"I was on the far courts practicing my backhand. I thought if I spent all day on it, it would improve. It didn't, of course, but hope springs eternal."

Susan got up again from the couch and leaned across the desk to look at the notes they were writing on the list.

"I saw both Julia and Charline there. They were together leaving the bar when I went in for my tea. And Fanny and I sat and talked for a while inside. In fact, she was with me when I choked . . ."

"Choked?" Brett was immediately interested.

"Just a small piece of ice caught in my throat." She suspected that he was disappointed that the accident had been so minimal.

"Who else?" Ellen prompted.

"Let me think. Nancy was there. And Kevin was wonderful getting the kids out of the way after Paula's death, you know . . ."

"Kevin's her husband?" Brett asked, making a mark on the list.

"No, Kevin is her son . . ."

"The son of her husband by his first marriage," Ellen elaborated. "He's working as a pool boy at the Club this summer."

"Yes, Mrs. Henshaw told me about the family's rather old-fashioned values," Brett acknowledged.

"They may be old-fashioned, but they work," Ellen responded, a touch of asperity in her voice. She had similar values and preferred to think of them as standards, and high ones at that.

"Of course," Susan continued, "Paula was there . . ." She hurried on with the list. "Martha Hallard was there; she stopped by to tell me about the dinner party she's having tonight. The mayor's coming and she wants a promise of financial support from the town for the school's participation in the centennial celebration—or something like that. I wasn't paying much attention. Although, come to think of it, it's surprising that she's sleeping late the day she's giving a party.

"Anyway, Carol Mann stopped in later in the afternoon. The shop has shorter hours in the summer and she's been getting the kids to the pool around one every afternoon. I didn't see Angie Leachman, though," Susan finished.

"I can help you there," Ellen interjected. "She was in the clubhouse changing when I was getting on my shorts. That was around noon. She was putting on her swimsuit."

"She probably stayed next to the kiddy pool watching her younger ones," Susan suggested. "I didn't get over there."

"So everyone on the board who was at the luncheon was also at the pool yesterday?" Brett summed up.

Ellen and Susan looked at each other before answering. Ellen spoke first. "But there must be some other suspects: teachers, or administrators, or someone from outside the group."

"Well, let's think about that." He yawned. "Could you get us some coffee or tea, Mrs. Henshaw?"

Susan leapt up. "Of course. Do you want some, Ellen?"

"I shouldn't, but I will. I didn't sleep very well last night and I was up baking early this morning. Do you need any help getting it?"

"No, of course not. It'll just take a second." Susan hurried from the room. She was in the kitchen filling the teapot with water and examining the not-too-careful job of cleaning that Chrissy had done on the floor when she began asking herself some serious questions.

So whom do I suspect? She put the pot on the stove, turned off the water, sat down at the table, and thought. All this time, she hadn't seriously considered the identity of the murderer. Oh, she had thought about the deaths, and the loss of her friends, but she hadn't considered the murderer. And that it must be someone she knew: one of the names she and Brett and Ellen had just been discussing.

But there was no one on that list of eleven people who could have killed twice. Okay, so she had been rather a Pollyanna when describing them and their families to Brett Fortesque; it was true, and everyone knew it, that Nancy Dobbs drank more than was good for her, but the other thing everyone knew was that her husband had never really gotten over the death of his first wife. Competing with a tragically dead young woman would drive anyone to drink. And if Carol Mann was less than a bright young person, well, she didn't come from the same background as the rest of us. She hadn't even gone to college; had married her husband (then an MP on an army base somewhere in the South) right out of high school and had gotten pregnant immediately or sooner. If even adding up figures on the sales slips in the shop would have been impossible for her without a calculator, well, everyone understood, and knew, that it was very difficult to be an outsider in a town as homogeneous as Hancock. Certainly no one would mention that the Manns could never have belonged to the Club if John Mann hadn't acted as security guard at all club functions. And everyone did feel more secure with an armed and trained person around, even if he was socializing in the clubhouse at the same time as he was "keeping his eyes peeled." (His words.)

And, of course, to suggest that Martha Hallard was pushy would be an understatement to the point of absurdity, but she did get things done. And, when you think of pushy, wouldn't Julia and Charline come to mind more quickly than anyone else in their group? She wondered if she or Ellen should mention that election for the presidency of the PTA a few months ago. That had been back before the luncheon, and Paula, if not Jan, had been a part of the nominating committee that had made such a fiasco out of the whole thing, besides picking the wrong people to run the PTA. It wasn't as if Julia and Charline had done such a great job this past year that they deserved a repeat performance. But the whole story was petty and bitchy, if true. And she and Ellen had agreed that the best thing to do would be just to avoid the subject if it ever came up. Surely it couldn't possibly have anything to do with murder. After all, if Carol had gotten over the hurt of being rejected, she and Ellen could do it, too.

So just what was Ellen telling. . . ?

Loud sizzling sounds and steam rising from the top of her range informed her of the overflow of the teapot and she rushed to get the mess cleaned up and the coffee, filter, and water mixed together in the top of a small Melitta. She had always wondered why she had two coffeepots; the theory was that she could brew decaf and regular for dinner parties, but she never had that she could remember. Anyway, the spare would be handy now, if she could find it. She knew it was somewhere in the back of one of the—

"Susan, what are you doing up on that stool? You look like a cartoon of a housewife who just saw a mouse. You didn't, did you?" Ellen asked, entering the kitchen.

"Of course not. I was just looking for my extra coffeepot. This morning I broke the one I usually use and—"

"Instant will do. Get down from there and get out the mugs," Ellen ordered, going to the cupboard where Susan kept coffee and tea.

Susan was relieved, and not a little irritated. Why did she always make such a big fuss when, of course, instant would be fine? And why did Ellen always seem to know what to do?

61

"Did you tell the officer about the PTA elections this spring?" Ellen's voice was a semiwhisper and she looked toward the door while speaking. "It's not, of course, that I want to keep any secrets from the police, but I don't think that's part of this and—"

"I didn't say anything. Don't worry. I agree with you. That couldn't have anything to do with the murders. Although Paula was on the nominating committee—the chairman of it, actually, and—"

"But the only person who would have wanted to murder the chairman of that committee was one of us: you or me. And I know it wasn't me."

Susan stopped in the middle of putting her best cups and saucers on a tray and turned to her friend, "You don't think it was me, do you?"

"Of course not. Just kidding. But as long as you didn't mention it . . ."

"I said I didn't . . ."

"Can I help with anything in here?"

Susan wondered if they both had guilty expressions on their faces when Brett Fortesque entered the kitchen. She didn't dare look at Ellen's face, but she knew that her own left something to be desired.

"We were just getting the coffee. Do you take cream or sugar, Detective Fortesque?" She quickly turned to the refrigerator for supplies, without waiting for an answer.

"Black, thank you. Could we get on with this, though? I have to meet one of my colleagues for lunch and . . ."

"Of course. Just sit down at the table and Susan will finish getting the coffee. You don't mind talking in the kitchen, do you? I feel more comfortable in here myself, and—"

"Anyplace is fine with me," he assured Ellen. "Now, about the rest of the people who were at the luncheon as well as at the pool yesterday. Did either of you remember anyone else who was in both places?"

So they hadn't been discussing that while she was getting

the coffee. So what had they been talking about? Susan asked herself. "Let me think," she said aloud.

"Well, there's Mr. Johnson, the gym teacher," Ellen began. "He might have been there."

"Oh, I don't think so," Susan said. "He was out of town at a convention or meeting in the City. I heard two of the lifeguards talking about it."

"He's a member of the Field Club?" Brett wanted to know.

"Of course not. He runs the athletic program for the kids in the summer," Susan corrected before she realized what she was saying. "Not that a teacher couldn't join the Club . . ."

"Of course they could. Our teachers are wonderful people. And we would love to have them as members; it's just that most teachers have to work in the summer . . ."

"Hancock has the highest starting pay of any school district in the state, Detective Fortesque. Don't think that we are underpaying our teachers, because we're not . . ."

"I don't think anything of the kind," he assured the two women. "So Mr. Johnson wasn't at the Club yesterday. Does anyone else from the faculty work at the Club?"

"No, but Dr. Tyrrell was there yesterday . . ."

"Who?" Brett asked.

"Dr. Charles Tyrrell, the principal of the school," Susan reminded him.

"Are you sure, Susan? Why would he have been there?" Ellen asked.

"I have no idea. I saw his car drive up right after I got there."

"And what time was that, Mrs. Henshaw?"

"I think about noon. That's the time I usually go, and Chad had swim-team practice at one-thirty, so I know we were there by that time. He was driving into the parking lot while I was getting the kids' towels and things out of the trunk."

"You're sure it was him?"

"Yes. He drove right past me and we waved to each other."

"Did you see where he went?"

"No, I got the kids inside before he had parked his car. He parked down toward the clubhouse, not near the path to the pool, so maybe he was meeting someone there."

"That's interesting, Mrs. Henshaw. Anyone else?"

"Not that I saw," Susan answered.

He looked at Ellen.

"No, I didn't see anyone else either," she answered slowly. "But we wouldn't have seen everyone at the Club. It's a big place and anyone could have been out on the golf course and we would never have known they were there. You'll be checking with other people?"

"Certainly." He stood up. "In fact, I should be getting on with that now." He moved toward the door. "You've both been very helpful. I'll call on you again when I need more information, if I may?"

He had almost left the room before Susan had a chance to stand up. "Let me see you out."

"Don't bother. You've done so much already. I can see myself out. Sit back and have your coffee."

There wasn't much Susan could do except take his suggestion, but neither she nor Ellen even so much as filled their cups until they heard his car start up, and neither said anything until a few minutes after it had driven off down the street. Then Susan poured the boiling water into the porcelain cups she had waiting, picked up the sugar bowl, and, placing all this on a tray, carried it over to the table where Ellen was sitting. And even then, neither woman knew where to begin.

"You went over the names of everyone on the board with him?" Ellen asked, stirring two teaspoons of sugar into her coffee.

"Yes, that's what he came back for this morning."

"Came back? When did you talk to him the first time?"

Now that it was sweetened, Ellen appeared to lose interest in the brew, and pushed it aside. "Was he in town after Jan's death in June?"

"No. I don't know that anyone but the local police were involved then." Susan took a big gulp from her cup. She realized it was the first coffee she'd had all day.

"So when did you first talk to him?" Ellen persisted.

"Last night. He came here right after I had finished cooking the kids' dinner . . ."

"Oh?"

"Yes, he said that in the reports of Jan's death, the reports that the local police made, I guess, my name came up several times. You know I'm an officer and I run the library." She didn't think Ellen would take kindly to the idea that Susan was considered an authority on something that she herself wasn't, and offered her positions as an excuse. "And, of course, I was at the teachers' lunch and sitting in a chair right next to Paula yesterday—"

"You weren't just at the lunch. You were standing right next to Jan when she died. Remember?"

Could she forget? But there was no time to answer before the phone rang. It was within grabbing distance of her chair, so she didn't have to get up. "Hello? It's for you." She handed the receiver to Ellen, and then she sat and drank her coffee. A mother didn't need privacy to speak to one of her children. From the sound of it, Ellen had forgotten one of her daughter's commitments.

"Can't your father take you? He's what? Okay, sweetie, don't get upset. I'll come home, but you better think of something to give her that we can pick up quickly on the way. I don't know what. Well, we'll just have to skip wrapping it. But that isn't very important, is it? Just get into your pink dress and brush your hair. I'll leave now." She hung up.

"Bethany is going to be late for Cindy Silverstein's birthday party, and Bob had to go into the office on some sort of emergency. I'd better scoot. I hate buying gifts for kids I

65

don't know." She stopped rushing to give Susan a hug. "You won't forget about the food for the Porters, will you? I'll call this afternoon."

But before she got to the door, she turned back to Susan. "I really would like to know what Dr. Tyrrell was doing at the Club yesterday. I don't think I've ever seen him there. Oh well, I'll call."

Susan drained her cup and placed it on the tray. She picked up Ellen's untouched coffee and put it beside hers, then carried both back to the counter. There waited the detective's cup: still empty. If he hadn't wanted coffee, why had he asked for it? She opened her dishwasher and started putting the dishes inside. The answer came to her, so obvious it couldn't be refuted.

He hadn't wanted coffee, just a chance to talk to Ellen alone.

So what had Ellen told him?

Six

───◆◆◆───

"And how do you know this Mrs. Henshaw isn't just feeding you a lot of misinformation? How do you know she's not the murderer? She was the closest person to both the victims when they died, as far as we know. What reason do you have to trust her?" The questions were coming from Officer Kathleen Somerville and directed at Brett Fortesque. She was sitting in the passenger's seat of the car he had driven away from the Henshaws. If she had expected another leisurely meal like breakfast had been, she was disappointed. Brett had picked her up at the Hancock municipal building and driven her straight down the street to Burger King. And if she was disappointed, she wasn't showing it, nor was she showing a continued dedication to the healthy way she had begun her day. She munched her Whopper and large fries as though she had never heard of cholesterol.

"I don't know she isn't the murderer," he admitted slowly. "My instincts tell me she isn't, but they don't necessarily count. I could be wrong."

"You could be," she agreed, scrounging around in the paper bag. "Any more catsup in here?"

He handed her a small metal packet that had fallen on the floor beside his seat, noting her cheerful willingness to accept the possibility that he was mistaken. "I'm trying to get some impressions from her. Not facts."

"And what are your impressions?" The catsup had squirted

out the wrong end of the container and she was busy trying to rub some of the sticky red goo from her skirt.

He took his time answering. "I'm not sure. She's not being totally open with me . . ."

"Well, that's significant. Is she hiding something specific? Do you think she knows who did it?" She balled up the dirty napkin and threw it into the bag.

"No, I don't think that. I think she's being too nice. She doesn't want to say exactly what she thinks about the other women. She shies away from any disclosure about disagreements or competition within the group."

"Competition? You mean like who wears the most expensive clothes? Whose husband is cutest? Real serious stuff, right?"

"Hey. How come all the prejudice? What's wrong with being a suburban housewife?"

"Everything. These women don't work for what they have. Their husbands buy it for them. They don't have anything real to do. It's like the women's movement passed them by. Look at where the murders took place: a ladies' lunch and a discriminatory country club. How nineteen-fifties can you get? These women are thirty years behind the times. It's not that I don't like them. I just can't take them seriously." She took an angry sip from her coffee.

"You'd better. One of them is probably a murderer." He crumpled his Styrofoam containers angrily. "This is not the time to let your personal feelings interfere with your judgment, Officer Somerville."

She didn't look at him, but emptied the last of her drink out the open window. "I won't, sir."

It was interesting how much sarcasm she could pack into the three-letter, one-syllable word. Brett decided to ignore it. "So what did you learn this morning? I hope the locals keep good records."

"Actually, they do. I was surprised, considering the way they bungled the aftermath of Mrs. Porter's death yesterday."

"And?" he prompted.

She pulled a couple of sheets of legal-size lined paper from her briefcase and began. "The town of Hancock has one dispatcher and one emergency number for all situations: a police problem, a fire, or a medical emergency. At two-eighteen P.M. on June second, Officer Craddock was answering the phones and received a call from Julia Ames requesting that a paramedic team come to her home at 144 Grant Place, that a woman had choked. A tape recording of all calls is made automatically. Because of the seriousness of this crime, the day's tape was saved and is available.

"The dispatcher sent out a call for the paramedics from the hospital in Cranport and they responded in an emergency vehicle with respirators, et cetera. At the same time, she called out the local volunteer first-aid squad and alerted all the police via their car radios."

"How many police cars responded?"

"Three. Hancock has a very well-equipped department. There are six cars—five of them on the road at all times—and three shifts of six officers each. Anyway, two of the other officers were busy with a stakeout of some sort. It had to do with a drug problem in the high school. I can find out more about that." She made a note in the margin of the sheet from which she was reading. "A patrol car was cruising just around the corner and answered the call first. I have a copy of the report the officer in that car filed here." She pulled it out of the briefcase. "It's very complete. He arrived at the scene at two twenty-two and proceeded to the back of the building. A large Georgian home on two acres was the description given in the report. There was a woman standing on the curb who motioned to him that he had the right place when he got there."

"Any idea who that was?"

"A Mrs. Carol Mann. It seems her husband is a police officer and she knew that there should be no time wasted by any emergency personnel peering up the wide lawns for the correct address, so she ran out front to signal. Good thinking, I thought."

"Go on."

"Well, Officer Harvey, the policeman who arrived first, was waved around to the backyard by Mrs. Mann and he found three or four dozen people. Wait, I want to quote him: '. . . standing around with their mouths open and their plates in their hands, staring at a woman lying on the ground . . .'"

"Like they had just received a shock while eating," he said without a smile.

"Uh, yes." She noticed his expression and put an equally serious one on her face before answering. "Anyway, Officer Harvey ran over to the woman lying on the ground, and, he says, she was already dead as far as he could tell. There was no movement, no breathing . . ."

"All signs of death, in fact."

She heard his impatience, but checked her annoyance at it. If he could spend a whole morning and most of an evening "getting impressions" from a housewife, he had time for her report.

"He didn't do anything to her. He reports that he was just bending over the body when the Cranport Hospital emergency vehicle arrived. Unlike the police cars, it came right up into the driveway and kept its equipment available."

"Mrs. Mann again."

"Yes, she did a good job. She directed the ambulance into the driveway and kept all the police cars out. That way, the respirator was available to Jan Ick and no one blocked the ambulance, which was presumably going to be making an emergency run to the hospital. Well, it didn't take long for the paramedics to see that there was really no reason to bother with the respirator. As a matter of form, they kept her on it all the way to the hospital emergency room. But she was obviously dead before they got her into the ambulance."

"But did they know she had been poisoned at that time?"

"No. According to other reports—"

"You don't have to quote. Just tell me the gist of them."

"Well, they knew that she hadn't had a heart attack, which is what they see the most of, and they knew that she was dead, but cyanide poisoning is a little out of the league of most paramedics. Their poisoning cases are usually kids who decide to drink a bottle of sweet cough syrup while Mommy is busy, or once, I understand, a suicide who downed a whole bottle of ammonia." She stopped and shuddered.

"So they didn't know until the autopsy what had killed her."

"Right, but someone did have the sense to stop everyone from eating any of the other food, even what was on the people's plates at that time. That was an Officer Richards. He had them put down their plates and then the police gathered up the food later—while they were questioning guests—to be analyzed for poison."

"And where else did they find it? Besides in the—was it a sandwich that Mrs. Ick was eating?"

"It was just in that sandwich. The small bit still undigested in her stomach and the tiny dab of filling that had fallen out on the plate she was holding were the only two places poison was found. Aside from that, there was no sign of cyanide anywhere." She looked at him and shook her head. "It doesn't make any sense, but there's no hint that they missed anything."

"They checked the kitchen scraps, the garbage?"

"Everything, as far as I can tell. They even took food that belonged to the Ameses out of the refrigerator and checked that. The garbage cans were emptied, but it was pretty early in the party and there wasn't much waste yet. Also, all the women were searched and their possessions were checked.

71

There was no sign that anyone carried poison into the group. You can read the reports for yourself."

"I will. Go on."

"Well, the paramedics took Mrs. Ick to the hospital. The police kept everyone else there until they got organized . . ."

"And then?"

"Then they took statements from all present. I have copies of them here. I know, you'll read them later." He nodded. "Well, it's quite a job. There were eleven members of the PTA board there—not counting Mrs. Ick, of course, and eighteen teachers and administrators . . ."

"Eighteen? I thought this was a kindergarten-through-fifth-grade elementary school?"

"Yes, but there was the gym teacher, the art teacher—"

"The librarian, et cetera," he finished for her. "Of course, I was forgetting that modern education can't get along with just a teacher in each classroom. Sorry I interrupted."

"No problem. The statements were taken according to procedure. Each person was interviewed separately and all the interviews were taped as well as taken down in short-hand."

"By whom?"

"Well, that part wasn't quite regulation. It seems that no one in the police department is trained to take dictation, and so they called for a volunteer. Mrs. Ames said that she could do it and so they asked her to."

"Mrs. Ames? The president of the PTA?"

"One of the co-presidents, yes. So they—"

"You're telling me that one of the members of the PTA sat in on every interview? That no one was interviewed with only the police present?"

"Well, that's how I understand it," she admitted. "You think that may have caused a problem or a bias of some sort?"

"Unless Mrs. Ames is universally loved and trusted by

every member of the PTA board and by all the teachers and whoever else was there, yes, I think it may have made a difference." He sighed. "But I don't suppose there is anything we can do about that now. It does seem to me, however, that the Hancock police department has gone out of their way to obfuscate the facts in this case."

"Do you want me to go on?"

"Did anything in particular stand out in the interviews?" he asked.

"Just that no one could see how it was done. Mrs. Ick went up to the table for seconds after the majority of people had served themselves and gone off to eat and, evidently, took a sandwich from the tray, ate it, and died. The person closest to her at that time was your Mrs. Henshaw. And it happened so quickly that no one really noticed very much."

Brett ignored the possessive pronoun in front of Susan's name. "Were there any theories as to the reason for her death?"

"I know what you mean. Usually everyone has an idea why the dead person was killed. But in this case that doesn't seem to be true. And the local police are baffled. There appears to be no motive as to why it happened and no way that anyone could possibly know that she was going to pick up that particular sandwich. Unless . . ."

"Unless?" he prompted, when she didn't continue.

"Unless she didn't pick up the sandwich. Unless it was put on her plate by the person who had put the poison in it—the only person who would know which sandwich had poison in it on a trayful of identical sandwiches. And the only person who could have done that was your Mrs. Henshaw. She was the only other person up at the table when the death occurred."

"And how did she keep someone else from taking that particular sandwich the first time everyone came up for food?"

"Ah . . . well, I don't know," admitted Kathleen who had been growing fonder of her theory every second.

"The food came from where? A caterer?" Brett asked.

"Oh, no. It was brought by the parents. That's the point of the lunch—the PTA makes it for the teachers. I understand that everyone brings a dish. I don't know whether they're all homemade or not."

"Can you check that out?"

"Of course." Another note.

"And will you find out the arrangement of tables and chairs, who was sitting where and how the food was placed on the tables?"

"Oh, I have some of that. I have a diagram of the food on the tables—it was made before the stuff was taken off to the lab. But there's nothing about where everyone was sitting. Maybe we could piece that information together from the interviews. Most people mentioned where they were sitting. The layout of the whole yard is easy. It's about two hundred feet square. There is a rectangular pool at the side farthest from the house. Perpendicular to that to your left as you face the pool is a long perennial flower garden running the entire distance from the patio to the pool. The food was set up on tables on the other side of the lawn. Three tables for the salads and main dishes and one round table for wine and coffee. Then the tables themselves—the ones the people sat at to eat—were set up in three rows of two tables each, perpendicular to the pool and the patio. I understand there is shade in that part of the garden during the early afternoon and it was a warm day."

"The food on the lawn was in the sun?"

"No, there are large trees over that area also, as I understand it. Shouldn't we go and have a look at the scene of the crime?"

"Yes, and soon, but first I want to spend some time going through these statements."

"And I . . . ?"

74

"How far away is the Ames house?"

"From where we are now? About five minutes, I'd say. Nothing is very far from anything else in this town."

"Tell you what. Why don't you drive back to the municipal building and we'll see if the autopsy report on Mrs. Porter is in. Then you can drive us to the Ameses'. I'll take the time to read through this. Okay?"

"No problem." He got out and she slid across the seat to the driver's side, her skirt catching on a piece of loose vinyl and sliding up her thigh as she did so.

Hmm. A garter belt was holding up those sheer stockings, Brett noted. He wondered if that meant anything.

"But I don't think the report's due until this evening," she told him, jerking down her skirt.

He shrugged. "We may as well give it a try." He was already skimming through the inch-thick pile of Xeroxes and continued to do so after their return to the municipal building, while Kathleen went inside. Part of the reason Brett had risen so quickly in his department was this ability to concentrate totally on something, no matter what was going on around him. But Kathleen Somerville did not just run into the building and back out, and after she had been gone for about five minutes, he completed the last page of the pile and put the whole thing back into its manila folder. He looked out the window at the curved beds of geraniums and white marigolds that swirled up and around the wide lawn before the building, but he didn't see them.

Either these women were extraordinarily serious about their positions in the PTA, or something else was going on here.

"It doesn't make any sense," he mumbled out loud, but to himself. "Why would there be so many lies?"

Seven

———◆◆———

"Maybe we should have called ahead and let them know we were coming." Kathleen brushed her hair off her forehead and turned the police car into the long flower-lined drive to the house.

"Maybe . . ."

"No, there's a van back by the garage. Someone must be here."

"Drive up closer. We may as well park there too. I doubt if anyone really wants a marked state-patrol car in front of their home. Especially a home like this one. Looks like one of the houses in the Cadillac ads."

She followed his directions and soon their vehicle was stopped beside a truck belonging to the Haskill Pool Service—"Cleaning—Repairs—Maintenance." When they got out, they could hear the voices of the employees of Haskills' coming from the back of the house.

"Wait. Let's look out there."

"But . . ."

"Come on," he insisted, starting without her. He knew that they could use the work crew as an excuse to look at the property without the owner's permission. How were they to know that it was merely the workmen's voices they heard? Although he doubted very much that the pool's owners inspected every little bit of maintenance . . . The two police officers walked through the opening in the tall hedge and entered the well-kept yard. Everything was as the description in the police reports had led them to expect, except more luxurious. The emerald grass was obviously receiving a great deal of care; there was not a weed or bare patch to be seen. The flower bed running along the far side of the lawn was an abundant display of various varieties, all seemingly at peak bloom. The patio, covered with an awning of thin multicolored stripes, was brick. And all around sat unusual redwood furniture, cushioned with plump pads that matched the fabric overhead. Here, too, flowers rioted in pots of clay, brass, copper, and ceramic. At the opposite side of the space was the pool: a large expanse of water, surrounded by gleaming ceramic tiles and more furniture. Four men, dressed in matching overalls that proclaimed their alliance with the Haskill Pool Service, were clustered around one of the ladders by which swimmers entered and exited the water. Their positions and the seriousness of their expressions reminded Brett of doctors consulting over a critically ill patient.

"Do you think it could possibly take four men to do whatever they're doing?" Kathleen asked, more to say something than because she was at all interested.

"In Hancock it always takes large crews to accomplish anything. I know it sounds like one of those horrible Polish light-bulb jokes, but there is a good reason behind it all. If it takes four men to do the work of one, then the bill can be four times higher." This was spoken by a tall, striking blond. "Hi, I'm Julia Ames." She held out her hand to Kathleen.

"Kathleen Somerville, Officer Somerville," she corrected herself. "We're from the—"

"State police," Julia finished for her. She was now shaking hands with Brett Fortesque. "And you're?"

"Detective Fortesque. Brett Fortesque," he said, impressed with the almost professional poise of the woman before him. How many other people had he met who would take the presence of two police officers in their backyard on a summer Saturday with such aplomb?

"Of course. I saw your car in the driveway. And I've been expecting you. What do you think about the scene of the crime?" She smiled and waved her arm to encompass the entire area.

"It's hard to imagine a less likely place for a murder," Kathleen answered honestly.

"Well, I don't know." Julia Ames laughed politely. "If those men don't fix that ladder correctly this time, I may murder them. Twice this season I've slipped off that thing into the water. And yesterday my son hit his head on the side of the pool when those steps shifted. Someone is going to get killed unless they find a better way to anchor them. Oh well, that's not what you came to talk about, I know. Why don't we all sit down?" She motioned to the chairs. "I could get us something to eat or drink, if you're hungry."

"Nothing, thanks." Brett declined for them both. "We would like to talk to you, though, if you have the the time."

"Of course. I've been waiting for you to come ever since I heard you were in town."

"You were?" He didn't bother to ask how she had heard of their presence. He knew that in a town this size and an organization this tight, word would travel quickly.

"Yes, because Jan was killed here, of course. And because I was at the Club yesterday when poor Paula died. That was murder too, wasn't it, Inspector?" She turned all her attention and charm on Brett.

"We think so, Mrs. Ames. And the title is Detective, not Inspector."

"Well, why don't you call me Julia and I'll call you Brett and we won't have to worry about titles? Now"—she sat back in a lounge, placing her well-tanned legs on a small footstool before her—"just what do you want me to tell you, Brett?"

"How did it happen that you were the person who took notes when the police interviewed everyone after the PTA lunch, Julia? Did someone on the force know that you knew shorthand, or was there a general request for help to the group from one of the police?"

"No, it wasn't like that at all. Let me think for a while. You know"—she directed her wide blue eyes at Kathleen this time—"I've kept going over that afternoon in my mind. Over and over. But I hadn't thought about that part of it before. You work with a very interesting man, Officer Somerville." A shy, almost coy glance at Brett followed this remark. Not allowing time for Kathleen to answer, she continued, "What happened was that after the body—Mrs. Ick—was taken away in the ambulance, the police requested that everyone gather here on the patio. I guess they wanted to keep us away from the food, although at the time no one was thinking about it. We were all so upset. Some of us were crying, some acting almost like they were in shock—just going through the motions, but not really aware of what was happening around them. Do you know what I mean? After all, Brett, a PTA lunch is not the type of place you expect a murder . . ." She paused for a second before continuing. "I remember that we all did just what the police asked, although a lot of the people were here already. I remember Miss McGovern was almost passed out on this lounge. We were really worried about her. She's one of our third-grade teachers and quite elderly."

"And so the police asked you all to gather here and then they asked for a volunteer to . . ." Brett prompted, trying to return to the subject.

"No. We all came here and sat around. No one really knew what to do or say. And the police were at that end of the yard"—she nodded toward the pool—"and they stood around talking.

"And then Carol Mann—her husband is a cop in town and she was—well, she must have been at that end of the lawn talking to the police—she came over and asked me if I knew shorthand. Well, I do. I think everyone in the PTA knows that I write notes in shorthand at all the meetings, but maybe she didn't know how fast I was or anything, so I told her yes. And she went back to the men—her husband was there, of course—and then an Officer Harvey came over and asked me if I would mind taking notes while each person was interviewed. Naturally I said yes."

"Naturally. And you didn't feel very uncomfortable listening to the statements of the others? It didn't put you in an awkward position?"

"No. Why should it have? We're all friends in the PTA, Officer Somerville, and at the time, it just seemed like a formality. It wasn't until that evening, after we heard that the paramedics thought the death was caused by poisoning, that I realized that one of us had to be a murderer."

"It's—"

"It's not the type of thing you think about one of your friends, or the teachers of your children, Brett."

"I'm sure it's not." He fingered through the papers he had been carrying. "Would you go over your own statement with us?"

"Of course. Oh, you have it right there. Could I look at it just to refresh my memory?" She held out her hand, obviously not expecting to be turned down.

"You took notes on your own statement as well as on everyone else's?" Kathleen asked, watching the bits of sunlight that the awning allowed through shine on Julia's hair as she bent over the document. Had the colors been chosen because they complimented the mistress of the house so well?

"Yes. Who else? I can assure you that I did not change anything on the statement. After all, it was made in the presence of two officers."

"Where?"

"Excuse me?"

"Where did the questioning take place?"

"I didn't understand. In my husband's study. It's that room—right through the French doors there." She pointed to glass doors leading off the far side of the patio.

80

"So each person who was questioned was alone with two policemen and yourself?"

"Yes. I remember now," she added. "But I don't know what you want me to add to it or say about it. It seems very clear to me."

Brett held out his hand and took the document from her. Without comment, he began to read aloud.

"'My name is Julia Ames. I'm thirty-three years old and my husband and I have lived at this address for nine years. I have two children ages six and eight, both of whom attend Hancock Elementary School. I'm co-president of the PTA at the school. Charline Voos is the other co-president and we've had the jobs this whole year. The PTA lunch was held at my home today, starting at noon, and it was supposed to end at three. I was sitting at one of the side tables, near the flower garden, when Jan died. The other people at the table, besides Jan, were Charline Voos, Dr. Charles Tyrrell, the school principal, Linda Smith, the kindergarten teacher (my son had her last year), and Beverly Anderson one of the teachers for first grade this past year. Also, Corrine DeAngelo, the art teacher. My daughter Constance is an excellent art student and Corrine teaches art for all grades.

"'I was the first to get my food. As usual, everyone was hesitant to be first in the buffet line—no one wants to look piggish—so I thought it was my duty as hostess to start the ball rolling. Charlie—Dr. Tyrrell, that is—was right behind me. In fact, most of the people at my table selected their food first, except for Charline. She waited until everyone was finished to get hers. That way she could keep an eye on things: to see if we needed to bring out seconds from the kitchen or if more wine needed opening, stuff like that.

"'I chose our table because it was an outside one. I wanted to be able to move easily between the kitchen and the phone and the buffet tables. Usually, at these functions, someone's child or housekeeper has an emergency and needs to get hold of a parent. Also, there was a dessert to come out after the main course. But I had planned for it. The lunch was held at my house before, last year, when I was vice-president of the PTA, so I was familiar with the things that could happen. We ate our meal rather slowly. Partially because we were first to get it and didn't have to rush, and partially because we were listening to Corrine describe the trip she is taking this summer to Europe. Part of the trip is being funded by a grant that the PTA gives a teacher each year to study or to work on a specific project. I helped Corrine get that grant, in fact. Not that I have more than one vote on our board, but of course there are lots of people who come to meetings who really aren't very involved in the school, not like board members are, and it is sometimes easy to convince them what is important and what isn't.

"'Anyway, we all had finished eating when there was a scream. I think it was Susan Henshaw who screamed, but I'm not sure. And everyone ran to the food tables. My table got there later than everyone else—we were farthest away—and then we saw Jan. She was lying on the ground. I think Nancy Dobbs was the person to say that she was dead, but really we could all see that. No one touched her. I think Charlie ordered everyone away from her, but I'm not sure. And I ran into the house to call the police. I don't know why I didn't use the extension on the patio, I just didn't think of it, I guess. Anyway, I called the emergency number and heard the sirens go off and in a few minutes the police were here. They were followed very shortly by an ambulance. Jan was put on some sort of machine and then taken off to the hospital. That's all I know.'"

"Is there anything you'd like to add to that statement, Mrs. Ames?"

"No, nothing," she answered, either not noticing or choosing to ignore the more formal address.

"What can you tell me about the rest of that day?"

"I don't understand." Her confusion appeared real.

"What happened after you ended your statement? How

long was it before the guests and the police left? When did your family come home? Or were they here all along?"

"Oh, I see. Of course, I remember that. Let me think for a minute, though." She stared out at the pool men still busy with the broken ladder.

"My kids were at Charline's house with her housekeeper. Actually, they didn't come home until quite late that night. They stayed there for dinner."

"And that had been planned that way?"

"No, but it took quite a lot of time to pack up. And they didn't just take the food on the buffet tables, but all the desserts in the kitchen and the bottles of wine—even the unopened ones. Anyway, there were police in my yard and my kitchen for hours. I think until five or six o'clock, so we decided to keep the kids away."

"We?"

"Charline and I. She was one of the last to leave, but she called her housekeeper about the change in plans."

"Any reason why she was here longer than most?"

"Nothing significant. She stayed to help."

"Why Charline and not someone else?"

"Because she's my best friend and she's in and out of my home all the time. She knows her way around here; she could show the police where everything was. And then she helped get cold drinks for everybody who had to wait to be questioned."

"From where?" Kathleen jumped in, having been silent all this time.

"From the refrigerator and freezer in the basement playroom. We had to convince the police that nothing had been moved from that floor of the house all day long, but then they let us serve cold soft drinks and lemonade. It was really a very hot day, and with the shock and all, everyone was very thirsty. The police, too."

"And your husband?"

"He came home early that night. Probably he remembered

that the lunch was going to be here and he came to help clean up. I don't remember . . ."

"How early?"

"Between four and five, I think. And he pitched right in helping the police get everything loaded into the vans they had brought and making sure that everyone who was too upset to drive home had a driver. He even drove Mrs. Clancy home himself, and she lives over in Westchester."

"And you?" Brett didn't seem terribly interested in the good deeds of Mr. Ames, especially those that took him on a drive of less than ten miles into the neighboring state.

"Well, everyone was gone by five-thirty, I'd guess, and the police had taken everything they needed, so I left Gertie to straighten up the kitchen and—"

"Gertie?"

"My housekeeper. Anyway, she's been with us two years now and I knew I could trust her to do everything right, so, since Charline had the kids, Miles and I went out to dinner at the Hancock Inn. We picked up the kids on our way home. And that's it, as far as I can remember." She recrossed her slim ankles and looked from one police officer to the other. "Is there anything else?"

"What does your husband do for a living?" Brett asked.

"He's in the import/export business. Mostly clothes and yard goods, but also some hard goods. He's very successful." She looked around her home as if to prove it to herself and the others.

"And what did you do before you were married?"

"Why," she looked surprised and answered with a slight laugh. "I was his secretary, of course. Why else would I know shorthand?"

Brett considered Susan's assumption that Julia Ames had had a glamorous job designing clothes and then decided that there was a great need to double-check everything in this case. "You've been more than helpful, Julia. I think that Charline Voos is next. Would you mind taking the time to call her and see if she is home for us? We'll walk down to the back of the yard while you're doing that, unless you'd rather we didn't?"

"Of course not. I'll just be a second." She got up and walked purposefully into the house.

"Come along, Officer Somerville." Brett got up and left the patio in the opposite direction, Kathleen following.

"Why did you give her a chance to warn her friend that we were coming?" she asked quietly.

"Shhh. Did you think that she wouldn't phone to her best friend the moment we left anyway? And I want to see that ladder before the workmen actually fix it. Just follow along, pretend you're casually going through those statements because there is nothing else to do, but check to see if Gertrude was questioned. See if there's a statement from her in your notes."

"I . . ."

"Please do as I say. I'll be right back." And he strolled over to the workmen.

She sat on a small bench under a large larch tree and thumbed through the papers. She was quick and was finished by the time Julia Ames returned.

"Men!" Julia said, coming up to Kathleen. "Just look at them all standing around talking about that ladder. If my husband were here, he'd be back there with them, talking and waving his arms just like they are."

"Detective Fortesque is very good at these things," Kathleen said, not knowing if it was true or not.

"I hope so. The men from the pool company sure don't know what they're doing. Oh, here he comes. Maybe he can tell us what is going on."

"They're waiting for a cement worker," Brett explained without being asked. "Those poles are going to have to be reset permanently. They're very dangerous the way they are now, you know."

"That's what I told Miles, but he was always too busy to

do anything about it." She sighed. "We'll just have to use the stairs on the other side for a while, I guess."

"Did you reach Mrs. Voos?" he asked, turning his back on the pool and its problems.

"Yes, and it was lucky I called. She was just leaving the house. But she's going to put off"—she paused—"put off whatever she was going to do until you have questioned her."

"Wonderful. It's fabulous how cooperative everyone has been, isn't it, Officer Somerville?"

"Wonderful," she agreed, trying to sound a little less cloying than he.

"Well, we'll be on our way . . . oh, one more thing, Julia."

"Yes?"

Kathleen wondered if that was apprehension in the other woman's eyes; she had seemed so calm until now.

"Why wasn't Gertrude asked to make a statement the day of the murder?"

"Gertrude?" She sounded as if the name were foreign.

"Gertrude. You said that was the name of your housekeeper," he reminded her.

"It is. But no, she wasn't. Why should she be? She was in the kitchen all the time. All the serving and everything was done by PTA members. We do the luncheon for the teachers ourselves."

"Of course. I was forgetting. By the way, were you at the Field Club yesterday?"

She smiled. "I met Charline there for lunch. Both of our oldest children are on the Club's swim team, and their practice is at one-thirty on Fridays. So, since the kids had to be there in the afternoon, we met for a long lunch in the clubhouse. And then spent the day going over some plans for next year. We're going to be co-presidents again and everyone will be expecting us to outdo ourselves."

"I'm sure you will. Now, if you'll just tell us how to get to the Voos house?"

Charline Voos, it turned out, lived just three blocks away, but Hancock wasn't Manhattan and the blocks weren't square and there were, even in that short a distance, many opportunities for them to get lost. They found most of them. But the mile or two that they went out of their way gave them a chance to chat.

"What did you think?" Kathleen asked, looking ahead for legible street signs. The town tradition of placing the street names on discreet cement posts instead of standard metal rectangles made it very difficult to know where anything was.

"She's an awfully organized person to forget that there is a phone on the patio in an emergency and go all the way into the house to use one."

"You noticed that too," she said. "Who do you think she called before the police?"

"Well, we don't know before or after, but I'd say that the call was made to her husband to get him home."

"Why?"

"I don't know."

"I worked on the narcotics task force before this assignment, you know," she told him. "Import/export is a convenient business to be in if you want to get illegal things in and out of the country."

"Sure would be," he agreed. "And I wonder just what was in the house that he didn't want the police to see."

"You think drugs?"

"These days I think drugs first, last, and always, but that doesn't mean that it couldn't have been some other type of contraband."

"Do you think we should get a warrant and search the house?"

"Absolutely not. In the first place, I think it would be a waste of time. The man has had two months to find a new place to stash anything. Besides, we have only a suspicion, no evidence of any sort. And we're looking for a murderer, not a pusher, remember?"

"I remember. Hey, here it is: Yale Terrace. Turn left, Mrs. Ames said, and then it's the third house on the right . . . two . . . three. Looks like this is it. Our two co-presidents sure live on the ritzy side of town, don't they?"

"The ritzy side of a ritzy town," he agreed. "That must have been Charline Voos at the window."

"Where?"

"You just missed her. The curtain is back in line."

Kathleen pulled the car around the semicircular drive in front of the impressively large Tudor house. The lawn swept beyond them to a small stream, furnished with a tiny rustic bridge and an equally rustic gazebo. The two stepped out of their vehicle onto the cobbled walk that led to the door.

"It's funny, isn't it?" Kathleen commented, ringing the discreetly placed bell.

"How so?"

"There's no logic to the placement of houses. A Tudor sits next to a contemporary, a Colonial next to a fifties ranch, a very large fifties ranch, but still—"

"You must be Brett Fortesque. And you're Kathy Somerville," the woman who opened the door identified them. "Julia called and told me you were coming. But you must know that, of course. Please come in." She stepped back to allow them to enter while she held open the door. They walked into a hall that rose up two stories to a beamed ceiling; a dark wood stairway spiraled up the same distance, carved and picked out in gold.

"What interesting carvings," Brett noted.

"They were copied from the grand stairway at Knoll in England. At least that's what we've been told. You may find them interesting, if you like that sort of thing." She led him to the stairs, leaving Kathleen standing at the door. She took the time to examine their hostess.

As much as Julia Ames fit into her environment, Charline Voos didn't fit into hers. Like her friend, Charline Voos was a beauty: chic, well-groomed, and expensively dressed. Her year-round tan was maintained in tanning parlors when she couldn't get away in the winter, nails were done once a week, and her permanent was touched up every few months to maintain its artless crinkling, and her dark good looks contrasted nicely with Julia's cool blondness. But her house demanded a romantic type, not the best of Saks Fifth Avenue.

"This was all done before we moved in," Mrs. Voos was saying as they rejoined Kathleen. "We're in the middle of redoing the living room right now. Come on in."

The room they entered was exactly as Kathleen would have expected, had she thought about it. Here the beams, though present, had been bleached or painted or otherwise covered with a light material, the delicate details wiped out. Here Charline Voos was right at home. She sat down on a paisley couch against one wall, offering seats to the others. Two crystal pitchers sat on a tray in the middle of the large marble coffee table between them.

"Iced tea or lemonade?" she offered.

"Iced tea," Brett responded, without waiting for his partner to answer. "This is a wonderful room, Charline," he added, as she handed him the glass, a sprig of mint decorating the drink.

"Thank you. I think the decorator has improved it immensely. You're sure?" she checked perfunctorily at Kathleen's refusal of her offer.

"Kathy's fine," Brett insisted, ignoring her fuming at his shortening of her name. "I'm sure Julia told you what we're doing, Charline. First, we'd like you to read over your statement of June second and see if you remember anything you'd like to add, if you will." He already had the paper in his hand.

"Of course, Brett." She read it aloud. "'I'm Charline Nelson Voos. I'm thirty-six years old and I've lived in Hancock for eight and a half years. I live at eight Yale Terrace with my husband Lars Hansen Voos and our two children: Peer, who's eight, and Kristen, who is three. Peer is in third grade at Hancock Elementary and Kristen is at the Montessori preschool in Darien. My husband is in the import/export business . . .'"

"Excuse me," Brett interrupted. "Kathy, did you say something?"

"I just choked. I have a dry throat. I'll just have some of this tea, if I may . . . I can pour for myself."

"Fine. Let me see, where was I? Oh yes, right here. 'I've been co-president of the Hancock Elementary Parent Teacher Association for this school year and I will be again next year. I suppose Julia told you about that? I'm talking about Julia Ames—she's right over there taking notes.

"'I was sitting at a table on the side of the lawn when Jan Ick died. Did—did Julia tell you I was the last to get my food? Well, I had only been seated for a minute, but I didn't see anything that happened. I heard a cry and then rushed over to where Jan lay. She was already dead, anyone could see that. I told everyone to stay away from her and give her air—not that it was going to do her much good at that point. Julia ran to the phone to call the police. The town's sirens went off and the police and ambulance were here almost immediately. The paramedics did their job and tried to revive Jan, but of course it was hopeless. They spent about fifteen minutes on her and then took her away in the ambulance. I'm sure she was pronounced dead by the first doctor who saw her at the hospital. No, I don't know anyone who would want to kill her and I didn't notice anything unusual about the food except that it killed one of us.' That's all." She looked at Brett as she handed him back the statement. "I can't think of anything else to add."

"What did you do after making that statement, if you can remember?"

"I went back out onto the patio with the other PTA mothers and the teachers. Everyone was allowed to leave after making their statements, but I was the first to make mine, so everyone was still there, except for Dr. Tyrrell. He went into the house to be questioned as I came out."

90

"Was there any order in which people were questioned?" Kathleen asked.

"I don't think there was, at first. I was called because I was nearest the door or something, but I don't know why Charlie went next."

"Charlie?"

"Dr. Tyrrell's first name is Charles. We call him Charlie. Anyway, after he was questioned, I think he insisted on the teachers' being questioned first. I wouldn't guarantee it, but they all went in right after him and before all the mothers. Charlie probably thought that they should be allowed to leave first, since most of them—well, all of them, in fact—live out of town."

"Did any of the mothers object?" Brett asked.

"Well, I don't think anyone said anything about it at the time. We were all pretty shocked by Jan's death—the hospital called right away to let the police know that she was dead, so we heard almost immediately and no one was thinking about anything else. Except for the normal things."

"I don't understand," Brett replied.

"You know, the normal mother worries. What is going to happen if I get home late? Will the sitter stay with the kids? What am I going to fix for dinner? Things like that. In fact, we spent a lot of time thinking about how this was all going to be explained to the kids."

"Mrs. Ick's kids, you mean?"

"Yes, them, of course, but also our own kids. Hancock is a pretty small town, you know, and our elementary school has only around two hundred and twenty kids, so most of them know each other, at least to say hello to. And they know the parents too. We were worried about the effect a violent death would have on the children. We knew that it couldn't be kept from them. In fact, we were even talking about the PTA sponsoring a psychologist to come in and speak to the kids, but decided that it was too late in the school year. Of course, now with Paula's death, maybe we should do something in September."

"So you stayed with the people waiting to be questioned. That's very interesting. Could you tell us your general impression, besides the obvious shock and grief, and the more, uh, practical concerns of the mothers and their children? Did anyone in particular seem more upset than anyone else, I mean?"

"I don't think so." She paused. "I don't think there was very much talk at all. We were all thinking our own thoughts, I guess. I'm afraid I can't tell you anything else."

"How many people call you Charlie, Charline?" Brett asked.

"A few. My husband and Julia and some old friends from college. I was a tomboy when I was growing up, and the nickname was obvious. But I thought I had outgrown it when I graduated from college and started calling myself Charline."

"So you knew Julia in or before college?"

"No, she picked it up from my husband."

"Then the four of you socialize outside of the PTA and school functions? At the Club, I guess?"

"Of course, we socialize most of the time. It's important, since Miles and Lars are co-owners of Farnsworth Import/Export."

"Farnsworth Import/Export?"

"Their business. Didn't Julia tell you? Lars and Miles are business partners . . . you really should get a doctor to look at that throat, Kathy. A persistent need to clear your throat could be serious. You don't smoke, do you?"

"I'm fine," Kathleen insisted, gasping for breath. "I just need some more tea." She poured herself another glass.

Brett gave his partner an annoyed look and continued his questioning. "Julia told us that you were a big help to her and to the police that afternoon."

"Oh?"

"She said that you showed the police around the house, and things like where the rest of the food was in the kitchen, where the phones were located, and helped convince them that refreshments could be safely served from the refrigerator in the basement."

"Yes. Things like that."

"What did you think I meant?"

"I didn't think you meant anything. I just didn't know what you meant when you asked that question, but yes," she hurried on, "I helped the police. I know Julia's home as well as my own and I was certainly more than glad to do what I could, of course."

"And your housekeeper kept Julia's kids for her—all evening, I understand?"

"Yes . . ."

"Mommy, Mommy! Peer hit his head on the diving board and he bleeded all over the pool. You should have seen it! The water was pink, pink, pink!" A blond, blue-eyed nymph jumped into the room, hopping from one foot to the other, dripping water from her very pink swimsuit onto the wood floor and waving a beach towel with a picture of Kermit the Frog at the room. "It was pink, pink, pink," she repeated happily.

"Kristen. Shut up. You'll scare your mother to death. Your brother is just fine now." A tall man, presumably the origin of Kristen's fair coloring, entered the room. Even in his madras slacks, his Adidas sneakers, and his faded purple Ralph Lauren polo shirt, he looked like a sixth-century Viking.

"Mommy. Daddy said 'shut up' to me. Daddy said—"

"Your father is right, Kristen. Stop yelling and tell me where your brother is." Charline Voos had leapt up from the couch, obviously alarmed at her daughter's words.

"It's okay, Charlie, he's gone home with one of the other kids on the swim team. . . ."

"If he hit his head, he should be home resting, Lars. Where is he? We'll go get him and bring him home this minute!"

"Charlie, he's fine, I tell you." He paused and looked at his upset wife. "Okay, I'll go pick him up. He's at the Henshaws with Chad. You look after your guests."

"Oh, I forgot . . ."

"There's no reason to look after us, Charline. We were done anyway. I'm Brett Fortesque, Mr. Voos, Detective Fortesque from the state police. This is Officer Somerville."

"Then it's your car that I saw out front. Do you think it's a good idea to keep police vehicles parked in front of the homes you're visiting? Who knows what people will think?"

"Lars, please." The worry was obvious in her voice. "I think we'd better call right away and let the Henshaws know we're coming to pick up—"

"No need, honey. You look after Kristen here and I'll go get him. They live over on Mackie Place, right? Stay with your mother, Kristen. Daddy will be right back."

Charline Voos put her arms around her daughter as her husband turned and left the room.

"I'm sure he's just fine, Mrs. Voos." Kathleen offered these comforting words.

"Are you a policewoman?" the child asked, untangling herself from her mother's arms. "Like on TV? Do you shoot people and kill them?"

As the child's mother stood staring at the door, Kathleen allowed the wet child to plop onto her lap and insist on an answer. "Do you have a gun? Do you have a gun?"

"No, honey, I'm not carrying a gun. Your name is Kristen, right?" She tried to rearrange the child so that the towel was placed between the two of them, but the little girl lost interest in her lap at this answer.

"No gun? Even my daddy has a gun. Mommy, the policewoman doesn't have a gun. And my daddy has a gun, doesn't he, Mommy?"

Charline, who had still been staring after her husband, seemed to pull herself back to the present. "Don't be foolish, honey. Of course your father doesn't have a gun. Now you march up to your room and get dressed. Not another word," she added as the child seemed likely to protest. "You do just as I say. Mommy's not happy with you for scaring her like that about your brother."

"But, Mommy!" Her voice rose an octave for authenticity. "He did bleed. I was telling you the truth."

"Kristen. Go!"

The little girl reluctantly left the room, dragging her soggy towel along behind her and, Kathleen thought, muttering something that sounded suspiciously like "shit" under her breath.

"Does your husband have a permit for a gun?" Brett asked, as Charline came back and sat down on the sofa, pouring herself a drink.

"Of course not. I mean, he doesn't even have a gun. Why would he need a gun? You know how children talk. Kristen just likes to get attention. She's at that age, I'm afraid."

"We'd better leave. I'm sure you'll want to take care of your son when he gets home." Brett stood and Kathleen quickly joined him.

"Thank you so much for the tea. Oh, and one other thing. How long were you and Julia at the pool yesterday?"

"The pool? Oh, you mean the Club. I don't remember. Julia is better at those things. What did she tell you?"

Kathleen looked at Brett, wondering what he would say in answer to that. His comment disappointed her. "Something about the time of the kids' swim practice. It probably doesn't matter. You've been a big help. We do want to thank you for your time."

The three of them headed out the door and into the monumental hallway. As they left the room, Lars Voos and his son entered the house. Even with the white bandage around his head, the boy could be mistaken as no one else's child, the resemblance to his father was so great.

"Peer!" Charline Voos rushed to her child and wrapped him in her arms. "How did you get home so quickly?"

"I'm fine, Mother." Peer drew himself up to his full height and flung up his arm to ward off her caresses.

"I told you, Charlie. The kid is okay. I met Jed Henshaw in the driveway—he was bringing Peer home. There's no reason to worry. You know mothers," he added for the benefit of his guests.

"Let me look at your head, then you can lie down and watch a video tape, sweetheart," Charline persisted.

"*Rambo*. Yeah, I want to see *Rambo*!"

"Anything. Just lie down in the family room. You'll understand if I leave you here?" she asked, suddenly remembering the others.

"I'll show them out, honey," her husband offered, but she had already left, still trying to comfort her unwilling son. "That Charlie. She overprotects the kids, but she's a good mother. You can tell she is by the time she puts in at that PTA of hers." He led them out the front door and to their car. "Did she tell you about that PTA group? She's co-president of it, you know, along with Julia Ames. And those two do a lot for that PTA."

"I'm sure they do," Kathleen agreed politely, getting into the passenger's seat, since that was the door Lars Voos was holding open for her.

"Yeah. And they love doing it."

"Of course," Kathleen said, pulling her legs quickly out of the path of the car door as he was slamming it shut.

"Sure they love it. Why else would they want to be co-presidents for two years in a row?"

"Why else indeed?" Brett asked rhetorically, starting the engine.

Eight

———•••———

"Write us a note, Kathy. We need to find out if, in fact, Lars Voos has a permit for a gun." He easily maneuvered the car out of the wide driveway.

"Kathleen," she corrected. "You think that the kid was telling the truth?"

"What reason would a little kid like that have to lie?"

"I don't know. To get attention?"

"Well, maybe, but I'll bet Lars does have a gun around and I'll bet we don't find any record of a permit for one."

"So where do we go next?"

He stared through the windshield at the street signs. "Do you have any idea where this Field Club might be?"

"None at all, but maybe we should go back to the municipal building and get a map, check on the gun, and, while we're at it, see if the autopsy report on Mrs. Porter has come in."

"Good thinking."

They had planned to dash into the building and right back out, but it turned out to be bicycle registration day in Hancock. A line of kids, mixed with a few adults, stretched around the police department. They stood beside expensive BMXs and ten-speeds waiting to have the serial numbers registered and identification numbers etched onto the frames. Brett and Kathleen had to wade through this line to get inside and, once there, they couldn't find anyone to help them.

"I know that Sergeant Mann left an envelope for you, but I don't know where he put it," explained the harried receptionist in the hallway.

"We can see that you're busy. Could we just make a few calls to our headquarters? And, if you could take a moment, could you find us a map of Hancock and the surrounding area?"

"No problem," she lied, and excusing herself from two eleven-year-old boys who were busy ramming their bikes into each other's, she rushed into the main office behind her. "There are the phones, help yourself. I think we have a map. Here it is." She held up a sheet of paper. "This is a small town, you won't have any trouble finding your way around. I'd better get back outside now . . ." She looked out the door at the boys who, no longer satisfied with bike combat, were kicking each other's shins.

"Fine. We'll just make our calls and leave. You've been very helpful," Kathleen assured her.

Brett got his information quickly, despite its being a weekend, and then relayed it to Kathleen. "There's no record of Lars Voos ever having had a permit to own a gun, nor his wife, nor Miles Ames. Julia Ames does have a permit for a pistol, however. She got it three years ago. July of eighty-four, to be more exact."

"That's interesting. I wonder if it means anything. And the results of the autopsy on Mrs. Porter?"

"They haven't finished the procedure, but they've done enough to know what killed her. Cyanide again. A huge dose in her stomach."

"And in her glass of iced tea, I assume."

"Yes, so all we have to know is how someone placed it in her glass and when and—"

"And we have our killer. You think that's going to be easy?"

"It depends on who was paying attention to what was going on at the Club yesterday. Did you look at the map? Is the Field Club marked?"

"Sure is. Shall we go?"

"I can't think of a more logical next step."

If their police car had looked out of place near the Ames and Voos homes, it was even more so here. The parking lot of the Field Club was directly adjacent to the clubhouse, an imposing Colonial structure of white-painted brick, dripping ivy from its walls and surrounded by beds of white flowers.

"Somehow I had envisioned a more casual atmosphere than this," Kathleen commented as they got out of their car. "You're not locking it?"

"I can't imagine that there is any need to here. Let's go to the clubhouse and see what we find, shall we?"

They headed up the brick path, also painted white and kept that way, no doubt, with no little effort on someone's part, and walked in through the front doors. They found themselves in a large reception room, the muraled walls showing Revolutionary War battle scenes.

"May I help you?" The man who greeted them was well over six feet tall and had an air of authority, even though he was dressed in the madras slacks and polo shirt that seemed to be the uniform of the day.

"I'm Detective Fortesque, and this is Officer Somerville. We're from—"

"The state police," he finished for them. "I've been looking forward to meeting you. No need to show your identification. I figured you'd be around here today."

"And you are?"

"Sorry. No reason you should know who I am. I'm Jack Mann."

"Of course. Sergeant Mann, we've been wanting to meet you." They shook hands. "Are you on duty here, or can we go and talk someplace where we won't be overheard?"

"No problem. I have an office here. Right this way." And he guided them through a door discreetly hidden right in the mural. "Do you want anything? I can call the bar or the club-house coffee shop from here." He motioned to a system of buttons on his desk. "Nothing? You're sure? Well, if you don't mind, I'll just sit here and keep an eye on the monitors while we talk." He flipped a switch and a wall covered with TV screens lit up. There were views of four or five indoor rooms, as well as shots of tennis courts, the pool, an unused skating rink, and four different views of the greens of the golf course. There were also two screens with pictures of the entrance drive. The three of them watched a Rolls glide by one of the cameras.

"Very, very impressive," Kathleen said.

"Does the local police department do all the security for the Club, Sergeant Mann?" Brett wanted to know.

"Call me John. Nope, this is a private club. The local police get called in if there's a problem, but the security is private. I'm off duty now. I work here when I'm off duty."

"Did you set this up?" Brett continued questioning.

"Sure did. Nothing like having unlimited funds, is there? We spent two hundred thousand dollars on this project. The Club even paid for me to go to New York City and check out the security setup of the various apartments and the clubs there. We've got the best of everything. Well, almost," he added with a smile. "They wouldn't let me have a camera in the women's dressing rooms. Not that I didn't try hard . . . oh, excuse me, ma'am. No offense meant."

"None taken," Kathleen said sincerely. "Do you have a camera in the men's dressing room? I don't see one."

"Sure do. I just didn't turn it on in honor of your presence." He waved at the blank screen at the bottom of the tiers of pictures. "And we do have a microphone in the women's dressing room." He pressed a button and some loud giggling and a muffled comment about George's something filled the room. He pressed it again and the noise went off. "The ladies know that it's in there, but they don't seem to care. You should hear some of the things they say . . ." He stopped talking and seemed to remember something. "Some of it is a little private," he explained, "but everyone knows I'm discreet. And a lot of the Club's problems take place in the locker rooms . . ."

"Like what, John?"

"Oh, mostly petty thievery. We had a lawyer here a few years ago who was stealing watches and sweatbands. That's it—just watches and sweatbands. But some of those watches were pretty expensive and no one likes to think of a stranger meddling around in their stuff. He left town, though. It didn't go to court or anything, seems a shrink was already treating him for kleptomania or something."

"What other problems have you had?"

"Nothing like the murder of Paula Porter, if that's what you're asking, Officer Somerville. I suppose you got the information on the autopsy from the coroner?"

"We know the preliminary results," Brett said. "You didn't happen to be here watching what was going on, did you?"

"Yeah, that would be a help . . . for me to have watched someone put the poison in her tea, but no such luck. I was here part of the day, but I didn't see anything. I'm not a full-time employee, of course. I work weekends here, eight hours a day, but they're flexible. I'm here for the day today because the kids' swim team had a meet—that brings in kids and their parents and coaches from other clubs and we always worry about who else might come in with them, if you know what I mean. It would be a good chance for someone to just wander in and start stealing things or causing trouble—"

"Aren't things kept pretty well locked up here?" Kathleen asked.

"No way. The members like to think of this as an extension of their homes. You should see the stuff they leave around. After one big party, one of the clean-up crew came to me with a diamond necklace—he had found it hanging out of one of the lockers in the dressing rooms—seems someone had found it was too hot and had stashed it there instead of bothering to bring it to me for safekeeping. I do have a safe here for valuables."

"So you have to keep track of strangers at all times," Kathleen said.

"Well, we're pretty lax except for special events. I change my schedule according to what's going on—like next week I won't be here during the day on Saturday because there's a big dance at night—a club-sponsored dance—and I'll be working from about two in the afternoon when the caterers usually start to set up and bring in their supplies until anytime: one, two, even four o'clock in the morning—when the last people leave and all of the clean-up people are finished."

"That's just for club-centered events?" Brett asked.

"Yup. The clubhouse is rented out for parties, but only to members, of course, and they're required to hire their own security people and post a bond to keep the Club from being liable for any problems."

"It sounds like a pretty good arrangement for you, John."

"It sure is. I get paid for this work. And the wife and kids get club membership free, too. And they're treated just like everyone else, no matter what Carol thinks."

"What does Carol think?"

"Aw. She thinks some of the other women look down on her because I'm a cop and we don't have the money of the other members, but I think she's just oversensitive. Everyone treats me real well, and without the money from this job we couldn't live in Hancock—not on a cop's salary. And the schools here are great. Both Janie and John Junior are straight-A students. They'll go to good colleges and they'll be doctors or lawyers or anything else they want, and they'll be able to live in this town without doing all the extra work!" He smiled with pride.

Kathleen found herself smiling back. What a nice man, she thought.

"I've got to make my rounds. And we've got a new pool crew coming in later this afternoon. The kiddy pool is cracking and I like to be on hand to meet new workers. Helps prevent problems if they know someone is watching them. I'll be back in half an hour, if that's okay with you both." He checked his watch. "At about five?"

"No problem. We may not even need to talk to you again today. Don't want to interrupt your work. Do you mind if we wander around?"

"Fine. I do keep my office locked, however . . ."

"Then we'll leave with you so you can lock up behind us," Brett offered. "Just one more thing. Do you have a printed layout of the Club so that we can figure out where we are and where we're going?"

"I have some brochures here in my desk that'll help you." He took two thick color pamphlets out of the top drawer and handed one to each of them. "These are given to prospective members. In the middle of each you'll find a fold-out map of the whole Club. Keep them. You're going to want to refer to them, I'm sure." He stopped with his hand on the door. "We're not used to murders here in Hancock. We really don't know how to handle them."

"You've been a big help, John. And I'm sure we'll be getting back to you soon." Brett followed Kathleen and the policeman out of the office.

"Well, good luck to you with your investigation. Oh, wait one second, there's someone you should meet." He waved to an elderly man on the other side of the room and urged the two of them over to him.

"This is Dr. Grayson; he's president of the Field Club. Dr. Grayson, these are the detectives from Hartford. They're here to find out who killed Mrs. Porter, sir."

"Well, I'm very glad to meet both of you. Does this mean that they're sure it's murder, Mann?"

"It looks like it, sir. But they'll tell you about that. I'll be off, if you don't have anything for me to do."

"What? No, nothing." The elderly man was directing all

his attention at Brett and Kathleen. "So when are you going to find out who did it?"

"Just as soon as we can," Brett answered politely.

"Well, it sure better be soon. We're not used to things like this happening at the Club. Not in Hancock, either, for that matter. I've lived here all my life and I've never seen anything like it. Don't think anything like it has happened since the Revolutionary War."

"Since the Revolutionary War?" Kathleen repeated, giving an involuntary look at the murals around her.

"That's right, young lady. A grocer in town then sold the British bags of rotten potatoes, with just a few good ones on top to disguise the contents. Made money and helped the war effort for the Colonists. Good thinking, I've always thought. Seems the British didn't agree. They killed him one night for revenge."

"How do they know the British killed him?"

"Stands to reason. He was killed when he lit a candle to take up to bed with him. Seems the top was a wick surrounded by wax, but hidden an inch or so down was gunpowder surrounded by paraffin. Poor fellow splattered all over the walls of his own bedroom. Always thought it was an appropriate way to die after what he did: hid the bad with the good, right?" He chuckled gleefully.

Kathleen thought the whole story a little morbid, but cops don't have the luxury of getting queasy over two-hundred-year-old murders.

"There's a picture of that grocer on the mural that's over the door to the Club Room. That's our bar. Not many people see that part of the picture. It's too high up. But me, I just like knowing that it's there. But I don't like having a real murder at the Club—not at all. Always telling people that this town is changing and not for the better. Lots of New Yorkers moving in. Businessmen in all sorts of businesses. And look what happens. First that Jan Ick is murdered at a PTA lunch of some sort, and now Paula's killed right here at the Club. What is Hancock coming to?"

104

"I don't know, sir," Kathleen replied, wondering why she was calling him "sir." Just because everyone else did was no reason for her to continue the tradition.

"Well, it's your job to find out, young lady. I'll be on my way." And off he marched.

"Old windbag," Kathleen muttered.

Brett was studying the map. "Well, this won't take much time. The grounds are extensive, but except for the golf course, everything is pretty much right here. Let's start at the pool, shall we?" And he opened the nearby door to the right, walked through it, and ran smack into another person coming from the opposite direction.

"Mrs. Henshaw. I'm sorry. I idn't see you coming."

"Detective Fortesque. What a surprise. Oh, you're here to see where Paula died, aren't you?"

"Yes. Kathleen and I were just on our way to the pool."

"Kathleen?"

"Oh, I'm sorry, she was working downtown when I was at your home. Let me introduce you. This is Officer Kathleen Somerville, Mrs. Henshaw. Kathleen, this is—"

"Of course, you must be Susan Henshaw. I'm very pleased to meet you. Brett says you were a big help in giving him background information."

Susan said all the right things, even offered to show both of them the pool and the place where Paula had died, but all the time she was watching the policewoman. This was not quite the image she had in mind when Brett mentioned the colleague busy down at the local police offices. Not to be sexist, but she hadn't imagined a woman. But she could deal with that if the woman were ordinary. This woman? This woman could be on the cover of some magazine, not running around investigating a murder. Now, that was sexist. And stupid of her. Shape up, Susan, she lectured herself, turning her back on Detective Fortesque and concentrating on Officer Somerville. It's time to stop acting childish.

"Officer Somerville . . ." she began her maturity campaign.

"Why don't you call me Kathleen?"

"Thanks, I will. Do you need to see anything besides where Paula lay?"

"We'd like to see most of it: the clubhouse, the pool. Actually, everything but the golf course."

It didn't take long, and when they were done, the three of them sat down at a table near the spot where Paula Porter had died.

"I'm thirsty. Can I get you all something?" Susan offered, once again the hostess.

"Let me," Brett offered.

"Actually, that would be great. Tell them at the bar inside the door what you want and have it charged to my account. You'll have to do it," she added, when she saw him hesitate. "Nothing here is on a cash basis."

"How is your investigation going?" she asked Kathleen, more to make conversation than from genuine interest. "I'm sorry," she interrupted herself. "I should know that you can't talk about it."

"There's really very little to talk about at this point, Susan. We're collecting information, visiting the places where the murders took place, trying to get impressions of the people involved."

"Well, you're here now. Does that mean you've been to the Ameses'?"

"Yes, we spent the morning there. And we went to see Mrs. Voos also," she added, deciding that if Brett had the feeling that every step of the way they were being followed by phone among the members of the PTA, then there was no harm in talking freely about their travels.

"What did you think about them?"

"Well . . ." This was moving beyond simple curiosity, Kathleen thought.

"They're interesting women, aren't they?" Susan was answering her own question.

Again Kathleen didn't know how to respond. Was Susan trying to direct her attention to the PTA's co-presidents because she wanted them considered as prime suspects? Did she have some reason for disliking Charline and Julia that was so serious that she'd be happy to see them arrested for murder? Or was she trying to deflect attention from her own guilt? Maybe she should start asking the questions.

"Is it usual for the same people to run the PTA for two years in a row?" she asked, thinking of Lars Voos's contention that it was his wife's love of children that made her want the job. Somehow that didn't seem right to Kathleen, and she remembered Brett's disbelief. "Didn't anyone else want the jobs?"

"Oh, someone else wanted them, but Julia and Charline made damn sure that no one else would get them."

"Oh?" Kathleen kept her voice noncommittal and prayed: please go on. It was these girlish confidences that sometimes led to information.

"Oh, it was constitutional, but it was rotten, nonetheless."

"Constitutional?"

"The rules were followed," Susan admitted. "Even Julia and Charline knew that they had to follow the rules."

"Could you explain what you're talking about?" Kathleen asked, beginning to doubt that she was going to hear anything worthwhile.

"Our local PTA constitution says that there's to be an election of officers each year, with nominations for each office coming from a nominating committee."

"So the nominating committee picks a slate, is that it?" Kathleen asked.

"Yes, but—"

"And who runs against that slate?"

"Well, no one, really. The slate the nominating committee picks is voted on at a general meeting of the PTA, and of course, the people on the slate get the jobs."

"There's no real election," Kathleen asserted.

"Not really, but you're missing the point. The point is that the nominating committee was fixed," Susan replied, realizing as she spoke that she had gone too far.

"You're telling me that Julia and Charline fixed the nominating committee so that they would be co-presidents next year? Why would they want those jobs so much?" she continued, when Susan nodded yes.

"Well, I don't know. And, of course, if Paula knew, she can't tell us now."

"Paula Porter? The woman who died here? What does she have to do with all this? Was she running for an office?"

"No," Susan answered. "She was the head of the nominating committee."

"And as chairperson of the nominating committee she had the power to pick the officers? By herself?"

"No, but as chairperson she was responsible for choosing her committee members—of course they're all members of the PTA—and some of our less-involved members would have voted for whoever they were told was the best person for the job—whoever the chairperson told them was the best person, that is."

"Julia Ames and Charline Voos."

"Yes."

"Instead of?" Kathleen asked.

"Instead of?" Susan repeated the question, knowing perfectly well what was meant, but not wanting to answer.

"Who else wanted to be officers?" Kathleen asked patiently, becoming interested because of Susan's discomfort. She thought she could guess . . .

"Ellen Cooper and myself," Susan admitted. "We put our names in to the committee and were shocked when we weren't picked. It's not as though we haven't done everything on the PTA. Between the two of us, we've run all the major committees. And that isn't all that went on," she continued. "Carol Mann told Julia Ames that she was interested in being vice-president next year—she just mentioned it one day at the Club—and within the hour Charline Voos was on the phone to her explaining that she really didn't want that job—that there were other, more important things for her to do in the PTA. And poor Carol has such an inferiority complex that she just backed out and didn't even turn her name in to the committee."

Kathleen wasn't surprised about that. She had seen enough of Julia and Charline to guess that together they could be more than a little intimidating. But, as for this woman and Ellen: just how much did they resent being left out? And did they do anything about it?

"Listen," Susan went on urgently, "I really want you to understand. It's probably all just silly, but it did hurt our feelings. Of course it's not Paula that anyone got mad at. She wasn't out to hurt anyone. Paula is just the type of person that other people get to do things . . . she was that type of person, I mean."

Kathleen looked out over the pool. She knew that Susan had said more than she meant to and that she wouldn't add anything useful, just make excuses for what she had said. But was there anything in this that could explain a murder? Before she could figure out the answer to that, Brett returned with a trayful of drinks.

"I wasn't sure what everyone wanted, so I brought two iced teas and a Coke. Ladies first," he offered, laying the tray before them.

Both women took tea and left him the Coke. "Did you bring any sweetener, by any chance?" Susan asked. "They usually hand it out with the tea. And it's usually on the tables; they must have had a party last night and everything was cleaned up."

"Those little packets of stuff. I forgot." He jumped up and went back to the clubhouse.

"I hope he brings back some artificial sweetener," Kathleen said.

"He probably will. Around here, more people use it than sugar. They don't even give out sugar unless you ask for it."

Brett returned more slowly than he had left, and he was fooling around with the little blue packets of sweetener as he approached the table.

"Find something interesting?"

"I was just wondering if these things could be opened and then resealed so that no one would notice."

"Packets of artificial sweetener?"

Kathleen was quicker than Susan to see what he was getting at. "You mean that's where the poison came from? Like Tylenol capsules filled with cyanide, only this time it was sugar-substitute packets?"

"I don't know, but it is possible."

"But you open the packet and add it to the tea; it's not like pain pills that you just gulp down without looking in them," Susan protested.

"Cyanide is a white powder," Brett explained.

"Then it is possible? But does it make any difference?"

"Sure it does. Because if the cyanide was placed directly into the tea, then it had to have been placed in it between the time that it was poured at the bar and the time when Mrs. Porter drank it. But if it was in the packet, then it could have been put in there at any time and—"

"That means more people could have done it," Kathleen finished for him. "Good. Nothing like more suspects rather than fewer."

"And just how many suspects is that exactly?" Susan asked, stirring her tea with great concentration and hoping no one could see her face.

"Everyone at the luncheon who was also here yesterday," Kathleen answered.

"There could be even more," Brett added. "It could also be anyone who put cyanide in the sweetener and who put the poison in the sandwich. We still don't know it wasn't someone else."

"But then how would the killer know who was going to

get that particular sandwich or that particular packet of sweetener?"

"Maybe he didn't."

"You mean maybe we have a madman around who is killing without caring who is killed?" Susan dropped her glass of tea onto the tabletop.

"It's posssible," Brett answered, reaching over to mop up Susan's spilled tea with her napkin.

"And how will we know if the packet contained the poison?" Kathleen asked.

"I put in a call to the lab while I was up. They're going to get back to me."

"When?"

"Right away. They have the information, but it had to be found. Seems the local police did turn in a couple of empty sweetener packets that were lying next to the body, along with everything else, for analysis . . ."

"Mrs. Henshaw. Phone for Mrs. Henshaw." The public-address system blared out over the patio.

"That may be the answer to our question. I told them to page you."

"Well, then let's get it." She hopped up and he joined her on her way to the phone. It turned out that the call was, in fact, from the state lab, and Susan handed the receiver to Brett. He took it and listened for a minute or two. "Thanks a lot," he said and hung up.

"Well?" Susan asked.

"Well, first, we're almost certain from lab evidence that both murders were committed by the same person or persons."

"How do you know that?"

"I'll explain later, but the good news is that the poison was in the packets. Let's go back and tell Kathleen."

They found Kathleen and her response was the same.

"Good news," she said to Susan.

"I don't understand," Susan replied. "Why should that be good news?"

The two police people looked at each other before Brett answered.

"Because if it hadn't been in the sweetener, the murderer would have to have been you."

Nine

———◆◆———

Kathleen's work with the narcotics unit had accustomed her to days when all three meals came through a drive-in window and had taught her to eat them quickly for whatever nourishment was available and then forget about them. Brett seemed to have picked up the same philosophy: he ate his food speedily, without talking, without paying any attention to the roomful of chattering people. When he had demolished everything edible on his tray, he stood up, dumped the contents into a waste container, and looked at Kathleen, as though he had just remembered she was there.

She wasn't a woman who needed constant male attention. Luckily. "Where are we going now?" she asked, her own tray of Styrofoam and cardboard following his into the trash.

He smiled. "I was afraid you might be a nine-to-five person. Glad you're not. We should take the time to look up Dr. Charles Tyrrell."

"The principal?"

"Yes. He lives in Barnes, but that's only a twenty-minute drive from here. You've got his telephone number in the statements the police took after the PTA lunch. Why don't we give him a call and see if he's going to be home this evening?"

"Great idea. Here, let me just find it in this stuff. Look at that: right on top."

"There's a phone near the rest rooms." Brett leaned across the table and copied the information he needed on a napkin. "I'll be back in a few minutes."

While he was gone, Kathleen read through the statement she had found:

I'm Dr. Charles Tyrrell and I live at 208 Glenhaven Boulevard in Barnes, Connecticut. I'm principal of the Hancock Elementary School and I have been for nine years. I cannot tell you what a tragedy this death is. I've known Mrs. Ick for four years now and worked closely with her on many PTA projects. She was a wonderful woman and a good mother and, certainly, an asset to the school.

I was sitting at the far table. The others at my table were the PTA co-presidents, Mrs. Julia Ames and Mrs. Charline Voos. I was sitting between them. There were also three of my teachers at the table: Mrs. Linda Smith, our kindergarten teacher, Mrs. Beverly Johnson, one of our first-grade teachers, and Miss Corrine DeAngelo, the art teacher. The first I knew of the tragedy was a scream—I think it was Susan Henshaw, but I'm not sure—but I know that we all rushed over to where the noise came from—and Charline Voos said to stay away and give her room, so we stood back. But Jan was lying so still and her face was so white that I think I knew then that she must be dead. No, I don't know what could have killed her, I'm sure.

I'd appreciate it if you would question the members of the staff of Hancock Elementary first. Not because I think they deserve preferential treatment, but because most of them have a longer way to go to get home. None of the teachers lives here in Hancock. Thank you.

It was a most concise report, with very little information, Kathleen thought. This Dr. Tyrrell was going to be a very interesting person to interview.

"Ready to go?"

"You got through?"

"Sure did. He was on his way out to a party but agreed to

wait and meet with us first. I don't know if he liked the idea, but I didn't have to insist. He offered.

"I'll drive and you navigate, okay?"

"Sure," she agreed, getting into the car and pulling out the Connecticut map from under the seat. "I looked over Dr. Tyrrell's statement while you were calling . . ."

"Brief and to the point, wasn't it?"

"Just professional?" she offered.

"Careful, I think. The best way to get caught saying something you don't mean is to keep talking. He made his points and shut up. It's smart."

"You think he has something to hide?"

"I don't know. But if he does, we're going to have a more difficult time finding it out than with someone else. He said all the right things about Mrs. Ick, but he also remembered his job and to protect his teachers in what must have been an emotional, if not hysterical, atmosphere. He doesn't lose his head easily. That's all that statement says . . . Do I turn left here?"

"No. Right. That's it. Looks like we have about five miles on Route 78 and then we turn off to Barnes. I hope there's a sign."

"I wonder what Dr. Tyrrell thinks about Julia and Charline?"

"You think he might not like them or something?" She put down the map. "Why wouldn't he?"

"Well, I'm not sure, but I get the impression that the PTA presidents are pretty powerful people in the parent group. Remember how Julia Ames got the grant for her daughter's art teacher? And that table was filled with the teachers of Mrs. Ames's children."

"You think the parents are using their positions on the PTA to help their kids get something the other kids don't?"

"I don't know what to think, but I would love to know what Dr. Tyrrell thinks."

"You're never going to find out if you turn left. Barnes is to the right. That's it. And then left here. It should be along this street somewhere. . ."

"He said it was a small Cape Cod sided with light green aluminum siding. Number 208. That's it. I'll just pull into the driveway."

"That must be him coming out of the house now. Heavens, he looks like an elementary school principal."

The man coming down the walk to their car did, Brett agreed, look like a school principal: tall, gray-haired, and with a certain academic dignity that was evident although he was wearing a sport shirt and Bermuda shorts rather than a Harris tweed with leather patches on the elbows. It was easy to picture him sitting behind a desk waiting to find out from little Johnny or Freddy or even little Brett just how that ball happened to go through the window of the classroom when everyone knew that there was no ball playing allowed indoors.

"Detective Fortesque? Detective Somerville? I'm Dr. Tyrrell. Come in, won't you?" He led them both toward the house. "My wife has left for the party without me, so there's no one home and we won't be disturbed. Please come in."

"We're very sorry to have upset your evening, Dr. Tyrrell. We certainly never planned to split up your wife and yourself. If you would like us to come back another time?"

"Certainly not. We've got a serious problem and the sooner it is solved, the better. Now come in and sit down and tell me what I can do for you."

Kathleen looked around the book-filled living room with delight. It might not be fancy and someone else might scoff at the lack of pretense, but to her this was charming: deep armchairs, just a little grubby and worn, lots of pillows, needlepointed by hand, footstools, pictures, a lamp and a table at your elbow no matter where you might sit. At the far side of the room in a window alcove, a large loom had been left in

116

the middle of a project. Yarn was piled in baskets around and under the equipment. But the most important thing about the room were the books. Books on shelves, around the walls, and under the windows; books piled on tables and chairs; books even stacked up on the floors. "What a wonderful place," she exclaimed.

Dr. Tyrrell's smile was warm. "The books are mine, but the silk screens on the wall and the loom all belong to my wife. She's an enthusiastic amateur craftsman. It does make for a nice mixture, I've always thought. And it never hurts for a person who deals with things intellectual to be grounded by someone involved in the material. But you're here about these murders. What can I do for you? Do you have any suspects?"

"Then you do know about Paula Porter's death," Kathleen said.

"Yes, I was at the Field Club yesterday, in fact."

"At the time of the death?"

"Yes. I didn't go out near the pool, but of course you'll have to verify that in your own way."

"Do you mind if I ask if you're a member of the Field Club?" Brett asked.

"It's your job to, isn't it?" responded Dr. Tyrrell.

"Yes, of course it is," said Brett, trying to shake himself of the feeling that he was the little boy and this man the authority figure.

"Well, for your information, I am not a member of the Field Club. School principals aren't affluent enough for things of that sort. But I was there at the time Mrs. Porter was killed, to answer your question. I had met Martha Hallard for lunch yesterday around noon—at her invitation. We were still talking when Mrs. Porter's body was found. Naturally, we hurried to the pool area immediately upon hearing the news."

"And the reason for the meeting?"

"The stated reason was because I'm looking for a new

house. Oh, we wouldn't leave here unless it was necessary," he added, seeing the startled look on Kathleen's face. "But this is a rental property. We have been very lucky in our landlord and we've been here for sixteen years, but the owner died last winter and his heirs are interested in selling. And we're not interested in buying. I'm going to retire in three years and then we're moving to Maine. We've a home on Deer Isle that we'll move into. So a rental is what I need. And soon, I might add. There is a buyer with cash in hand waiting to close on the house. The new owners are very considerate and they haven't been pushing too hard, but I'm sure they will be pleased to see the last of us."

"And Mrs. Hallard, being a real estate agent . . ."

"Is looking for a home for us. Exactly."

"You said that was . . . I believe you called it . . . the 'stated reason'?" Brett pressed on.

"I'm afraid there were ulterior motives. Not that I don't need a place to live. I do, and I have complete faith in Mrs. Hallard's finding something for us. She's a very efficient person. And she's a wonderful source. She knows an amazing amount about what is going on in Hancock. And I was looking for information."

"About anything in particular?" Brett asked and immediately wished he had asked slightly differently.

"Of course," came the decidedly indignant reply. "I was interested in the investigation of Mrs. Ick's murder. I thought that having the case unsolved in the fall would have a definite effect on my school."

"In what way?" Kathleen asked.

"Firstly, our concern is the children. Mr. Ick and his children Robbie and Sandy have remained in town and will be attending school in the fall. That could be awkward, of course."

"Because of what the other kids might say to them?"

"That, yes, but children are creatures of the moment. A murder that happened three months ago isn't likely to interest most of them, but there is my staff to consider."

"In what way?"

"It would seem to me that they are all suspects in a murder case."

Kathleen and Brett exchange glances.

"Well, sir," Brett began, "I have good news and bad news for you."

"Good news and bad news, eh? Now where have I heard that before?"

Kathleen thought she detected a twinkle in his eye. If so, Brett missed it.

"Good news first, I always say," Dr. Tyrrell continued.

"Well, sir, unless your teachers were at the Field Club yesterday, they've pretty much been eliminated from our list of suspects."

"You mean that the same person committed both crimes?"

"We're not absolutely sure, but it's a reasonable guess."

"Please explain, Detective Fortesque."

"The poison, cyanide, that was used to kill Mrs. Ick, was from the same batch as that used to murder Mrs. Porter. You see, our toxicologists tell us that there was an extra ingredient, a contamination of the pure poisons, in both the stomach of Mrs. Ick and in the packet of cyanide that was masquerading as sugar substitute. It's not all that unusual to find trace elements of other chemicals in cyanide. It's not meant for ingestion, after all. Now, it is just possible that two people got the poison from the same place with the same contamination and then proceeded to kill off two different people within the same two months, but . . ."

"Of course, it's very unlikely. So you're saying that yesterday's murder of Mrs. Porter eliminated from the list of suspects everyone who was not present in both places. I assume you possess lists of those present at both events?"

"Yes, and they indicate that none of your teachers was at the Field Club yesterday. Your phys-ed teacher, Mr. Johnson, is employed there in the summer, but he was in New York City at a sports equipment show for the entire

119

day. So, unless someone hid from the police who compiled the names of those present, your faculty is cleared of all suspicion." As he spoke Brett had a sudden image of Miss Pinksnap, his own third-grade teacher, crouching low in the shower of the ladies' locker room of the Hancock Field Club.

"I agree that's unlikely, but you, of course, must consider all the possibilities," Dr. Tyrrell urged.

"But for all practical purposes, we've eliminated your teachers from our investigation. Of course, things may change, but for now I think you can stop worrying about them."

"That is the good news? And the bad news, I gather, is that you can't eliminate me from the list of murder suspects. Am I correct?"

"Yes." Brett couldn't think of anything else to add.

"Well, this will be a novel experience. I've never been a suspect in a murder case before. Is that what you want to talk to me about? You want me to make another statement?"

"Do you have anything to tell us about Paula Porter's death that you haven't already?"

"No, Detective Fortesque, I don't. As I told you, Mrs. Hallard and I were inside for the afternoon."

"Did either of you leave the table? You were there for about. . . ?"

"At least three hours, I'd say. And yes, we both left the table, although at different times. Mrs. Hallard went to the ladies' room between lunch and dessert. I myself went to wash up after the entire meal was over. We did have another cup of coffee somewhat later in the afternoon. But neither of us was gone from the other for more than ten minutes. And that, of course, is time enough to slip poison into someone's drink. I assume that's what happened?"

"Possibly." Brett saw no reason to elaborate. "The local police are looking into the facts of the crime. They haven't been here?"

"No, not yet. Is this all you want?"

"No, Dr. Tyrrell. We're hoping you'll be willing to tell us some more about the PTA and the women in it. Of course, everything will be confidential."

"I don't understand what you want. Are you looking for some sort of personality profile of each woman who was on hand for both murders? Or are you looking for a description of the PTA and its offices?"

"Well, both," Kathleen answered.

"I still don't understand, but I'd be glad to help you. But this is going to take a while, and if you don't mind, I'll call my wife and let her know that she's going to be the lone representative for the Tyrrell family this evening. The phone is in the kitchen. I'll be right back."

He was barely out of the room when Kathleen slipped out of her chair and went over to Brett, but any idea she had of a hurried conference was squelched as he got up and began to peruse the largest of the bookshelves in the room. Kathleen, not wanting to show any hurt feelings, picked up the closest magazine and feigned an interest in it. Unfortunately she had chosen *Early Childhood Education*. She was trying to figure out some graphs about math problems when Dr. Tyrrell returned.

"My wife is having a wonderful time without me, so I thought we might have a little treat without her. I've brought tea and brandy." He placed a tray containing both on the buffet under the bookshelves and turned back to them. "Who would like what?"

"Brandy," Brett answered firmly.

"Brandy, please," Kathleen echoed. She needed it.

"Good. Three brandies." He passed out the snifters and resumed his seat. "You'd better start with the questions because I don't know how to begin." He sipped his drink and looked at Kathleen.

But it was Brett who answered. "Does the PTA help you or cause you trouble, Dr. Tyrrell?"

"Whew. That's some question. You did say all answers would be confidential?"

"Meaning that they cause problems?"

"All groups cause problems."

"But this group more than others?" Brett persisted.

"This group has raised major amounts of money for my school, Detective Fortesque. They have caused things to happen that have been of great educational importance for our students . . ."

"We're not interested in a press release on the wonderful things the PTA does, Dr. Tyrrell. We need to know how they function and why these particular women have chosen to become involved in this group instead of spending their time on something else."

"That's easy to answer: their children. They're involved in the PTA because they are interested in getting the best education possible for their children. That's almost always the reason for the initial commitment." He paused.

"And later?"

"Well, there are always people who feel the need to run for office, not necessarily because they want the responsibility but because of what the office brings with it."

"Such as?"

"Well, some people need to be in control, of course. And some people are looking for benefits from the position—for professional contacts or even just acceptance by the 'in group,' if I many use a colloquialism."

"Does this have anything to do with Mrs. Ames and Mrs. Voos being elected for a second term?" Brett asked.

"Oh, you've heard about that, have you? I'll give you credit for having good sources. I thought the women involved were keeping quiet."

"We know that there was some discontent, and that Mrs. Porter was chairperson of the nominating committee," Brett said. "We would appreciate knowing the whole story."

"The whole story. Well, I'm not sure that I know the

whole story, but I'll be glad to tell you as much as I do. But not everything gets back to the principal of the school. The PTA is an autonomous body, although they very kindly defer to my judgment about many things."

"But about the nominating committee?"

"Well, first you have to understand that while the nominating committee's job is to search out the best candidates for each position, in reality they sit and take volunteers for the various offices as well as suggestions from members. For instance, who has some training in accounting for treasurer?—things like that. Some years this works out well. Most years, in fact, groups will get together and decide who wants what job and they will call the chairperson of the committee and then the committee will meet and vote to elect those people to the jobs that they want. Some years it works less well; a few years ago, no one wanted to be president and the nominating committee had to beat the bushes, as it were, to find a person willing to put in the time and effort. The job may be unpaid, but it is hard work and everyone who does it puts in many, many hours. The organization of the PTA is terrific, and in some ways, the president is responsible for everything that happens during her term in office."

"But this last year?"

"This last year, when the time came to set up the committee—that happens at the last meeting of the year—Charline or Julia, and I don't remember which, asked for volunteers to chair the nominating committee and Paula Porter raised her hand. No one else said anything about wanting that particular job and so she got it. I don't think anyone thought anything about it at the time. Well, I shouldn't say that. It is possible that Paula had been prompted to volunteer ahead of time . . ."

"By whom?"

"Possibly Charline Voos. She and Paula are—were—good friends. But I don't know about that. You'll understand, if you let me finish."

"Certainly. Go on."

"Well, there were four volunteers for the office of president: Julia Ames, Charline Voos, Ellen Cooper, and Susan Henshaw. They volunteered in pairs: Julia and Charline and Ellen and Susan. So, although it is nice to find such enthusiasm in our parents, the nominating committee had a mess on its hands. I don't think that Paula expected to find herself in this situation; she came to see me in my office at the school and she seemed honestly confused at the time. And she did what I thought was the sane thing. She got her committee to offer the candidates a compromise: two co-presidents and two co-vice-presidents."

"And who was suggested for each office?" Brett asked, looking at the loom.

"I think Julia Ames and Ellen Cooper were offered president positions and Susan and Charline the VP jobs. By mixing them up, I think the committee thought it was being fair."

"But that didn't suit them?"

"No, not at all. But you know, there was something interesting. Ellen really wanted the job and I think Susan just went along as a friend. And Ellen absolutely refused to work with Julia. But . . ."

"But?" Brett pushed.

"Well, by insisting that she work only with Susan, it was Ellen who really refused to accept a compromise and thus, in the long run, gave the jobs to Julia and Charline. But that's not what bothers me."

"What does bother you, Dr. Tyrrell?" Kathleen asked, wondering why this could possibly be important.

"This is just a gut feeling, you understand. But I thought that Julia and Charline wanting a second year in office didn't make sense. They had had a good year, but nothing spectacular. I didn't get the feeling that they were having a great time. I honestly don't know why they would want to be co-presidents again."

"Possibly they don't like anyone having something they don't have," Kathleen suggested, thinking that she had summed up the personalities of these women pretty well in that sentence alone.

"They are quite competitive, yes. And that might account for it. But I can't help thinking that there's something else there—some stronger motive."

"Was Paula Porter the type of person who would arrange an office like that for a friend?" Brett asked.

"Yes, possibly. Paula was a nice woman. A hard worker, but, well, easily manipulated. The person who gets left holding the wrong end of the stick sometimes. That's probably why people suggested that Charline had put her up to the whole thing."

"You think that's what happened?"

"I don't know. But you have to remember that no one knew who was going to throw their hat into the ring for offices."

"Except that Carol Mann had already told Mrs. Ames that she wanted to be vice-president. And was promptly discouraged from putting her name forward," Kathleen said.

"Did she? Well, that something I didn't know. And it does surprise me. Mrs. Mann wouldn't make waves as vice-president. I don't know what objection they could have had to her holding office."

"Maybe because she isn't in their class?" Kathleen suggested.

"Possibly. Mrs. Ames and Mrs. Voos aren't above being snobs, if that's what you're saying."

"You really don't believe that anyone would kill Mrs. Porter because they objected to her choice for president of the PTA, do you?" Kathleen asked a little sarcastically.

"Definitely not. And I don't believe that I said that."

"We understand that," Brett said. "Did you like having Mrs. Ames and Mrs. Voos as co-presidents? Would you possibly rather have worked with Mrs. Cooper and Mrs. Henshaw?"

"I try not to get involved in this type of thing. Of course, if I had found it impossible to deal with either woman . . . But no, there was no reason not to want them as co-presidents again."

"But would you rather someone else had been?" Brett persisted.

"You must understand my position, Detective Fortesque, I have to get along with whatever the PTA decides."

"And you must understand our position, Dr. Tyrrell. We have to know everything about anything that might have to do with these murders. And it should be obvious to anyone who has looked at the suspects that the members of your executive board of your PTA are well represented. I'm not suggesting that we have decided that the political maneuvering of these women had anything to do with the murders directly. But I won't be able to eliminate that possibility until I know more. Now will you please answer a question: Would you rather have had Mrs. Cooper and Mrs. Henshaw for co-presidents?"

Dr. Tyrrell took a few moments before answering. "Okay. Yes, I really don't like Julia and Charline. Maybe it's personal prejudice on my part, but they do seem to want the office for the status and not because they want to contribute to Hancock Elementary. Actually, I had thought that being in office once would have been enough for them. I was very surprised to find that they wanted to do it again."

"So . . ." Brett began.

"But," Dr. Tyrrell raised his voice and interrupted, "I want to make this very clear. While it may be true that Paula Porter and her committee didn't pick Mrs. Henshaw and Mrs. Cooper, I cannot, I repeat, I cannot believe that either of them would kill Paula Porter out of revenge or for any other motive." He looked at them sternly.

"We understand that, sir," Kathleen assured him, noticing that Brett seemed involved in his own thoughts.

126

"Do you have any other questions?"

"Well, do we, Brett?"

"Not that I can think of." He picked up his glass and drank down the contents and then stood up. Kathleen hurried to follow.

"Oh, Dr. Tyrrell." Brett stopped on his way to the doorway. "Do you have any drug problems at your school?" he asked casually.

Ten

———◆———

"Well, now we all know how to offend an elementary-school principal. Just ask him if his school is loaded with little addicts," Kathleen said, getting into the passenger side of the car.

"You were on the narcotics squad. Are you telling me you haven't heard of drugs being taken by fifth graders?" he replied, putting the key in the ignition and starting the motor.

"I worked in the city. This isn't exactly the poverty-plagued urban area that breeds dependence on drugs," she protested.

"That shows how little you know about it," Brett argued. "You think there's less cocaine use here than in the city? These kids certainly have enough money to get the stuff. And if they can't get it right here in town, New York City is only thirty miles away."

"I know that," Kathleen said, indignant. "But not fifth graders, not in this environment. If you want to suggest that there are drugs in the high school here, or even the junior high, I won't argue. But not these little kids, I don't see it. And where are we going?" Just because he was in the driver's seat didn't mean he could take off wherever he wanted to, did it? Well, actually, of course, it did.

"I'd like to clear up this story about the presidency and—"

"You're kidding me. You really think that a woman would kill someone just because she's not getting to run the PTA the way she wants to?" She flung her head against the head-rest and closed her eyes. "I cannot *believe* . . ."

"I think we should clear up any area in which we know people were unhappy and that there was conflict. That is what I think. You may think what you want. You may . . ." His voice trailed off; her skirt was hiked up above her knees and there were those garters again . . .

"And just how are you going to clear up these things?" She glanced over and saw what he was looking at. "Just keep your eyes on the road. You don't want to get us lost again, do you?"

"I don't think I was the only one to get us lost today. I believe you were driving when we tried to find the Ames home." He sounded more sure than he felt; in fact, he felt he was lost. Well, maybe if he turned here . . .

"Left, not right. This is where you almost made the wrong turn on the way to Dr. Tyrrell's house. Left, I said."

"This is a short cut," Brett said firmly, and then changed the subject, since she would never believe that one. "Did you notice the phone in the living room?"

"No, why should I have? Just because he said he was going to make his call from the kitchen? He probably just wanted some privacy. Are you sure you know where this short cut is taking us?" she demanded.

"I am on my way to Susan Henshaw's house," Brett insisted, doubting the truth of his own words. "If you prefer to pursue some other line of inquiry or even to quit for the day, I'd be happy to drop you off somewhere else."

"I think I'd like to stay with you, if you don't mind." She stared in stony silence out the window.

At least she didn't seem to realize just how lost they were getting . . .

"Well, I'll admit it. I'm impressed," Kathleen commented.

"You're what?" Just in time, he saw the municipal building loom up on the right. What luck. "I won't say anything," he said, turning the correct direction to get to the Henshaw home.

His luck continued and he found the Henshaw place easily. A baby-sitter with platinum-blond hair, blackened eyes, and more holes in her earlobes than he would have thought possible explained that the Henshaws were out for the evening. A party next door, in fact. When he showed his identification, she offered to give him the phone number, but Brett resisted the offer, thanked her warmly, and suggested to Kathleen that they call it a day.

But his decision not to interrupt the party was a mistake: except for Dr. Tyrrell, all the suspects in the case were there. It would have been very informative.

Susan Henshaw was having a third glass of sangria, on the theory that if you can't get a little sloshed on the evening of the day that for a while, at least, you were the main suspect in a murder case, then when can you?

Besides, she reminded herself, looking around from the sofa on which she sat, doesn't everyone get drunk at a wake? And this was either a wake or New Year's Eve, because most people were doing some serious drinking. Certainly more than was normal for this crowd.

Nancy Dobbs came and plunked herself down next to Susan, some of the drink she was carrying sloshing out of the glass and dripping down onto the skirt of the sundress she was wearing.

"Damn. Oh well, no one will notice. And it's washable."

Susan frequently found herself tongue-tied when it came to party small talk. She had a tendency to forget everything about the person next to her and always hoped the other person would start the conversation. Nancy did.

"Wasn't Kevin great yesterday? The way he gathered up the kids and got them away from Paula's body? I've been telling Doug how wonderful he was. Don't you agree?"

"He did some quick thinking. Doug must be very proud of him."

"Well, you know Doug. He's sometimes a little hard on the kids. Not that he doesn't want the best from them—I mean, for them—but sometimes he doesn't see just what good kids they are. Say something to him about Kevin, if you get the chance tonight."

"Of course," Susan agreed, knowing she could do that without lying or exaggerating. It really had been remarkable of Kevin to think so quickly, and wasn't it interesting that Nancy was willing to be even this disloyal to her husband? She had always thought that Nancy was something of a stick about her marriage: never a word against Doug, even when all the other women were sitting around sharing complaints. It had always been "dear Doug, how lucky I was to meet him," instead of how lucky he had been to meet a woman who would raise his three kids and then have five more.

"I really shouldn't have this drink," Nancy was saying, her voice surprisingly coy.

"I can't imagine why not." Susan looked around the room. "It seems to me that everyone here is drinking. Why should you be different?"

The response was a giggle.

Susan looked carefully at Nancy. Maybe she shouldn't have a drink if it was going to make her act like a forty-year-old teenager.

"Can't you guess why not?" Nancy asked, putting the glass, still full, down on the table beside the couch.

"Aren't you feeling well?" And was this Twenty Questions?

"Well, sometimes a little queasy in the morning. But you know how that is."

"Not really. I usually get up, grab a cup of coffee and go. There's no time to feel queasy. Of course, when I was pregnant . . . You're not!"

"I am." There was that giggle again. Look pleased, Susan ordered herself. Just because you'd slit your throat if you found yourself pregnant again doesn't mean that Nancy feels the same way. "How wonderful." Say the same things you always say to pregnant women, you idiot, she ordered herself. You haven't had that much to drink. "When are you due?"

"March thirtieth. I just hope it isn't late and turns out to be an April Fool's baby, don't you?"

"I'm sure it will be right on time. Or maybe even early," Susan assured her, knowing just who she thought the April fool was going to be.

"I really do hope it's on time. Doug always goes down to Key West fishing in April and I would hate him to miss the birth again."

"Oh, but he'll stay around for that," Susan assured her.

"He never misses his fishing trip," Nancy insisted. "And I wouldn't want want him to. It's important for him to relax. His work is very exacting, you know. And Doug always says that women make too much of pregnancy and birth. That they used to go out into the fields and have babies and get right back to work before Lamaze—"

"Oh, there's Doug," Susan interrupted. "I must go congratulate him. You sit right here and rest." And she abruptly got up. Nancy's queasiness seemed to be catching. But she didn't head for Doug Dobbs, but in the opposite direction. Whenever she heard a man talk about giving birth in the field and getting right back to work, it made her want to take that man out into a field somewhere and make sure he didn't father any more children.

"Susan. Did you hear about Nancy?" Ellen grabbed her arm as she pushed through the crowd.

"If you mean the news that she's going to go out into the field and give birth while her husband is relaxing fishing for marlin somewhere on a tropical island, then yes. And I don't want to talk about it." She knew that Ellen also considered every baby a blessing and she really wasn't able to deal with that attitude now.

"Well, you don't seem to be in a very good mood. Come into the kitchen with me." She pulled her through the swinging doors.

"Oh, excuse us." Ellen was surprised to find the caterers lounging around the kitchen, munching on canapés and sipping something that looked very much like wine. "Shouldn't you be . . ." she began.

"We're just on our way to the patio," Susan said, before Ellen could interfere in the workers' habits.

"They shouldn't—"

"It's not our business," Susan interrupted. "Let Martha Hallard worry about it. It's her party. Now what did you want to see me about?" She sat down on one of the lounges and breathed in the cool night air.

"Everyone knows you've been with the state police detectives more than anyone else. What's going on?"

"What a beautiful night. I wonder why Martha decided to hold the party inside. It's lovely out here. Ouch." She slapped her arm.

"There's one answer: mosquitoes. Now tell me what is going on," Ellen nagged.

"I don't know. The police have been very nice. They've asked me a lot of questions and—" There was a scream from the other side of a nearby boxwood hedge. And then a muffled giggle. Susan stood up. "Who was that?" she whispered to Ellen.

"I don't think we're supposed to know. Let's find a quieter place."

Ellen hustled back to the house and Susan followed, looking over her shoulder as she did so. They hurried through the kitchen door. This time the kitchen staff didn't even bother to stop their drinking and chatting. They went into the hall, where Ellen opened a door and pushed Susan in front of her into the bathroom.

"What are we doing here? Shouldn't we go back outside and see what's going on?" Susan insisted.

"I know what is going on and if they wanted us to see it, they could have rented a video camera and made an X-rated home movie."

"But . . . Then who was it back there?"

"How should I know?" Ellen sat herself down on the closed toilet seat and picked at the tissue box. But Susan had more immediate concerns. She grabbed the door and started to leave, issuing directions as she went. "Don't move. Lock the door behind me and I'll knock five times. When you hear me, let me in." She rushed back out into the party.

The Hallards' house had been designed for large gatherings. The living room opened into the dining room and that opened into a large family room filled with expensive video equipment and a gigantic stereo.

Off that room, two French doors led to a large solarium. It was there that she found her husband talking to Bob Cooper.

He turned and smiled when he saw her. "Susan, where have you been? I was looking for you before . . ."

"Were you outside?" she asked quickly.

"Outside? Why would I go outside? Bob and I were just talking about the trip he and Ellen are planning to St. Barts. What was the name of that place we stayed at two years ago?"

"The Mermaid Club."

"That's it. I knew it was a dumb name, but the place was great, Bob. Best damn scuba diving . . ."

Susan left them to their vacation plans. She really hadn't thought that it was Jed back there in the boxwood, but it never hurt to check.

"Susan, have another drink." It was Martha Hallard, followed by a good-looking young man from the caterer's staff. "What do you want?" The tray he was carrying hovered by her right hand.

Why not? It was a party, wasn't it? "I'll have another glass of white sangria, if you have one there."

"Of course." Martha took the glass from the tray offered and handed it to her. "I'm so glad you could make it to the party. And I love that dress. Did you get it down at the Country Cross? I was in there the other day and they have

134

the most fabulous things. Bloomingdales had something similar, but not nearly so nice . . ."

Susan sipped her drink and listened to Martha's chatter about clothes and New York shopping as compared to the local stores. When it came to shopping, Martha was a chauvinist.

"I really do think that we should support the local merchants, don't you? Especially now. It's only a matter of time before the press picks up the story of these murders. I turned on the local news in New York tonight, sure that I would hear something about the Hancock murders or something like that, but nothing. But it is, you know, just a matter of time. I was talking to the mayor about it just a few minutes ago. We really should form a committee and try to do something."

"Do something? What can we do?" Susan asked, paying very little attention to the conversation. She had spied Carol Mann over in the corner talking to Angie Leachman. Carol wasn't usually invited to these parties. She wondered if Martha had hired John Mann for security. With all these murders around, it might be a good idea. Angie was looking wonderful in a silk dress of shimmery peach. She really should move closer and get a better look at that fabric.

"We have to put out some good publicity to counter all the bad things that are going to be said about Hancock if the situation doesn't end soon. I don't know what I worry about more: that we'll look like a town harboring a mad killer or a town full of suburban women bored with their husbands and playing around with high school kids while their husbands commute to the city."

"Fooling around with who? Who's fooling around with high school kids? Marty, what are you talking about? What does this have to do with high school kids? Marty, what are you talking about? What does this have to do with the murders?"

"Paula Porter and Kevin Dobbs."

"They were having an affair?"

"Didn't you know? I thought everyone knew about it. It's been going on all summer. That's why no one used the shed for the tennis equipment in the afternoons—everyone knew they were likely to be in there wrapped in each other's arms. Don't tell me you didn't know!"

"I don't play tennis."

"Oh? Well, you can see how this is going to affect the town when it all gets out, can't you? I hate to think what it will do for property values. Oh, there are the Bermans. Fanny called and said they were going to be late. Some sort of sitter problem. I had better go greet them. You'll think about that committee, won't you? We're going to need a lot of workers if we're going to help Hancock."

Martha rushed off and left Susan standing in the middle of the floor, no longer sipping, but now gulping her drink. Did everyone know about Paula and Kevin? Well, not everyone, certainly, she assured herself, thinking of the conversation she had had with his stepmother earlier. She wondered if Ellen had known. Ellen! My God! Was she still waiting in the bathroom? She put down her empty glass on a table and hurried off to find out.

"They'll be going in the bushes if we don't get out of here," Ellen greeted Susan when she returned to the bathroom. "And there's probably a rumor going around the party right now that I'm lying dead drunk on the floor in here after locking myself in. Come to think of it, you might have brought me another drink. You must have had time to stop at the bar, you've been gone long enough."

"Sorry. But listen, Ellen, did you know that Kevin Dobbs and Paula Porter were having an affair at the Field Club?"

"Of course. Didn't everyone? Everyone except his parents, of course. I was just telling Bob the other night that Kevin's had to work too hard for everything and he deserves a little pleasure. I believe in raising independent children, but poor Kevin has been pushed too hard. I could kill that Doug

Dobbs sometimes. He's such a male chauvinist. He sits and does some sort of esoteric surgery and gets paid millions, probably—or close enough, anyway—and then his kids have to work and he doesn't think that Nancy needs household help or even an au pair.

"I don't know about Paula. If I were a sixteen-year-old boy, I don't think I would choose a milquetoast like that to sleep with. She never struck me as sexy, but then what would I know? I guess I've had a hard time seeing her clearly ever since the PTA elections. I still have the feeling that they were rigged by Charline in some way. And Paula must have been in on it, don't you think?"

"I wonder if the police know about Kevin and Paula?" Susan said.

"The police!" Ellen hit her forehead with her palm. "That's what I wanted to talk to you about. Do the police know about the elections?"

"The PTA elections? What difference would it make if they did? You keep asking me the same thing. They can't think that we killed Paula because she didn't nominate us for co-presidents." I hope, she added silently. "And anyway, they think the same person killed Paula who killed Jan, and Jan had nothing to do with the nominating committee. I really think you're letting this presidency thing get to you. What I want to know is what did you and Detective Fortesque talk about while I was in the kitchen? What's that noise?"

Both of them stared at the door, which was being slowly lifted up and into the room, apparently on its own power. Then appeared a hand holding a screwdriver, and a face peered through the opening.

"Ellen? Susan? We don't mean to interrupt, but, well, I couldn't imagine what was going on. If you're okay . . ." Martha Hallard asked, looking confused. Dan Hallard put down the door, dropping the screwdriver he had used to release it from its hinges.

"We were just looking for a quiet place to talk. Nothing

serious," Ellen insisted, getting up from her perch on the john. "Sorry to cause so much trouble."

"Well, I guess you can put the door back, Dan," Martha said. "I think that there must be better places to talk, Ellen. This is a big house."

"Yes. But what I want now is another drink." Ellen walked past Dan and the door as though this happened every day.

"I guess I'll get something to drink, too," Susan said, smiling uncertainly as she squeezed out of the room, past Martha Hallard and the group that had gathered to see what was going on. What had they expected to see? Two bodies writhing on the floor? Everyone knew that type of thing didn't happen in Hancock. Except, she reminded herself, choosing seltzer over something alcoholic, it had been happening at the Club all summer long and it seemed she was the only one who didn't know about it. Boy, Detective Fortesque had sure come to the wrong person for information.

She stopped, glass in hand, to repeat the question: Why had he come to her?

At that moment, Detective Fortesque, in room 214 at the local Holiday Inn, wouldn't have appreciated more information. He was having a very difficult time handling what he had. He took a sip of watered-down Scotch. No room service here; luckily he'd brought his own supplies. The room had come equipped with its own small refrigerator, hidden under the bathroom sink, but the ice cubes must have been in it since the day it was installed, he decided. They gave his good Scotch a soapy aftertaste.

He had come to his room without stopping for a nightcap in the bar, thinking that a few hours spent alone with a pad and pencil might help sort the facts into a pattern. He didn't know what Kathleen was doing. She had also returned to her room: next door, number 216. Was she also sitting and thinking about the murders? What else could she be doing? Rinsing out her stockings?

Well, those thoughts were going to get him nowhere. He picked up his pen and started making lists: lists of people at the PTA lunch; lists of people at the Field Club the day Paula was killed; lists of suspects they had questioned; lists of those they hadn't. Lists of motives.

Because, he thought, that was what he was looking for here: a motive. Or two motives?

He threw down his pen and picked up his drink, thinking how he'd felt two days ago, before he had even seen Hancock. He'd been so optimistic then, so sure he could walk into a roomful of middle-aged PTA mothers and they would . . . would what? Throw themselves at his feet and confess? Throw themselves into his arms and undress?

He could see his reflection in the mirror without moving much. He'd always been good-looking. When he was a kid, he'd thought that maybe it helped make up for his lateness in learning to read and his general slowness in the rest of his schoolwork. But as he got older and school became so easy that he could expect an academic scholarship to college, he found that he was, if anything, even better-looking. And he had developed a charm to go with his looks. Sure, he used it, but he didn't depend on it. He had come to depend on hard work and clear thinking. And, at times, bursts of inspiration that combined all the facts into a pattern that revealed the truth.

At least, that's how it had worked before. He had solved bank robberies, complex cases of fraud, even a kidnapping. But this case he couldn't sort through. His job was important to him. He wouldn't let this one go down in the file as unsolved. He was lucky the press hadn't gotten hold of the story yet. That would put extra pressure on him, and that he didn't need.

Oh, hell. He put down his drink and yanked off his clothes. He'd shower in the morning. As he checked the small travel alarm already in place on the table next to the

139

bed, pausing to turn off the light before he slid down under the covers, a quiet click near his head caught his attention. It was a muted echo of the switch on his own light in the room next to his. Kathleen was also getting into bed. He imagined what she must look like. . .

Shit. He was never going to get any sleep.

Eleven

———◆◆◆———

The next morning, Brett's first words were (after hello) the standard "We don't give out information during a murder investigation." It had happened; the press had heard about the murders. Now they would be all over everyone involved for the slightest lead, the least bit of information that could fill out a story. Forgetting that some of these same members of the press corps were his friends when they weren't on the same case, he sat up in bed and cursed at them in absentia. What a lousy way to start the day!

Of course, he couldn't warn the members of the Hancock community not to speak to the press, and he hoped Kathleen had more sense . . . but he'd better check. A call to her room only told him the line was busy. The question was, was she calling home or accepting a call from the *Daily News*? The *Daily News*—oh hell, at the end of August with no real news, they'd blow up this story until it looked like another Son of Sam thing or the Tylenol murders. Whom was she talking to? He shook the receiver as though it could answer.

Well, he'd be stupid to take any chances. Forgetting his shower, forgetting even to shave, he pulled on yesterday's clothing, found lying crumpled by his bed, and knocked loudly on the locked doorway between the two rooms.

There was some banging around, a small crash or two, some rattling of the doorknob, and then the door opened. Kathleen, wrapped in the bedspread, inappropriately printed with gargantuan Hawaiian flowers, stood before him. The lamp next to the bed, as well as the ashtray, had been knocked on the floor, the result, no doubt, of her desire to use the bedclothes as a wrap. She looked tousled and beautiful and her phone was off the hook.

"You were talking to someone?" he asked, nodding at the phone.

"So?"

Well, she didn't wake up in a very good mood, did she? "Not the press, I hope," he said.

"You think they should get all their information from the victims' families and people like that? You think there's something wrong with the honest dissemination of the news? You think—"

"I think we don't talk to the press during an investigation. We let the public-relations flaks in Hartford do it for us. That's what I think." He walked across the room and smacked the receiver back onto the phone.

"You had no right to do that!" She almost sprang at him.

"I had every right. I'm your superior officer on this case. You had no right to go talking to the press without me saying so." He glared at her. "I'm going to shave and shower and dress. We can talk about this in the coffee shop. I'll be there in fifteen minutes." He slammed the door behind him on the way out.

He thought he was quick, but Kathleen was already sitting at a table for two by the window, sipping steaming coffee, when he arrived. No longer sleepy and sexy-looking, she had pulled her hair back into something resembling a bun and was wearing little, if any, makeup. Her clothes were what fashion people called oversized and he called too loose.

"Coffee?" a young waitress asked cheerfully, putting a menu down on the table across from Kathleen.

"Please." He sat and picked up the menu. Technicolor visions of too-yellow eggs and gleaming French toast didn't tempt him. Oh well, he had to eat. "Cheese omelet, sausage patties, and English muffins," he ordered.

"Right away, sir." Had she winked at him? Kathleen thought so.

"You've made quite an impression in a very small amount of time," she said, looking into her coffee.

"The hell with her. She's not out of high school. Listen," Brett insisted. "I'm sorry if I jumped on you this morning. I was pissed at those reporters. I should have known they were going to hear about this, but their involvement is going to make our jobs harder."

"How so?" She still didn't look up.

"Well, they'll ask every one of the suspects about the two murders and people will exaggerate and other people will read the exaggerations and it will become harder and harder for us to find out the facts. And then headquarters will start getting political pressure. Politicians pay us nothing and then panic when we can't do everything instantly. And that pressure will come down to us. We'll be expected to pull the murderer out of thin air, the sooner the better. Nothing good ever comes out of press involvement. Believe me, they're worse than leeches."

"My fiancé writes for *The New York Times*." The face came up from the coffee mug and the look suggested that he just try and make something of it.

"Oh, I didn't know you were engaged. No ring," he explained.

"It's unofficial. Uh, he's still working out the details of his divorce with his . . . uh, his ex-wife."

"You mean almost ex-wife," Brett corrected.

"I mean that I intend to talk to him when and if I feel like it, and that it is no business of yours."

"I don't care when you talk to him, but I do care what you say," Brett said. "I expect you to be able to keep your personal and professional lives separate and not to pass on information to anyone. You are not to—"

"I am more than willing to keep police and personal business separate, and I certainly expect you to stay out of my affairs. What I mean is . . ." she started to correct herself, realizing she had used the wrong word.

"No problem," Brett replied, smiling at her slip.

The waitress slid their meals before them and they ate. Brett was thinking that, although he had scored a point, the news of a current attachment was a disappointment. More of a disappointment than he had expected.

"Are you Brett Fortesque?" Their waitress was back.

"Yes."

"There's a phone call for you at the desk," she said with a wiggle. "Oh, not a reporter. They've been calling all morning. It's been keeping Lucy on the switchboard very busy. This call is from a Mrs. Cooper. She said it was urgent and that you would talk to her. Will you?"

"Mrs. Cooper?" He remembered. "Oh, that must be Ellen. Yes, I'll talk to her." He speared one of his sausages and stuck it in his mouth. "Is there someplace private where I can talk to her without going back to my room?"

"I knew you'd ask that," she answered, obviously thrilled at her own perceptiveness. "You can use the phone in the manager's office. He never comes in on Sunday. I'll bring your breakfast and you can finish it while you talk."

"Excellent idea." He turned to Kathleen.

"I'll finish here," she said, looking out the window rather than at him.

He shrugged, waited for the waitress to reload a tray with his food, and followed her out of the restaurant, through the lobby, and into a door marked "Manager" in gold letters.

Kathleen had finished her own food and was debating the wisdom of a third cup of coffee when he returned.

"We're going to meet Ellen Cooper at the Field Club," he announced.

"I don't think I've met her," Kathleen remarked, ready to put this morning's argument behind them and get on with work.

"That's right. I talked to her yesterday morning. You were still down at the municipal building."

"Why did you interview her so early in the case?" Kathleen asked, signing her room number across the bottom of her check after adding a tip. "I don't remember who she is."

"To be honest, if I hadn't met her at Susan Henshaw's, I might not have done so, but she placed herself in the forefront."

"I don't understand." Kathleen swung her shoulder bag onto her shoulder and started to leave the room.

"Do you need to return to your room for anything?" Brett asked, following her.

"No. Unless you do, I'd rather just get on with it."

"Great. I told the girl on the switchboard to take messages for today. They'll probably all be from the press, but"—he paused, thinking himself on shaky ground again—"we should go through them anyway."

"Yes." She ignored his comment. "About this Ellen Cooper."

"What about her?"

"Why is she calling? How did you end up interviewing her early in the case? What did you mean when you said she placed herself in the forefront?"

"She's one of those people, I think, who hates to have something happen without herself being involved," he answered tentatively.

"Isn't she one of the women who wanted to be president of the PTA next year that I'm so tired of hearing about?"

"Yes, but that's not all there is to her. She came over to the Henshaw house while I was talking to Mrs. Henshaw on Saturday morning. And when she found out that I was there, she didn't excuse herself, she immediately became involved in helping describe the various PTA members and also the ones that were at the Field Club when Paula Porter died. And then she took advantage of the time when she and I were alone together—"

"When was that?" Kathleen interrupted, going through the door he had opened for her.

"When Susan Henshaw went to make some coffee. I suggested it more to find out if Mrs. Cooper would stay around than to get the coffee."

"And Ellen Cooper didn't offer to help get the coffee?"

"She may have offered, but it was a halfhearted offer at best. And I think that Susan Henshaw expected Ellen to insist. I think she's that type of person. But maybe I'm wrong." They had arrived at the car and he stopped talking to unlock it.

"And so?" Kathleen pushed, getting in.

"And so," he replied, putting the key in the ignition, "she took advantage of the time when Susan was out of the room to explain in long and repetitive detail how she never did anything for the PTA except for the good of the organization. That there was never any personal gain or greed or aggrandizement involved."

"And you knew she was lying?"

"No, I got the impression that she believed every word she said," Brett answered. "But, in fact, I think she was lying. I think she's unwilling to admit to herself just why she does the things she does, why she has to be involved in everything."

"Is this the amateur shrink hour?" Kathleen asked.

"Okay, you don't have to agree with me. Just see what you think of her."

"I will, if you've taken the right turn for once."

"The left turn is the right turn and here we are," Brett answered fatuously, but they were, in fact, approaching the Field Club's impressive gates.

"So where is she going to meet us? Or didn't she say?" Kathleen asked, as he parked the car.

"This is a very organized woman," Brett answered. "I don't think she leaves much to chance. Anyway, she said she would meet us in the clubhouse near the bar. She suggested we make the meeting look like an accident."

"Excuse me?"

"She didn't want it known that she had called us for a

meeting. She suggested that we act as though we were look-ing around the Field Club again and had accidentally run into her." He smiled. "I told you she was an organizer."

"Sounds pushy to me," Kathleen commented. Brett laughed, which irritated her; she didn't know why and she'd be damned before she asked.

As it turned out, they ran into Ellen Cooper as they were entering the clubhouse, and since no one else was around, there was no need to act as if this were anything other than a planned meeting. Refusing yet another offer of coffee or something to eat, they all sat down in the clubhouse meeting room; a large, intentionally imposing space with tables and chairs enough for a hundred people. But they arranged them-selves before a fireplace filled with fresh flowers at one end of the room.

"Well," started Ellen, sitting down. "How can I help you?"

"You called us" was Brett's response.

"Is there something you want to tell us?" Kathleen asked more gently.

"Well, I don't want to, but I believe that I should. I've thought about it and thought about it and I really feel that I have to tell you."

"Oh?" Kathleen made the syllable sound as gentle as possi-ble. Was this a confession?

"Of course, maybe you know already?" Ellen sounded cheered by the thought.

"We won't know if we know until you tell us what it is," Brett explained, none too clearly. "If there is anything you know that we might not know, then you should tell us."

"I really feel that it is almost a civic duty."

Well, thought Kathleen, it wasn't going to be a confession. Her next guess was that the information was more likely to qualify as slightly dirty gossip. Ellen Cooper's next words proved her hunch.

"Do you know that Paula Porter and Kevin Dobbs were having an affair?" Her eyes were open wide. "I'm not spreading gossip. I just think that you should have all the information available."

"Do you think that Kevin Dobbs killed her?" Kathleen asked, trying to remember just where she had heard that name before. He wasn't one of the teachers, was he? Maybe the gym teacher?

Brett's memory was more accurate. "You mean the young man who worked at the Club? The one who got the kids away from the body?"

"Yes, he took them to one of the back tennis courts. That's him," Ellen confirmed.

"His father is. . . ?"

"Doug Dobbs." Ellen supplied the name he had forgotten.

"Oh, that's right," Kathleen suddenly remembered. "His mother's name is Nancy."

"Stepmother," Ellen corrected. "She's pregnant again, you know." It was one of the big topics of conversation last night at the party. She'll be feeling tired very soon. I really should bake a cake and take it over to the kids some evening."

Brett felt she was veering off the topic. "Can you tell us how much you know about this affair, Mrs. Cooper?"

"Not very much," she admitted. "Everyone knows about it, I think. It's been going on all summer. That is, people have seen the two of them going into the storage shed out by the back tennis courts since spring . . ."

"The same tennis courts where Kevin took the kids after Mrs. Porter's death?" Brett asked, becoming more and more interested.

"Yes. I hadn't thought of that. Do you think it means something?"

"I don't know," Brett admitted, "but it is something to keep in mind. Go on."

"Well, really, that's all. I know people said that Paula was looking for an affair. That's why she lost all that weight in the spring, but I don't know if that's the case."

"What would you say the difference in their ages was?" Brett asked.

148

"Oh well. Kevin is going to college in the fall. Yale, you know. But he skipped a grade when he was in elementary school, so he's ahead of himself. He's sixteen. And I know Paula was thirty-nine. She's been talking about the party she was going to give herself for her fortieth birthday sometime in January. So she's twenty-three years older than he is. Or she was, rather."

"But just why did people think they were having an affair?" Kathleen asked. "Did either of them tell anyone about it?"

"I don't think they said anything. But what else would they be doing in the tennis shed every afternoon? Counting tennis balls? And everyone commented on how relaxed they both were when they came out." She shrugged; to her the answer was obvious.

"Do you think Dr. Porter or Kevin's parents knew about it?"

"Well, Jack Porter is a nice man, but a workaholic. I don't think he had the time to know about anything except his own work. I know Paula complained about how little time he spent with her and the kids. They had four kids, you know."

"And the Dobbses? Do you think they knew?"

"Not a chance. You don't know the Dobbses. If they had known about this, all hell would have broken loose."

"They would have been upset?" Brett asked, hoping for a better description.

"Would they ever. Well, not Nancy, probably. She's too wrapped up in love and motherhood and apple pie. You know that she's Dan Dobbs's second wife, don't you? I mean, Kevin isn't really her child. Not that you could tell that from the way she treats them. She's a wonderful mother. Always baking and sewing and taking care of those kids. You really couldn't tell which ones are hers and which are the kids of the first wife. She's done a great job."

"How many kids are there?" Brett asked.

"Eight."

"And how many are hers?"

"Five, and one more on the way. But I said that, didn't I?"

"And what do you think her reaction would be if she found out Kevin was involved with a woman so much older than himself?"

"I think she would be upset, but not mad. Not in the long run. She would probably be madder at Paula than at Kevin. She tends to think her kids can do no wrong. And it would be easy to think that Paula should have known better. But I don't think she would kill Paula. Not at all!"

"And her husband's reaction?"

"Well, that's different. Doug wouldn't have killed Paula if he thought his own son was sleeping with her, he'd have killed Kevin!"

"Really?"

Ellen Cooper shook her head, dismayed. "He is horribly strict with his own children. He has very firm ideas about the way his kids should and should not act. I don't know quite how to explain him. And I don't want you to jump to the wrong conclusions because of something I've told you."

Brett wondered if, in fact, she did hope they would jump to just the conclusion she had been telling them about, but did she realize that she was leading them into suspecting Kevin and not his father? "Don't worry, Mrs. Cooper," he said. "It's a little early in the game to expect any conclusions."

"You mean this investigation could go on for some time?" The thought obviously distressed her.

"Possibly. It's really too early to tell. But you have been a very big help." He stood up and Kathleen quickly followed. "We'll be getting back to you if we have any questions, if we may."

Startled that the interview was coming to such an abrupt end, Mrs. Cooper stood up herself and looked around the room as if in search of something. "Are you . . . are you going to question Kevin and his parents?" she asked, seeming to think of nothing else to say.

150

"Yes, right away, in fact," Brett said. "Could you give Detective Somerville directions to the Dobbs house? I'm going to use the men's room and wash up." He turned to Ellen. "Thank you for your information. We appreciate it. And now, if you'll excuse me?"

Kathleen stemmed the other woman's gushing reply long enough to figure out the drive to the Dobbses', all the time thinking that Brett had stopped this interview too quickly, that there must be something else to learn here. But what?

She didn't know. But there was something.

"She's trying to mislead us" was Brett's analysis, when they were alone again in the car.

"You think she's lying about the affair?"

"Oh, I don't think she would be making that up. She says that everyone knows about it, so we'll be able to check on the facts. I think, though, that she's hoping that we'll concentrate on this and forget about something else."

"What else?"

"I haven't the foggiest," he admitted. "But we'll find out eventually, whether the people of Hancock want us to or not."

"Twenty-two Grant Place, right? We're right down the street from the Ames house, aren't we?"

Kathleen agreed and then asked, "If you think Ellen Cooper was trying to mislead us, then why are we here?"

"Because the Dobbses' name has come up too many times and I want to meet them. Besides, maybe I'm interested in what sort of sixteen-year-old boy appeals to a thirty-nine-year-old woman."

"Sure." Kathleen didn't smile. "So why are you going to tell them we're here?"

"We're investigating a murder, remember? We have to check out everything. Well, I wonder if this is Kevin himself coming toward us?"

Kathleen looked out the window and decided that this

sixteen-year-old boy would appeal to most any woman. To her surprise, the first thing he did was open the back door of the car and fling himself into the back seat.

"Look, I'll tell you anything you want to know. Just get this car out of here before my parents come home from church. Please," the young man begged with an intensity that would have been hard to deny.

Brett responded by pulling the car out of the driveway and back out to the road without taking the time to ask questions. "Any idea where we can go to talk?" he did ask when they had driven a few blocks from the house.

"Turn left up there," the young man replied. "Then keep going. It will lead you to the old road that goes to the reservoir. It's the local lovers' lane, but no one will be there on a Sunday morning."

"Anything you say." Brett swung the car to the left and Kathleen turned and smiled uncertainly at the boy in the back. He was so nervous she felt miserable for him, and this, she guessed, would always be his effect on women. Here was a young man who attracted sympathy. She'd better leave his questioning up to Brett.

But Brett seemed in no hurry to ask anything. He drove the car along the street until they came to a dirt road. A sign indicated the way to the reservoir. Without questions, he followed that road until the imprints in the now dry dirt indicated the parking area the boy had spoken of. He rolled over into one of the spots with a view of the water, stopped the car, turned off the motor, and . . . nothing. He didn't ask any questions, he didn't say anything, but he managed to convey to Kathleen that he expected her to follow suit.

The silence was broken by Kevin himself.

"Thanks. I don't know what my dad would do if he knew you were coming to question me. I don't know what he'll do when he finds out about this anyway."

"About the affair you were having with Mrs. Porter?" Kathleen asked. Brett glared at her, but said nothing. Kevin seemed glad she had brought the matter out into the open and was almost anxious to talk about it.

"Yes, that's it. Our affair. My father is very old-fashioned. Not just about sex, but about everything. He'd kill me if he knew that Mrs. Porter and I were sleeping together."

"You were seen by many people going into the shed by the back tennis courts, you know. I mean, it seems that a lot of folks knew about you and Mrs. Porter. Your father may hear about it sometime," Kathleen suggested.

Kevin sat back and appeared to think about it for a minute. "Well, I would know if Dad knew about it already. And there's really no reason for him to know now that Mrs. Porter is dead, is there?"

"It may have to become common knowledge at the inquest, if it has any bearing on her death," Brett said.

"Oh, it doesn't, sir," Kevin said. "I'd know about that, wouldn't I? And I can assure you that this has nothing to do with it."

"When did your affair with Mrs. Porter begin?" Brett asked. Kathleen thought that he seemed almost indifferent to the question and equally disinterested in the answer.

"Let me think. April or May," Kevin answered. "No, I remember: April."

"You're sure?" Brett asked sharply.

Kathleen stared at him.

"April. I remember now. It was April."

"Were you a virgin?" Brett asked.

"Uh, excuse me, sir?"

"I asked if you were a virgin when you started sleeping with Mrs. Porter? Was she your first affair?"

"Yes." Kevin looked out over the lake, avoiding the eyes of those in the front seat. "I always liked her," he added, seeming to think that more was expected of him. "She approached me one day. When I was out practicing my backhand. She was a very attractive woman and I was curious and . . . well, it happened."

153

"And you've been meeting every day since then?"

"Well, no, not every day, but most days, I guess. Until she died, of course . . ." He still kept his eyes away from theirs. "I'll miss her," he added, but Kathleen thought that maybe he was more relieved that the affair had ended than he was willing to let them know.

"I'm sure you will," said Brett. Kathleen looked at him closely. Was that sarcasm?

"You were at the Field Club the day she died?" Brett asked.

"Yes. But I didn't go near the pool. I was assigned to look after the tennis courts. We all have posts. There are four boys hired for the summer. Just to look after things and generally be available to help out. Our stations are changed each week. This was my tennis-court week."

"But you have time to leave your station? To eat lunch and visit the tennis shed and things like that?"

Kevin looked down at his shoes. "Yes," he answered unwillingly. "But I didn't go near Mrs. Porter that day. I had brought my lunch and I was going to eat it near the courts. She was going . . . she had told me that she would join me at the shed later in the day."

"And she didn't show up?"

"No."

"So how did you find out that she had been killed?" Brett probed.

"I heard the screaming near the pool and I went to investigate. After all, we're hired to help out wherever there's a problem. I went to see what was going on. I didn't know that it had anything to do with Mrs. Porter."

"I see. And you took the kids back to the tennis courts when you discovered what had happened?"

"It seemed like a good idea to get them out of there. The courts were the first place I could think of. I could keep an eye on them all there, see? If I had taken them to the golf course—which is also away from it all—they would have

154

taken off and we would have spent a month getting them back. You know kids," he ended, the wisdom of being the oldest of a large family apparent.

"Yes." Brett didn't sound interested in the answers to his questions. "You didn't always call her Mrs. Porter, I assume?"

"No, of course not. But I always had to call her that in public. It's a habit. Look, do you think my dad is going to hear about this? Because if he does, it would be better if he heard it from me."

Kathleen jumped in. "I think it would be wise for you to tell him."

"I guess you're right." He sighed. "I'll do it now while I have the courage, if you don't mind."

"Of course not. We'll take you back home, won't we, Detective Fortesque?"

"Sure. Why not?"

No one said anything on the way back to the Dobbses' home. Kathleen thought that Kevin was probably trying to think of a way to tell his father of the affair. She couldn't help feeling sorry for him if his father was as horrible as everyone seemed to think. Brett drummed his fingernails against the steering wheel as he drove down the road, preoccupied or angry, Kathleen couldn't decide which.

"We could drop you off a block or so from your house, if you think your parents might object to your arrival in a police car," Brett offered.

"Thank you, sir. That would be great."

The car slowed down at the corner exactly a block between the Ames house and the Dobbses'. Kevin started to get out of the back seat.

"Kevin?" Brett stopped him.

"Yes, sir?" He stopped with one leg on the ground and one in the car.

"Do you happen to remember where you were the day that Mrs. Ick was killed?"

"The day of the PTA lunch?"

"Yes."

"I was at home. It was the week before finals. I was study-ing."

"Did you go over to the house anytime during the day?"

Kevin hesitated. Or did he? Kathleen asked herself. Was she imagining it?

"I was over there in the afternoon after the murder," he admitted.

"After the murder? Why?"

"Nancy—my stepmom—sent me over to see if there was anything I could do to help out."

"She sent you over and told you to offer to help?"

"Yes."

"And that must have been after she herself arrived home?"

"Yes, it was almost dinner time, I think," he added.

"And did you help out?" Brett continued his questioning.

"No. I found Mrs. Ames and Mrs. Voos and asked them if there was anything that I could do. You know, cleaning up and all that. And they said no, so I went back home.

"Can I go now?" he asked, still in his awkward position.

"Sure."

Kathleen and Brett watched him jog off toward his home.

"I wonder what he's hiding," Brett said.

Kathleen said nothing.

Twelve

———◆◆◆———

"You don't have to stop out here in the street. You're more than welcome to park in the driveway."

"Mr. Ames," Kathleen said, guessing the identity of the man looking in her window, "we weren't . . . that is, we weren't coming to see you. We were just . . ." What were they going to do next?

"Mr. Ames, good to meet you" was Brett's more hearty greeting to the man. "We could use some help."

"Yes? Get down, Champ," he ordered the very large, very hairy dog jumping up on Kathleen's window. "How can I help you?" he asked again, pulling back the animal's head.

"We seem to have lost our bearings. We're looking for the Henshaw house. Nice dog you've got there," he added, feeling he had to say something about the animal now straining on the leash to catch a squirrel.

"Dumb animal, you mean. Julia got it for the kids. Said it would teach them responsibility. So why the hell am I always the one walking the thing, is what I want to know. But you don't care about that," he interrupted himself. "You want the Henshaw house. It's easy to get to from here; you just turn right onto . . ."

Kathleen ceased to listen and she suspected that Brett did too. The only place they could get to in town without directions was the Henshaw house. She didn't think that they were going there anyway. Obviously Brett had just used any explanation he could think of to excuse their presence on this street. The dog, having lost interest in the local inhabitants, had resumed his interest in her. She moved her arm so he could no longer drool on it.

"Sorry about that. Down, Champ. Down, dammit. That's what I think we should have named this animal: Dammit. Cute, huh? I once knew a guy who had a dog named that and now I know why, but Julia would never stand for it."

"We appreciate your help, Mr. Ames," Brett said. "I'm sure we'll get there with your fine directions."

"Anytime, anytime" was the reply they heard before Brett pulled the car away from the curb and they were off.

"So where are we going?" Kathleen asked, watching Mr. Ames and his dog jog off down the street in her rearview mirror.

"To the Henshaws. I keep telling you that in a town like this, everyone knows everything about everyone else. If we don't go there now that we've said we're going, people will know about it and wonder why."

The young girl who answered the door to the Henshaws' was clearly thrilled to see Brett.

"Officer Fortesque, no one told me you were coming," she trilled, as she opened the door wider for them to enter. "Do you want to see my mother? She's in the kitchen, getting lunch. We just got back from church."

"Who's at the door, Chrissy?" Susan followed her voice into the hallway. "Detective Fortesque." She was surprised to see him. "Why are you here? I mean . . ."

Brett laughed. "You probably mean just that. We're here to talk to you, if you have some time?"

"Why not? Nothing else has happened, has it?"

"No one else has been killed, if that's what you mean. And we really don't have a lot more information. Just a few things we would like to check out with you, if you have the time."

"Sure. Come on into the kitchen. I'm finishing sandwiches for Chrissy. She has another swim meet this afternoon and I want her to eat early. Jed and Chad are off to a Mets game, so Chrissy and I are alone. You're used to my kitchen anyway, Detective Fortesque. And you don't mind, do you, Miss Somerville? I'm sorry, Officer Somerville."

"You'd better call me Brett and her Kathleen. And you know we don't mind your kitchen. Just lead the way."

Chrissy was left standing in the hall as the adults went back to their business.

Susan returned to the counter and her sandwich makings. "I'd offer you something to eat or drink, but something always seems to go wrong, Brett." She smeared mustard on some whole-wheat bread.

"I'm Susan's jinx in the kitchen," Brett explained to Kathleen. "And we don't need anything to eat. We just want to talk. What do you know about the affair between Kevin Dobbs and Paula Porter?" he asked, jumping right in.

"Boy, you've come to the wrong person to ask about that. Everyone seems to have known about that but me," Susan answered ruefully. "I was at a party last night and it was mentioned as casually as the weather. I honestly think I'm the only person in town who didn't know about it. And Doug and Nancy, of course."

"Well, we know that it's true. Kevin admitted it," Kathleen said, watching Susan put the food on paper plates, put the plates on a tray, and pour milk into a waiting glass.

"Let me take this out to Chrissy." Susan picked up the tray and left the room.

"Now why did you say that?" Brett's voice was angry.

"Say that Kevin admitted it? Why not?"

"We can keep what we know—or think we know—to ourselves. We're here to get information, not to give it."

"Well, I'm sorry. I didn't think I was doing anything wrong."

"You didn't think" was all Brett could say before Susan was back. She wondered why the two officers were glaring at each other. Maybe she should offer them some coffee?

"You said you were surprised to hear about the affair. Was that just because you didn't know about it?" Brett asked, perching on a bar stool.

"Well, I was surprised that everyone knew but me, yes. But I was also surprised that it was happening at all." She sat on an identical stool and started to clean off the counter. "It seems so unlikely, you know."

"Unlikely?" Kathleen thought she could ask and not risk censure from Brett. Her own opinion was that a thirty-nine-year-old woman's affair with a sixteen-year-old man was more enviable than unlikely. When she thought of Paula Porter, she thought here's a woman who didn't waste all her time doing cute little suburban things. Here was a woman with guts. Of course, look where it got her.

"Unlikely in what way?" Brett persisted, when Susan didn't answer Kathleen.

Susan stopped what she was doing, mayonnaise jar in hand. "I don't know the answer to that really. It just doesn't sound like Paula . . ."

Brett jumped out of his seat, interrupting her. "Could I use the phone? Privately, I mean. I just had a thought. It's not that I'm not interested in what you're saying . . ."

"There's a phone in the study," Susan said. She didn't have time to say anything else as he rushed from the room.

"Do you have any idea what that was about?" she asked Kathleen.

"I have an idea," Kathleen lied. "Why don't you tell me just why you think this was so unlikely? I don't understand that word myself."

"Well, you didn't know Paula, of course."

"Of course not, but wouldn't any woman have an affair under the right circumstances?"

"I don't know about that," Susan said. "It seems to me that some women would never have affairs and others may just be waiting for some man to come along and . . ."

Brett thought it was lucky that his call had been finished in so short a time, before these two really started to argue.

"I'm going to get a call here," he announced, reentering the room. "It should be soon. I hope you don't mind."

"Of course not."

"Now, you were saying?" Brett encouraged, resuming his seat.

"I was trying to explain to Kathleen that Paula wasn't the type of person to have an affair."

Kathleen opened her mouth, but Brett was there before her. "Why not?" he asked.

"It has nothing to do with her views on morality or her beliefs," Susan said slowly. She really didn't know how to explain. "It's just a gut feeling I have that she wasn't that type of person. I know, I'm not explaining well. Let me try again."

"Take your time," Brett urged.

"Paula was a very methodical person. If you gave her a list in ABC order, she would go straight down the list and do everything in sequence. And she would do it well. But she wouldn't do anything extra. She just wasn't a person with any flair or pizzazz." She stopped. If only she could make them see the Paula she knew. And why Kevin? That was it. Kevin.

"I know what I'm trying to say. I know what doesn't make any sense to me. It's not Paula; it's Kevin and Paula. If Paula had an affair, the man would have to come to her. She wouldn't be the one to start it: she just wasn't the person to start anything. And Kevin is a nice kid, but I can't see him seducing an older woman. If he was having an affair with an older woman, the woman would have to come after him, and Paula wasn't the type to go after anything. Am I making any sense at all?" she asked, knowing her syntax was lacking.

No, thought Kathleen, but kept it to herself.

"You're saying that if either Kevin or Paula were sleeping with someone, it would have to have been started by the other person."

"And since neither of them would have started it, then how could it have begun? Yes," Susan insisted. "But everyone seems to agree that they were spending every afternoon in the tennis shed, so I must be wrong."

The phone rang at her elbow. "Hello. Yes, he's right here." She handed the receiver to Brett. "Your call. Do you want to take it here?"

"No problem." His need for secrecy seemed to have disappeared. "Hello . . . speaking." He listened for a short time. "Very interesting. Thank you very much. You've been a very big help." He hung up.

"Well?" asked Kathleen. He'd better not leave her out of this in front of Susan.

"Well, it turns out that Susan may have very good instincts," he began.

"How so?" Kathleen asked, doubting it.

"That was the lab on the phone. I was checking on the autopsy. They routinely check vaginal fluids, you know."

"And?"

"And Mrs. Porter had no sexual relations with anyone within forty-eight hours of her death."

"They're sure?" Kathleen asked. "What if the man used prophylactics?"

"They can still find traces of either synthetic material or lubricant," Brett answered. "Yes, they're sure."

"So what were they doing in that shed?" Susan asked.

"An interesting question. And one we'd better find the answer to quickly . . ."

"Mom, company!" Chrissy's voice called from the front of the house.

"Susan. I saw the police car in the driveway . . ." A large, sandy-haired man entered the room. His clothes were definitely suburban-casual like those of the other men in Hancock, but with a difference: his madras shirt had epaulets on the shoulders and his slacks had more defined creases. There was a certain military air about the man. Kathleen had guessed his identity.

"Doug, hi. Yes, the police are here."

162

"There you are," Doug Dobbs said, ignoring Susan's greeting and directing his attention to the two officers. Kathleen thought that he probably was in the habit of ignoring things that didn't interest him.

"What are you going to do about my son?" Doug Dobbs towered over them where they sat.

"What do you think needs to be done about your son?" Brett asked quietly.

"I think you'd better find him and stop hanging about in kitchens, that's what I think."

Brett Fortesque stood up. "In the first place, we didn't know that he was missing, Mr. Dobbs. And in the second place, we're here investigating a murder, not looking for missing children."

Doug Dobbs wasn't going to let the power go quite that easily. "Are you telling me that you don't care if my son is missing?"

"Is he involved in this murder investigation in some way, Mr. Dobbs?"

"He was very close to Mrs. Porter. Hell, he was having an affair with Paula. Everyone knew that. You must know that by now."

"You knew?" Susan gasped.

"Sure did."

Why, the bastard is proud of it, Susan and Kathleen thought at the same time. "Damn chauvinist" was their appraisal and unknowing joint condemnation.

"But that doesn't mean that he had anything to do with her death. And I think you ought to find out just where he has gone."

"How long has he been missing, Mr. Dobbs?" Brett asked, unwilling to mention their interview with the boy, but wondering just where he had gone after they dropped him off near his home less than half an hour ago. How missing could he be in so short a time?

"I'm not sure how long. My wife and I took the younger

163

kids to church around nine this morning. Kevin said he had to work at the pool—and that was an untruth and my kids don't lie to me, officer. Anyway, we came home about ten minutes ago—"

"He's been missing ten minutes?" Kathleen's disbelief was apparent in her voice.

"I don't know just how long he's been missing, but I found this." He glared at her for the interruption and handed the sheet of paper he had just taken from his pocket over to Brett, asking, "I suppose now you'll do something about this?"

"Let me find out what this is first" was the impatient answer. Brett unfolded the sheet and read for a few minutes. "We'll certainly have to look into this as regards to the murders, but you'd better turn it over to your local police immediately. They'll know what to do with it."

"The local police? Are you crazy? What do they know how to do? They're paid security guards. They couldn't solve a crime if their lives depended on it. I want my son found and brought back home, and I want it now."

"It's not what we're here to do, Mr. Dobbs. I'm afraid I can't help you."

"You can't help me? You damn well better help me. If my kid isn't found, everyone in town is going to be thinking that he killed those women. And I won't have him accused of anything like that—even if it's just gossip. So you do as I say and find my boy. I did some very important surgery on the governor's son and I'll be happy to remind him that he owes me a favor. You'll be hearing from your superiors!" Doug Dobbs turned and stalked off, leaving the paper in Brett's hands. Kathleen took it from him without asking, read it through, turned it over a few times looking for identifying marks, and handed it to Susan.

"It's okay if I read this?" she asked, dying to do so.

"You might as well. You've probably figured out what it's all about" was Kathleen's begrudging answer.

"But this says he's run away from home" was Susan's surprised response to the letter.

"What did you think it would say?" Kathleen asked.

"I thought he had been kidnapped."

"You thought what— You know, that's an idea . . ." Brett changed his mind in the midst of his sentence.

Kathleen picked up quickly. "You think he might have been kidnapped and the kidnappers forced him to write this letter? Is that possible?"

"Well, the way things are going, I certainly wouldn't rule out any possibility. What I don't understand here," Brett continued, "is why Kevin was so worried about telling his father about the supposed affair. It appears that Doug Dobbs is almost proud of his son's . . . uh . . . conquests."

"Possibly Kevin didn't know how his father would react," Kathleen said.

"You know, I don't think that's it," Susan said. "I was surprised by Doug's reaction, but the more I think about it, the more I think that it is the only reaction he could have. The man is a lousy male chauvinist and everyone knows it. Kevin must have known too. Or does a son not know that type of thing about his own father?"

"If everyone knew it, you can bet Kevin did too," Brett said.

"So you think he must have been kidnapped, and forced to write this fake note. And that he wouldn't really run away to escape his father's wrath because his father, in fact, would have been proud of his affair with Paula Porter," Susan summed up.

"But that doesn't make sense either," Kathleen protested.

"May I ask why not?"

"Because we were with Kevin half an hour ago and he seemed honestly scared that his father would find out about Mrs. Porter," Kathleen explained. "Now, if we assume that the boy would judge his father's reaction to that news correctly—well, then what was he so afraid of?"

"That he would be kidnapped?" Susan offered.

"But he may not have been kidnapped," Kathleen protested. "And if he was, surely he wouldn't have known about it ahead of time."

"You know, there's something interesting here," Brett said, ignoring their speculation.

"What?" Susan asked.

"Are you going to tell us?" Kathleen questioned.

"Did you both read the note?" he asked, still looking at it.

"Of course," they answered together.

"And it says . . ." he began.

"It says, 'I feel like I'd better leave now. I'm going to hit the road. Please don't worry about me. I'm sorry for all the trouble I've caused. Love, Kevin.'" Kathleen had grabbed the letter from his hand and she had read out loud.

"Look at the outside," Brett ordered.

"'Nan!'" she exclaimed.

"It's addressed to his stepmother," Brett said, smiling.

"If it's addressed to me, don't you think I ought to be the one reading it?" Nancy Dobbs asked loudly, entering the room, followed by Chrissy Henshaw.

"Mommy, Mrs. Dobbs is—"

"I know, Chrissy. Thank you for showing her where we are. Now would you leave us alone?" Susan asked, waving her daughter away, and wondering just why the child was hanging around today. Usually she was more than happy to be with her friends, and she did have that swim meet.

"I repeat, don't you think you ought to let me read it?" Nancy Dobbs asked in a determined way when the adults were alone.

Brett handed over the note without saying anything, and Nancy took it in the same manner. Like the others, she read it through quickly and then went back over it more slowly. "It really doesn't say very much, does it?" she asked, folding it up and starting to put it away in her jeans pocket.

"Your husband left that with us," Brett forestalled her. "He wanted us to investigate the boy's disappearance."

166

"And you need this note to do that?" Nancy asked, putting her hand over it protectively.

"It might . . . that is, anything might help," Brett said honestly. "We certainly could use a few clues."

"Maybe you can help us," Kathleen suggested. "We could use more information, if you have it."

"I don't know what I can tell you," Nancy said. "There was a note on the hall table when we came home from church. That's nothing unusual. In a family as large as ours, keeping track of everyone could be an impossible task; our children have been brought up to write down where they are going and to leave the information in the hall when we aren't home. I left Doug to read the note and went upstairs to change my clothes and make sure the younger children got into play clothes before leaving the house. I didn't even know Doug had left the house until he returned. And then he said that Kevin had run away from home. When I asked him how he knew, he told me about this note and that he had given it to you both. So I came right over here to see it. You've read the note. What is there to add? Aren't you going to start looking for him? He's still young. He could be anyplace . . ." Tears welled up in her eyes.

Susan, knowing how protective Nancy Dobbs was of all her children, hoped that no one would mention the possibility of a kidnapping.

"We'll start looking for him just as soon as we have all the information we need," Brett said, ignoring his previous statement to the contrary. "May we ask you some questions?"

"Anything. Just ask me quickly so you can get started on your investigation. What do you want to know?"

"Why do you think Kevin was so worried that his father would be mad when he found out about the affair the boy was having with Paula Porter?"

"The affair . . . I . . ." Nancy seemed stunned, then she rocked slightly to one side. "I . . . I really don't feel very well . . ."

Instantly, Susan remembered Nancy's pregnancy. "Oh, sit

down," she urged, grabbing her arm and leading her over to the couch. "You should put your feet up, too."

Nancy Dobbs did what she was told, leaning against the back of the couch and closing her eyes for a few minutes. When she opened them, she seemed more resolved.

"I'll do anything I can to help. I'm sorry about that," she added. "I don't know if you know, but I'm two months pregnant. I guess it gets to me sometimes. I'm not as young as I used to be."

Susan handed her another pillow and pushed the coffee table more firmly under Nancy's feet. She was pleasantly surprised to find her vulnerable. She had always assumed that pregnancy was easy for her. "Just rest," she suggested.

But Nancy didn't stop for long. Putting her feet squarely on the floor, she sat up straighter. "I'm fine now. Ask me your questions, officer. Anything I can tell you about Kevin or about his affair with Paula Porter I will. Of course, he didn't speak about such things freely to me, but he knew I would always support him, regardless of what he did."

"Do you know why he ran away, Mrs. Dobbs?"

"No, I cannot imagine why, officer. Kevin is a good boy. Everyone in Hancock will tell you that."

"Then what is this reference to the 'trouble I've caused?' in this note?" Brett asked.

"I assume he is talking about his relationship with Mrs. Porter. Perhaps he thought it might reflect poorly on the family or something. I really don't know. Shouldn't you start looking for him, officer?"

"He's a detective," Kathleen said, referring to Brett's title.

"Then he'll be better able to find my son" was the complacent reply.

"You don't have anything to add to this note?" Brett persisted.

"Nothing. I don't understand it any more than you do."

"Do you have any idea where he might have gone? Are there any friends he could stay with?"

"I can't think of anyone." There was a slight pause. "Perhaps, Detective"—she emphasized the title—"I had better leave you to go on with your investigation. I think, if you have no objection, that I will go home and call one or two of Kevin's friends. They might have some idea of where he is. We may be worrying over nothing. You know how kids are. Well, you may not know, but we do, don't we, Susan?"

Susan smiled her reply, glad to see that Nancy was perking up.

"If you think of anything . . ." Kathleen started to say.

"I most certainly will get in touch with you. Thank you for so much of your time. Bye, Susan. See you at the pool tomorrow." She left the room, almost running into Chrissy, who had been sitting just outside the door.

"Well, she certainly did change personalities right in front of our eyes," Kathleen commented. "Is she always like that?" she asked Susan.

"Not really. I've always thought she was just one of those very maternal women, that there wasn't very much to her. But maybe I misjudged her," Susan answered absently. Just what was her daughter doing hanging around when she had been told not to?

"I wonder," Brett began.

"I can tell you something about Kevin," Chrissy offered, entering the room, hugging the wall as though ready to make her escape quickly if she was not welcome.

"Chrissy. What could you possibly know about Kevin and where he is?" her mother asked impatiently and, she thought, rhetorically.

"Oh, I don't know where he is" was the quick answer.

"Then we really don't want to know what you think you know. Now please leave us alone."

"No, wait, Susan. Maybe Chrissy does know something we should hear," Brett said.

"Ok, just be quick about it," Susan agreed, wanting desperately to keep her daughter out of this.

"I know that Kevin Dobbs is a druggie."

169

Thirteen

———◆◆◆———

"You know what?" Susan asked, standing up.

"I know that he's a druggie. You know, one of the kids who's involved in drugs," Chrissy said, with an attempt at a nonchalant shrug of her shoulders.

"Are you sure?" Brett asked, standing beside Susan.

"Sure. Everyone knows about it."

"I didn't know about it," Susan said.

"I mean the kids, Mom. We all know about it," Chrissy insisted. "He's been running around with that group for, well, for six months or so."

"Sit down, Chrissy," Brett said. "Tell us what you know and how you know it."

Chrissy did as she was told. "Well," she began, looking earnestly at the detective, "I don't know when it started exactly, of course, but he was hanging around with Stanley Gardener and Frank Bond and that bunch around Christmastime. I know that, and you know about those kids yourself, Mom."

Susan nodded her head. "I don't know either of the families well, but I do know that both Stanley and Frank have been involved with drugs. Frank was even arrested in the City for some kind of drug involvement. His sentence was suspended and he had to go to some clinic for therapy, I think. Stanley Gardener has been a problem to his parents since he was young. I'd heard the drug rumors there, too.

He's the type of kid . . . it would surprise nobody to hear that about him. I thought he was supposed to be working on some sort of dude ranch in Wyoming for the summer. But are you sure that Kevin was hanging around with that group, Chrissy?" She looked at her daughter anxiously, knowing this was an age when girls were apt to be dramatic.

"I'm sure of it," Chrissy said. "My friend Andrea at school?—you know her, Mom. Well, her older sister Betty was dating Kevin and her parents made her stop because he was taking her to parties where there were drugs. Andrea heard a big argument between her sister and her mom and dad late one night . . ."

"Do you have last names . . . phone numbers . . . so we could check this out?" Brett asked the child.

"Sure, Andrea and I call each other all the time. Her last name is Emery, and the number is 555-6161."

"Wonderful." He wrote it down on a piece of paper. "Go on."

"Well, Andrea said Betty told her that Kevin would get away with things that the other guys couldn't because he looks so clean-cut and has a good reputation. But Betty said it wasn't going to last long because when you get in with that group, everyone finds out about it and then your reputation is ruined. She's dating John Cavanaugh now. He's president of the debating club and star of the basketball team."

"Were there any rumors of drug use at the Field Club this summer?" Brett asked.

"At the Field Club?" Chrissy repeated. "Of course not." She was indignant.

"You've been very helpful, Chrissy. In fact, you may have been the most helpful person in town," Brett said, sensing she had told him all she knew. "We'll let you get on with your own life now. But please be sure to let us know if you hear any more about this, will you?"

"And don't go around starting rumors about Kevin or telling anyone what you might have overheard today," Susan said.

"I won't, Mom. I'm going over to Nickie's house. Her father is going to help us with our backstroke in her pool. Then he'll drive us to the swim meet. Okay?"

"Sure. Be home in time for dinner." Susan watched her daughter leave the room, shocked about how casually the child talked about drugs. She sighed. Just how good a job had she done raising her children? Were they protected from making these mistakes? She shivered.

"Don't worry," Brett said, reading her thoughts. "She was just parroting what she's heard her friend's older brothers and sisters saying. She really doesn't know what she's talking about."

Kathleen, who knew more about the drug world than her superior, was silent.

"I think we should find someone who does know what Chrissy's talking about," Brett continued. "I wonder where John Mann is this afternoon?" He turned to Susan. "Would he be at the Field Club on Sunday?"

"John Mann?" she repeated, trying to bring her thoughts back in line. "I doubt it. There's not much happening today. The swim meet is at another club."

"Then let's give him a call at home," Brett said, "Do you have a phone book handy?"

"If you just want the Manns' number, I'll give it to you." And she did.

From this end of the line, it sounded as if the person on the other end answered at once.

Susan was pleased when Brett, hanging up, said, "Let's go to the Manns. And could you come too, Susan? John says we might need help finding his house. It could save some time if we had a guide."

"Of course. Just let me leave a note in case Chrissy comes home or Jed and Chad get back from the game early." She wrote swiftly and hurriedly stuck the paper on the kitchen table, which served as the family's message center.

The drive to the Manns was as confusing as it was short. They lived in the converted coach house of one of the mansions that had once made up the town of Hancock. Their house was on a lane with no other buildings and behind some of the more conventional homes in town. There was a street sign, but since no one in his right mind would expect a road there, no one really ever saw the sign. Susan gave accurate directions from the back seat of the police car and they arrived quickly in front of a building more like a cottage than anything else in Hancock.

Like other buildings of that classification, it should have been charming. The windows were made of small glass diamonds. The slate roof slanted at every which angle. The walls were half-timbered. So where, Susan asked herself, was the charm? It was a question she asked herself each time she saw the building. The answer, she knew well, was that Carol, a woman of remarkably little talent, also had very little taste. She had done little to her home, and what she had done, she had done wrong.

Carol herself was waiting for them beside the front door. "Susan," she said, surprised, "I didn't know you were coming along. No wonder you found our place so quickly," she said to Brett.

"You certainly are hidden up here," he commented.

"I think of this as our secret garden," Carol said, as Susan had heard her say so often. And Susan thought again how little this plot of land, overrun with weeds and children's toys, broken and rusting from neglect, resembled the romantic spot created by Francis Burnette. Well, she reminded herself, Carol wasn't a natural housekeeper and they certainly couldn't afford to hire anyone.

"I'll wait out here with Carol," Susan offered unwillingly, as John came out of the house to greet his guests.

"Actually, I'd appreciate it if you sat in on this conversation," Brett replied. Kathleen didn't say anything.

"Oh, I'd be de—— happy to," Susan gushed. Now she could find out what was going on.

When they left the cluttered little house an hour and fifty-five minutes later, she wasn't so sure that she was glad she knew what was going on. There was a lot to be said for ignorance, she decided, as she said good-bye to Carol in the driveway.

"I hope you find this killer," Carol was saying to Kathleen. "And I'm so glad you came to John for help. He really knows what's going on in Hancock."

Carol rattled on and on, obviously proud of her husband. The detectives got into the front seat. Susan resumed her spot in the back and, with a final wave, they drove off, down the tiny road and back toward the Henshaw house.

"Well, what do you think?" Brett asked Susan, looking at her in the rearview mirror.

"I can't believe it" was the reply. "I mean, I knew that there were drugs around. That's the way the world is now. But so many high school kids with drug problems! Drug busts at graduation parties in the past few years. Our kids picked up at crack houses in the city slums. No, I didn't know that . . ."

"And you don't think anyone does?" he asked.

"No, of course not. We'd lock up our kids if we knew that."

"But there is a program in the PTA in the junior and senior high schools to inform parents about drugs," Kathleen said.

"I know. I went to one that was held Chrissy's first month in sixth grade. It described drugs, told about their effects, explained about alcohol use among teenagers. I thought I knew what was going on after that."

"But you didn't." Kathleen almost sounded sympathetic.

"Oh, no. I didn't know anything. I see that now."

"And your friends?" Brett asked.

"I can't believe . . ." she started. "Of course they don't know. If we knew about the things that John Mann was talking about, we'd . . . well, I don't know what we'd do. I still

174

cannot believe that nice boy who delivered for the cleaners was a drug dealer."

"But you knew that he vanished from the community pretty quickly," Kathleen pointed out.

"We were told that he got a job helping tag whales or something up on Cape Cod. Not that he was arrested in the City and was imprisoned somewhere in upstate New York. I can't believe it. And that Kevin and Stanley Gardener and Frank Bond had all been picked up by the local police for using drugs right outside the high school . . ."

"What I thought was interesting was that Officer Mann said that Kevin's arrest had been kept secret from his father. That his mother had come to pick him up and the whole thing was hushed up. That it never went to court or anything," Kathleen said.

"I thought that was very sensible," Susan said. "In the first place, his father would have killed—" She shut up. After all, this was a murder investigation. "You think this all may have to do with why Kevin was hiding from his father? That it didn't have anything to do with his affair with Paula?"

"That maybe he wasn't even having an affair with Paula? That maybe their meetings in the tennis shed had more to do with drugs than with sex?" Brett ended for her.

"That will be easy to get a handle on," Kathleen contributed, "We'll send in a forensic team. If they've been using drugs in there for a few months or so, there should be some evidence. I'll get right on that." She picked up the two-way radio and started talking to the voice that answered her summons.

"Having a hard time taking this all in?" Brett asked.

"Absolutely. I cannot believe it. First all this about drugs in Hancock—all over Hancock, in fact—and now thinking that Paula was involved in drugs. I just can't believe it."

"Can't you really?" Brett asked gently.

Susan thought back to all the things she hadn't understood in the last few years. Sure, there had been kids who disappeared off to the north or to the west to do unusual work or to stay with a family there. And Paula? Had Paula really been the drudge everyone said she was? Always doing just what her husband, her kids, her social group wanted? Had she been all that while waiting—waiting for years for the first escape offered? And when it came, it wasn't an affair with a handsome young man, but an escape into the world of drugs?

"I hate to admit it, but it does make some sense. I mean, once you put drugs into the picture, I guess it explains a lot of things. But we're forgetting Jan. She died and she wasn't involved in drugs, was she?"

"We don't know that right now," Brett said as he started the car. "We still have a lot of searching to do."

The police car started off down the drive.

Susan walked back into the house to a ringing phone. She rushed to pick it up before it stopped, assuming that it was Jed calling from the Mets game. She wanted to ask him to take Chad to dinner so she would have time for a quiet chat with Chrissy. She didn't know what to say to her, but she wanted to continue their discussion of drugs in Hancock. She knew now how important it was to score some points for her side.

But, when she picked up the receiver, the caller had hung up. Oh well, who ever it was would call back. She sat down on the couch near the phone and put her feet up. She'd wait right here in case the phone rang again. In a few minutes, exhausted from the strain and unhappiness of the past few days, she was asleep.

Hours later, the phone rang again, waking her up. She picked up the receiver in the middle of a ring.

"Hello?" If only he hadn't hung up.

"Hi, Sue. Have you been napping? You sound sleepy."

"No," Susan lied, recognizing Charline's voice and hating to admit her fatigue.

"Susan, I'm calling because I don't know who we can get

to run the fund-raising committee next year. Jan and Paula were going to do it again, you know."

They were? Then they were probably both glad to be dead, Susan thought. Anything to escape that responsibility two years in a row. Why would they volunteer to do it again?

"And we're going to have to look for substitutes right away. You know how long it could take to find someone willing to do it. Any ideas?"

This wasn't what she wanted to think about now, but Charline was right. It did have to be done. She tried to focus on the problem. "Well, who did you ask to do it before you talked Jan and Paula into doing it again?"

"No one."

"No one?"

"That's right. In fact, we didn't even have to ask them to repeat. Jan volunteered to Julia right before she died."

"Right before she died? How soon before she died? That day?" Was there some sort of pattern here? Something she should tell Brett?

"Well, it wasn't her dying words, if that's what you're getting at. She called a few days before the luncheon. I think the Sunday before. And she said that she and Paula had such a good time that they were willing to do it another year. At least, that's what Julia told me."

"Did Paula know that Jan had volunteered them both?" Susan thought about Paula last year: how tired and over-worked she had seemed, how endlessly she had complained about the hours she was putting in on the two school fairs, of the bitching about the phone calls that interrupted her family's mealtimes, of Jan's bossiness, and what an irritant it all was.

"Of course, we thought of that right away. But when Julia called her, Paula said she thought it was a great idea . . ."

"What?" Susan couldn't believe that.

"Honest. Julia called and told Paula that Jan had volunteered them both for next year's chairpeople and Paula said great. That the whole year had been a lot of fun and that it would be easier to do a second time. I was in the room when Julia called and she let me hear the answer. We thought that Paula had had a nervous breakdown after all the crabbing she did all year long."

"But you accepted her offer?"

"Of course we did. Do you know how hard it is to find someone willing to do that shit?" Her voice trailed off at the end of the sentence and Susan knew they were both remembering that Charline had convinced her to run the fundraising committee the year before—and had convinced her by telling her what fun it would be. Charline rushed back to the subject. "So, anyway, we never asked anyone else for next year. Do you have any ideas? Julia is going off to Rome in a week and we'd really like to get this settled before then."

"I can't help you, Charline. I really don't know anyone who's willing to take on that task." And I certainly wouldn't recommend one of my friends to do what you yourself call "that shit," would I? she added to herself. "But I'll think about it and if I get any ideas, I'll pass them on to you. Okay?"

"Fine." Charline sounded so complacent that Susan began to wonder if this really was the reason for the call. "So what's happening in your life?" Charline asked politely.

"Not too much. I was just thinking about . . ." She paused, wondering what she could say she had been thinking about. "I was wondering what to wear to the funeral tomorrow morning," she finished her sentence, as her eyes fell on the hand-written note left near the phone. It read, 'Susan, Paula Porter's funeral is being held tomorrow at noon at the First Presbyterian. Burial immediately after. Do I need to call in and tell them I'll be late for work, or can you do this alone? Love. Jed.'

"Oh, I bought a wonderful black sun dress last month. Not too naked or anything. I thought I would wear that," Charline said and then stopped suddenly.

She'd probably realized that the funeral of a woman who was willing to do "that shit" for two years in a row shouldn't be considered a fashion show, Susan thought.

"Whoever imagined that we would be going to two funerals for two PTA members in the same year?" Charline continued. "I get so frightened sometimes."

"Frightened?"

"Of course. Don't you think it's a little odd that two PTA members have been murdered? Two of us?"

"Well, I . . ."

"Two members of the board, not just members," Charline went on, warming to her subject. "Not officers, exactly, but they were chairpeople of a very important committee."

Susan had a sudden vision of masked men carrying machine guns bursting into a PTA meeting, crying, "Officers and committee chairpersons first!" She swallowed a giggle. She was tired, that's all, just tired. "I don't think they were killed just because they were PTA members, Charline."

"You don't? What else did they have in common?"

What else indeed?

"What do the police think?"

"The police?" Susan tried to sound noncommittal, now knowing why Charline had called.

"Susan, everyone in town knows that gorgeous Brett Fortesque has practically lived at your house ever since Paula was killed. Surely you know what their investigation is about . . . what they're thinking of?"

"They just ask questions, Charline. They don't give out information."

"But you must know something!" The voice implied that if she, Charline, had the same contact with the police, she would certainly know something—and probably quite a lot.

"Well, of course . . ." Shut up, Susan, she ordered herself. The only way to prove you know something is to tell her. Was she going to do that? She made up her mind. "Of course, I do know more than others in town, but the police, especially Brett, have asked me to be discreet." She smiled in a rather nasty way, but after all, she was human. "I would tell you if I could. You know that," she added, knowing that Charline knew just the opposite.

"Well . . ." There was a pause. "Let me know if you think of anyone to replace Jan and Paula. Ta."

There was a click and the phone went dead. Susan put down her receiver and she was smiling. It wasn't often that she got the best of Charline Voos, but oh, how she enjoyed it when she did. But that wasn't the point, she reminded herself. The point was that Jan and Paula had volunteered for a second year of the most thankless and hardest job the PTA offered. Why? Could it possibly have anything to do with their deaths? Deaths that followed—at least in Jan's case— within a few days of their generous offer to Julia. It was probably a coincidence that Brett and Kathleen should hear about. She reached out for the phone and then stopped herself. Wouldn't it be nice if she could give them more than a little bit of information? Maybe she should wait and see if she could come up with more.

What more?

Well, just how many people knew that Paula and Jan were going to do the same job next year? That was what the police would want to know, wasn't it?

And how would they find out the answer?

Good question. Well, maybe they would just ask people, and she could do that herself.

Of course. This time she reached for the phone with assurance. She would call Martha Hallard. Martha was pretty good friends with Julia and Charline. At least, she was closer to them than Susan was, and besides, Martha knew what was going on in town as well as anyone. And with a lot of luck, she might even find her at home.

She wasn't. Dan answered the phone. Susan had the presence of mind to remember the party last night gave her an excuse for calling. "Dan, I was just calling to talk to Marty.

180

But I may as well thank you for the lovely evening last night. Everything was wonderful. As usual," she gushed.

"Well, I don't know how Marty does it, with all that she has to do, but she always puts on a good party, I think," Dan said. Neither of the Hallards was ever loath to sing the other's praise. Reflected glory and all that, Susan thought.

"Well, we do thank you for asking us, Dan," she continued out loud. "And, by the way, I do have some questions for Marty. If you will just tell her that I called?"

"Thinking of selling your house? Need more room? You aren't going to add to your family without letting me know?" her obstetrician kidded.

This was one of the disadvantages of having your doctor as a personal friend, Susan thought. "Now you'd be the first to know, Dan," she answered as gaily as possible when she really wanted to gag. It was a good thing Dan Hallard was a good doctor because his jovial bedside manner was a little too fifties for her taste. "It's just some PTA business. I won't bother you with it."

"You gals. Still busy with school even in the summertime."

"You'll tell her I called?"

"Of course. Of course. Say hi to Jed for me, will you?"

After more small—very small—talk, Dan Hallard hung up. But Susan wasn't going to let things rest. If Martha wasn't home, she would have to wait. So who else would know? Possibly Fanny Berman, she decided. Not only had she been treasurer of the PTA last year, but she and Julia were good friends. So Fanny it was.

This time she was lucky. Not only was Fanny at home, but she had a ready answer to the question. No, she didn't know that Jan and Paula were going to repeat their posts.

"But that's good news," Fanny suggested.

"Why?"

"Because it means that none of the PTA members could possibly be suspects."

"Just how do you figure that?"

"Because we wouldn't want them dead. Now Julia and Charline are going to be calling around and trying to talk some poor sucker into that job. I don't know about you, but I'm not going to answer my phone until I hear that they've found someone. You know how persuasive they can be."

Susan laughed. "Then how are you going to hear that someone has said yes?"

"Good question. But I'd rather remain ignorant than be badgered to work. I was planning to cut back on my involvement next year. I'm going back to school, you know."

"No, I didn't." Their conversation changed directions and it wasn't until Susan had heard all about Fanny's plans to return to NYU and finish her graduate degree in social work that she hung up and returned to her investigation.

So whom to call next? she asked herself, her hand on the phone. Maybe . . .

There was a sharp pain in the back of her head and she knew she was falling to the floor.

Fourteen

On waking, her first thought was that it was true that people did see stars when they were knocked unconscious.

"I was hit on the head," she informed Kathleen, who was hovering above her. "I saw stars."

"I'm sure you did," Kathleen said. "Are you feeling nauseous or faint?"

"My head hurts."

"It must. Can you get up or shall we carry you to the couch?"

"I think someone hit me," Susan told her, putting her hand on the back of her skull. Was she going to have an egg just like a little kid? Well, why not?

"Yes, I think someone hit you," Kathleen agreed. "Why don't you just not say anything and let us get you off the floor? Unless you think we ought to call the doctor?"

"No."

"Or maybe you should go to an emergency room," she suggested.

"Just give me a few minutes and I'll get myself on the couch," Susan said. She lay back on the pillow that Kathleen had placed under her head. Out of the corner of her eye, she saw Brett talking on the phone. "Who's he talking to?" she asked.

"Hancock Police. We're putting out an all-points to find the man that hit you."

Susan sat up. "You mean you know who did it?" she asked, but the effort was too much for her and she was forced to lie back down.

"Don't overdo," Kathleen ordered. "No," she continued, "we don't know who it is, but we were able to send out a reasonable description: adult middle-aged male, Caucasian, blond hair, about six feet tall, wearing jeans, running shoes, polo shirt, with a cotton sweater hung over his shoulders . . ."

"But that description fits all the men in Hancock who aren't brunette or bald," Susan protested.

"Well, he can't have gone far. We might have a chance of getting him if he's hiding out in someone's yard. But, of course, if he lives nearby and just ducked back into his own home, well . . ."

"A car. How do you know he didn't just get into a car?"

"He ran off through your backyard . . ."

"Someone saw him?"

"I'm sorry. I thought you knew. We saw him, but just his back."

"You saw him and you didn't catch him?"

Brett had hung up the phone, and coming over to the two women, heard Susan's question.

"You mean saving your life wasn't enough? You wanted us to catch the potential murderer too?"

"Potential murderer?"

"Well, he would have qualified as a full-fledged murderer if he had succeeded in what he set out to do."

"We arrived here in time to scare away the man who hit you," Kathleen explained. "In fact, if you had locked your door or if you hadn't made so much noise when you hit the floor, you'd probably be dead."

"He tried to kill me by hitting me over the head?" Susan asked.

"Probably not, but look at this." Kathleen held up a long

slender strip of plastic that had once held packing cases together. "Whoever he is, he had this around your neck when we came into the room." Susan put her hand to her neck. She could feel no evidence of this story. "I was knocked out and then this man was going to strangle me?"

"It looks like that. When he saw us enter the room, he dashed into the hall and through the kitchen and out the back door."

"Which means that he knew the floor plan of the house. That he must have been here before. That he might even be a . . . friend." Susan closed her eyes and let that sink in.

"But you must have known that the person who killed Jan and Paula is someone you know, someone you see all the time, probably," Brett said.

"I've tried not to think about it," Susan answered. "I don't know how to deal with the thought that I know a murderer. And now I have to think that he tried to murder me." She struggled to her feet.

"You should lie down," Kathleen urged, but not convincingly. She knew that she wouldn't be able to keep still if she had just been told someone had tried to kill her.

"You think the man who tried to kill me is the same one who killed Jan and Paula?" Susan asked, standing shakily.

"There's no way of knowing that," Brett answered. "We've been assuming that the same person murdered both women because the method used was identical and the poison content the same."

"And this is different," Susan offered.

"Yes, and it isn't the same type of crime."

"I don't understand."

"Well, both Jan's and Paula's deaths were planned. It's not likely that someone just dropped by and put poison in their food. Those crimes were thought out. This seems more spur-of-the-moment. And there was a real risk that someone would just walk in on him, like we did. It's Sunday evening.

185

Most of your neighbors are home or coming home. Anyone could have walked in while he was sliding that piece of plastic around your neck."

"But neither of the other murders took place in private. That's one of the things I don't understand about them. They both happened in such public places," Susan said.

"I know. But think of it this way: a public place, especially when it's full of people, is a good place to hide. How many suspects do we have for the two murders? But if you come into a room with one dead woman and one very much alive man, you have a pretty good reason to suspect that the man is the murderer. And, as I was saying, anyone could have come into the room and found this man here. I think he took a great risk. He must have been desperate."

"Desperate?" Susan squeaked, supporting herself against the sofa with her hands.

"He must have a very good and immediate reason for wanting you dead," Brett explained.

"Why?" Susan sat down. There seemed little point to being brave and strong when the police were saying that someone was desperate to kill her.

"I don't know. I think you do, but maybe you just don't know that you know," was Brett's answer.

"You don't know that you know what?"

Susan and the two police officers looked up at Jed standing in the doorway. "What don't you know?" he repeated, entering the room.

"Oh, Jed, someone tried to kill me," Susan cried, rushing to him and relishing the security of his arms.

"I have a feeling that I've missed another exciting event in your life," he said, holding her tighter despite the half-kidding tone of his voice. "Is someone going to explain what's been going on?" he asked.

"Oh, Jed. Wait. Where is Chad?" Susan asked, thinking she didn't want her son to hear about this.

"He's over at the Rands'. We ran into Malcolm and Teddy

at the game and Chad was asked for dinner and to spend the night. I said I thought it would be okay, but that I would check with you and, if you agreed, we'd take his clothes over after our own dinner. I was hoping we could get rid of Chrissy and go over to the Inn, but I have a feeling that isn't going to work out, is it?"

"Actually, it's an excellent idea, if Susan's feeling up to it."

Susan stared at Brett. What did he have to do with this? Why should she go out with her husband? What about that talk she was going to have with Chrissy, come to think of it? But she reconsidered; she could use a good meal in a nice setting. "Why don't you call the Inn and make reservations, and I'll try to find someplace for Chrissy to stay? I'm not feeling that bad."

"Don't worry about Chrissy. Kathleen can fix her something to eat here," Brett offered. Kathleen gave him a dirty look, but said nothing.

"Well, then it's just a matter of getting reservations and going," Jed said, picking up the phone. "You can tell me what happened today while we eat," he added.

"I have to call Chrissy," Susan insisted.

"You can let us worry about her," Kathleen said. "You get your clothes changed and go. We'll make sure Chrissy is taken care of. Maybe I should help you get dressed . . ."

"No, I'm fine. A good meal will help, I'm sure." She didn't sound sure, but no one argued, so she got on with the job. But Susan wasn't going to ignore her daughter. One phone call and she knew that Chrissy was still with Nickie and was thrilled to stay there for dinner. So, with her children taken care of, Susan decided to ignore the horrors of the last hour and enjoy herself. She put on a new blue dress, fixed her hair, and spent a little extra time on her makeup, trying out the new eye shadow colors that she had received as a bonus with a recent purchase of cologne. When she was finished, Jed had showered and shaved and was ready to go.

"Ready?" she asked as he walked into the room wearing a navy sports jacket over his usual summer chinos.

"I sure am. New dress?"

"Yes, do you like it?"

"Terrific. We'd better hurry. I made the reservation for seven and that was five minutes ago."

But they were well known at the Inn, and arriving fifteen minutes late didn't keep them from getting a table in the better part of the room. The Hancock Inn was a direct descendant of the 1774 original on the outside. From its cobbled drive to its wooden gutters, it was as close to the Revolutionary original as money, time, and research could make it. Inside was another story. Shunning wide-planked floors, muskets over the fireplace, and wooden paneling, the Inn's most recent decorator had chosen to pickle the beams, lighten the floors, and scatter French country prints wherever possible. Susan loved it.

The food was as light as the decor, and Susan was just beginning her appetizer of bay scallops when she noticed that, around the corner, were two people she knew: Brett and Kathleen. From the position of their table, she knew that she wasn't supposed to see them, but that they planned on watching her. She put down her fork with a bang.

"Something wrong with the food?" Jed asked, looking up from his melon.

"It's fine," she replied, looking at him carefully. "You know, don't you?"

"Know what?"

"You know that I'm being watched. I was just thinking how nice it was that you weren't asking me a lot of questions about this afternoon. But you don't have to ask any questions, do you? Kathleen or Brett have told you everything. Including that they're watching me."

Jed surveyed her angry face and put down his fork. "You're

right," he said slowly. "I thought you might act this way . . ."

"This way . . ." Her voice was louder than she had meant it to be and some of the diners looked toward their table.

Jed put his hand over hers. "Susan, you couldn't expect me to ignore what's happened. Darling someone wants to kill you. Tried to kill you. You need protection."

She thought about what he was saying and then picked up her fork. The scallops were really too good to waste. She finished off her portion before looking at her husband. "Okay," she started, putting down her fork again. "But am I going to be watched forever?"

"Just until this maniac is caught. We were planning to tell you about it. Actually, we have to. Kathleen is moving into our guest room tonight. I just wanted you to have a good meal and make sure you were feeling better before telling you. I suppose it wasn't a good idea."

Susan sighed and watched Jed spoon melon into his mouth. She was going to say something, but the wine steward arrived with the list for Jed, except, since they were known here, he gave it to Susan. She was the wine expert in the family. She had taken a few courses in wine at the New School before the kids were born and Jed had happily left the selection to her after that.

"Chateau Gris seventy-six," she ordered. "How are you, Pierre?" she asked of the man writing down her order. His name wasn't Pierre except professionally, but in all the time they had been coming here, Susan had never learned his real name.

"We could ask them to join us," she suggested to her husband when they were alone again, nodding at Brett and Kathleen in case there was any doubt whom she meant.

"Not on your life. I want to be alone with my wife" was the answer.

"Because you think it may be a long time before we're alone again?"

"Not necessarily."

But his answer came too quickly for Susan to believe. "You do think that. You know it. We won't be alone until they've caught the murderer." But Pierre's return, the activity that surrounded opening a bottle of fine wine in a chic restaurant, and the arrival of their food interrupted their conversation. Around the corner, almost out of sight, but not quite, Kathleen and Brett were not to know the luxury of any break.

"You think she knows something?" Kathleen was asking, picking the Crenshaw melon, the same appetizer Jed had eaten.

"She must. Why else would she suddenly become a target for the murderer?"

"Why would she hide it from us?"

"I don't think she would. She just knows something that she doesn't know she knows, just like I was telling her when her husband came in."

"You mean . . ."

"Or maybe the killer just thinks that she knows something. But that's not what interests me most," Brett continued.

"What does?"

"Either she didn't know it until recently or else the killer didn't know until recently that she knew it."

"Because he just tried to kill her today," Kathleen confirmed, catching on to what he was talking about.

"Nothing, just iced tea for both of us." Brett interrupted their conversation to chase away the wine steward. "I know it seems a shame to have a good meal like this without wine, but I think we had better stay as clearheaded as possible. Do you mind?"

"No, I agree. I'm feeling a little strange about moving my things into the Henshaws' guest room without Susan knowing. I hope he's telling her now." She looked over her shoulder at the woman they were guarding.

"I'm sure he will. I've called the locals and there will be men stationed outside, too."

"You spoke to John Mann and told him what was going on?"

"Sure did. It surprised him, but he immediately called in some off-duty officers and will have the guards set up before we get back from here. He's really cooperating with us. The locals may not be as incompetent as I first thought . . . Thank you," he said to the waiter who was serving him. "No salad dressing?" he asked Kathleen, after their food had arrived and they were alone again.

"Only oil and vinegar and some herbs—more French," she explained.

So she ate in a lot of places like this, Brett thought to himself. Not on her salary. Must be the reporter. He sighed.

"Did you say something?" asked Kathleen, hearing his sigh.

"No. I was just sighing. You know," he added before she could ask why, "I was thinking. There's too much going on here: drugs, PTA jealousies, women having affairs with kids . . . I feel like I'm missing something. Something significant."

Kathleen looked down at her food: breast of duck, braised fennel, gnocchi. It looked wonderful and she knew she wasn't going to be able to concentrate on it. Alas. "Maybe if we go over everything in order?" she suggested.

"Excellent idea." Brett cut into his beef fillet and tasted it. Delicious. He'd eat in more places like this, too, if he could afford it.

"So we start with the murder of Jan Ick," Kathleen suggested.

"No, we start with two things: one, Kevin Dobbs became involved with a group of kids who use drugs sometime in the spring or late winter of the last school year; and two, Ellen Cooper and Susan Henshaw volunteer to be co-presidents of the PTA—"

"And before that, Carol Mann told Julia Ames that she was

interested in becoming vice-president, don't forget," Kathleen interrupted.

"Okay. Number two is that Carol Mann, Ellen Cooper, and Susan Henshaw all wanted to be on the executive board of the PTA, and all were turned down," he amended. "And three, Jan Ick calls Julia Ames and offers the services of herself and Paula Porter for the fund-raising committee for the following year."

"Wait! How do you know that?"

"What? Oh, you mean about Jan and Paula volunteering for the fund-raising committee?"

"Exactly."

"Easy. I read a note by the phone. Haven't you noticed how Susan always picks up a pencil or pen and scribbles while she's on the phone? Even during short conversations? Well, I noticed a freshly filled page of a scratch pad by their phone while you were checking to see if she had a concussion. The message was very clear." He stopped and took a second bite of his rapidly cooling meal.

"And?"

"Now wait for me to tell you," he insisted as she started to interrupt. "It said, and I quote, 'Jan Ick called and said that she and Paula Porter would repeat their jobs as co-chairmen of the fund-raising committee.' Exclamation point. Exclamation point. 'Without being asked.' Exclamation point. Exclamation point. Ex——"

"I get the idea," she interrupted.

"But not the whole story," he said, chewing the food her interruption had given him time to consume.

"What else was there?"

"Well, after the second series of exclamation points were four very interesting words: 'before the PTA lunch.' Then there were a lot more ex . . ."

"Exclamation points. Yes, I know. But let's go back to the beginning. I don't see how Kevin's involvement in drugs could possibly have anything to do with Jan's death."

"Neither do I, but I won't leave it out. It may be involved in some way. In fact, I think it was . . ."

"Possibly the murderer wanted to kill Paula the first time and Jan ate the poisoned food accidentally?" Kathleen offered.

"I don't think so," Brett said. "I think that food was meant for Jan. Remember more than two months went by before Paula was killed. There didn't seem to be much hurry to get rid of her, and there might have been if the killer had killed the wrong person on the first try."

"Okay. But the only things we can find in common between Paula and Jan is their involvement in the same committee. We don't know that Jan was involved in drugs in any way . . ."

"Let me write that down," Brett suggested. He took a small notebook out of his pocket and scribbled a few words. "That drug connection is certainly something we want to check out. And while we're at it, we could use more information about just what the fund-raising committee did last year and what it was planning to do in the coming year."

"You think the PTA activity had something to do with the murders?" Kathleen was incredulous.

"I don't see how it couldn't; it's a common theme running throughout this whole investigation."

"Well, okay." Kathleen conceded the point. "So what's next?"

"Well, number four is Jan Ick's murder."

"Okay."

"And next in order is that Kevin was at the Ames house the day of the murder. So Kevin is number five."

"Then he has to be number six, too," Kathleen said. "Because number six has to be that Kevin and Paula started taking drugs together—with or without sex. Because people talked about their affair starting in the early summer and the drug use must have begun at about the same time."

"Yes, so six is Kevin and Paula's involvement. And seven

193

is Paula's murder. And eight is Kevin's disappearance—whether he was kidnapped or ran away. And nine is . . ."

"Is the attempt on Susan's life," Kathleen finished for him.

"Right."

"And so what do we have?" Kathleen asked, eating more of her meal.

"Beats the hell out of me."

"Okay. If we're going to list events, maybe we should also list the questions," Kathleen suggested.

"I think that list would run somewhere close to a thousand items. I feel like all I have are questions."

"Like what? I'm not sure I even know what to look for anymore."

"You're not the only one." He stopped talking and started eating again, but the steak didn't seem quite as tender, nor the potatoes as flavorful. Damn. An investigation always did this to him. He hated unanswered questions. He was almost incapable of living with loose ends. And right now that was all he had. That and two dead women, one lost boy, and another woman with a lump on her head.

"Shit." He put down his fork.

"You don't know where to start," Kathleen diagnosed his comment.

"Oh, I know where to start. I just don't know how to find out what it is that Susan Henshaw knows that threatens the murderer so much if she herself doesn't know what it is."

"You think that's the most important part of this investigation?"

"I think that if we can find out what it is, even if it does not solve the murders, us knowing could keep Susan alive. And I'd rather be investigating two murders than three."

He returned to his food, and Kathleen, seeing that he needed time to think, returned to hers. And she was thinking too. Thinking hard, because she felt that she had been no help at all solving these crimes. She ate automatically and sifted through the information. Somewhere, she thought, somewhere there must be a connecting link between all nine events, but it wasn't until dessert that she had decided what it must be: drugs. Over vanilla mousse, she offered this suggestion to Brett.

"Yes." He agreed it did seem like the connection. "We still don't know how Jan Ick was involved—or the PTA—but it seems to me that drugs are the likely answer to a lot of our questions. You know," he continued, "I'd like to know more about the import/export business that the Ameses and the Vooses run. That might give us some information. I can get the people in Hartford to look around for us. Maybe the company isn't exactly what it's supposed to be. They'll have the contacts with the federal customs people who might know something."

"I'll check with my friends in the narcotics squad, too. There may be more there than we know. What else?"

"Let's find out more about Jan Ick. Maybe it's because her death is farther in the past, but I don't feel I know very much about her. Besides the fact that she was bossy."

"You know, I wonder if this doesn't go back to Jan. I wonder if Paula realized that she knew something—either about that death or about something going on in the fund-raising committee or just about Jan Ick herself, and that's why she was killed, Brett."

"Well, that's a possibility."

"It's more than a possibility. It's like Susan's murder attempt. I mean, the attempt on her life. You think she knows something and so she has to be killed to protect the murderer. Why not the same for Paula?"

"Well, Paula's death doesn't seem so impromptu. I keep thinking that the man who hit Susan on the head tonight took a terrible risk. Anyone could have walked in on him. But Paula's death was like Jan's. Someone placed the poison where they knew the victim would eat it and then the murderer walked back into the crowd and waited for it to happen."

"But how did they know it was going to kill the right person? How did they know Jan would eat the sandwich? Of course, Paula could be expected to drink the tea from her own glass, but how did that particular sandwich end up on Jan's plate?"

"I think," Brett said gently, pushing aside the remains of his cake, "I think this is where we came in."

Fifteen

———◆◆◆———

"You might glance over at who just came in yourself," Kathleen said. "And they're heading straight for the Henshaws."

"Well, look at that." His voice picked up interest. "Look at that. No—I was just using that expression—don't look! You look at me and, no, move a little to the left to shield me. No, I meant your right. Great, now stay there." He was silent for a moment. "I can't wait to hear what they're saying."

Brett was interrupted when the waiter appeared to refill their coffee cups. He noticed where they were looking. "Ah, I see the Vooses found the Henshaws," he commented casually.

"They were looking for them?" Brett asked, equally casual.

"Yes. I was at the desk turning in some charges a few minutes ago and the Vooses called. Actually, I believe it was Mr. Lars Voos who called and asked if the Henshaws were dining with us tonight. He said he needed to talk to Mr. Jed Henshaw about something. That it was urgent."

"And you told him that the Henshaws were here?" Kathleen asked.

"No, I was just there turning in my receipts. I told them nothing, but Mrs. Turner, she is hostess here, told them. Usually, of course, we keep the identity of our patrons confidential. Of course . . ." He stopped.

"Of course," Brett soothed, praying the man wasn't going to stop now. "But you know both these couples and so . . ."

The waiter was quick on the uptake. "Of course. That's right. We know both couples so well and we know that they are good friends and have many things to talk about, so of course we tell Mr. Lars Voos where he could find his good friends."

"That just shows what a friendly place Hancock is," Kathleen said, knowing it was an inane thing to say, but feeling someone had to make the effort, since Brett seemed to have shut up.

Brett appeared to wake up. "You're sure it was Mr. Lars Voos who asked about the Henshaws?"

"Yes. I remember exactly. Mrs. Turner said Mr. Voos's name several time on the phone. I'm sure of that." He suddenly grew suspicious and, perhaps, aware that he was not living up to the Inn's reputation for discretion. "You are friends of the Henshaws, too, are you not?" he asked hopefully.

"Yes, very good friends" was Brett's answer. "We were just giving them some time alone before going over to greet them. A couple deserves an evening out without everyone they know stopping at their table to chat, don't you think?"

"Of course, sir. We think that too at the Inn. It's just that the Vooses and the Henshaws, being such old friends and all . . ."

"Don't misunderstand me, Chan." Brett squinted to read the man's name tag. "I'm not criticizing. Not at all. Ah, the Vooses are leaving now. I think it's time we pay our respects, Kathleen. Do you mind bringing us two more cups of coffee—at the Henshaws' table this time?"

"Of course not, sir." The man rushed off to bring two clean cups and Brett and Kathleen got up and headed over to Susan and her husband.

"I thought you didn't want to be seen with Susan this evening," Kathleen hissed.

"I've changed my mind. Susan may be safer with a visible bodyguard."

"With a what?" Susan asked, hearing the last word. "Oh, are you joining us?" she continued, as the two police people pulled chairs out from the table.

"It looks like it," Jed commented dryly.

"We think you might need—"

"We were curious about what the Vooses wanted to talk about," Brett interrupted Kathleen.

"They just . . ." Susan started when Chan returned with the coffee Brett requested.

"I hope this is all right, sir?" he asked of Brett, but managed to include Jed in the question.

"Just fine," Brett said. Jed just smiled.

After fluffing out the flowers and checking to see if the ashtray had been touched, he left them alone again. "You were saying?" Brett asked Susan as soon as the man had departed.

"They just stopped by to say hello," Susan said.

"Hello?" Kathleen repeated.

"You know, 'Hello, how are you? What a surprise to see you here,' that type of thing," Jed said, a little angry that he and his wife couldn't have this time alone together.

"They really said that?" Brett persisted.

"They really said what?"

"They really said something about it being a surprise to see you?"

"Yes, they did," Susan answered. "Although, of course, it really isn't. All of Hancock eats here."

"But the point is that the Vooses called before coming to find out if you were here, so they shouldn't have been the least surprised to run into you," Kathleen said.

"What?" Jed leaned on the table, nearly upsetting his wife's wine. "Oh, shit!" He grabbed the glass. "What did you say?"

"I said that the Vooses didn't just *happen* to find you here. They came here to find you," Kathleen repeated.

"How do you know that?"

"We know, so if they actually said that they were surprised to see you—"

"They did," Jed stated emphatically. "They did," he repeated to himself. "So what does all this mean?"

"It means that they wanted to find you for some reason. Did they say anything that might give you some hint as to why?"

"Let me think. Can you think of anything, Sue?"

"No," Susan answered slowly. "They really acted like it was just a casual greeting. You know, two couples running into each other by chance and the one stopping to say hello to the other. It really didn't seem to be much more than that. Although . . ."

"Although?" Kathleen prompted.

"Although Charline seemed nervous. I thought so at the time. In fact, she seemed very nervous. And, you know, they made a big deal about running into us and we're really not very good friends. In fact, I've always felt that Charline looked down on me as being not quite in her class."

"Now wait. Let's take this one thing at a time," Brett came back into the conversation. "First they lied to you about the meeting being by chance, and then they acted more friendly than usual. How much more friendly?"

"Well, now that I think about it, much more," Susan answered. "They would usually just wave or say hello to us and then go to their table— Should we be seen together like this?" she asked, interrupting herself.

"Don't worry about it," Brett answered, not telling her that he was making his presence known quite intentionally. "Go on," he urged.

"Well, they really were much more friendly than usual. I can't remember them stopping by the table like that before. I don't know why I didn't think about it at the time."

"And Charline seemed uncomfortable, you said?"

"Nervous. She just rambled on and on about how we must get together more often and see more of each other. Were we going out on the Island this year?—that type of thing. Social chitchat, but not at all like her. Charline is usually quite businesslike and to the point."

"You know, the same is true of her husband," Jed added. "We meet around the kids' school and at some of the club functions, but I don't think he could possibly consider me his friend. I don't think of him as mine. And he was acting like we were old war buddies or something. You don't think that this has anything to do with Susan's hit on the head tonight, do you? You don't think that Lars Voos was the one who—"

"I don't think anything at this point. And you better not either," Brett interrupted, trying to calm the other man, who was getting furious at the thought that he might just have been with the person who hurt his wife. "What we do know is that the Vooses wanted to see you here and we still don't know the reason."

"Well, I can't think of anything they said to let us know why either. It was just like Susan said. Social chitchat."

"Did they ask you any questions?"

"Besides whether we were going to the Island this summer—they have a house in Montauk—nothing. Oh, and they wanted to know how Susan was feeling . . ."

"Just Susan?"

"Just Susan," Jed answered. "Just like they might know that there was a reason she might not feel very well," he added. "They must have something to do with this. I'll bet Lars Voos was the one that hit her on the head. He's the murderer." Jed rose from his chair and was grabbed by all three of his tablemates, Susan managing at last to spill the glass of wine that she had left untouched all evening.

"Look." Brett grabbed Jed by the arm and held him still. "This is not the time or place to make a stink. Understand? We'll take care of it, and I can assure you, if Lars Voos is in any way involved in this thing, if he did anything to hurt your wife, we will find out about it and see to it that he gets what he deserves. But you have to let us do this. Stay out of it." This last order was whispered as a battalion of waiters and busboys rallied around to clean up the spilled liquid.

"Tell your husband you're not feeling well and let's get out of here," Kathleen whispered to Susan.

Susan did as she was told and the four of them, bills paid, good-byes said, were out of the Inn in record time.

"Quick thinking," Brett complimented Kathleen as they had a private conference by the police car in the lot, Jed and Susan having gone off to find their Mercedes.

"You think Lars is our murderer?" she asked.

"No, but I wouldn't be at all surprised to find out that he did hit Susan on the head this afternoon."

"And you think he came to the Inn to kill her?"

"No, but I'll be damned if I do know why he came. Maybe he wanted to know if he had hurt her. Or, more likely, to see if she recognized him. That would account for Charline's nervousness. Whatever the reason, my intuition tells me that Lars hit Susan on the head this afternoon. Of course, if that's true, it's a relief."

"A relief?"

"Because I don't think he'll try again. I think it was a spur-of-the-moment type of thing. He was trying to protect himself from something and lashed out. But he won't do it again. It's time to get busy looking into his business. You go home with Susan and keep an eye on her. I may be all wrong about this and there may be dozens of men trying to murder her in the night. I've got some checking up to do."

"Do you want me to meet you someplace tomorrow morning, or will you come to the Henshaws'?"

"I'll be over first thing. We can talk then." A beige Mercedes pulled up beside them. "Well, here's your ride."

Kathleen got in, and watching them drive off, Brett got the distinct feeling that he had wanted to kiss her good-night.

You have work to do, he reminded himself, as he returned to his motel room and its overworked phone.

Kathleen was looking around the well-decorated guest room a few minutes later and thinking along similar lines. The drive from the Inn had been uneventful; most of the talk had centered around Jed's worries about his wife's safety and Kathleen's assurances of the police protection. Riding into the driveway of the house, she had spied two separate policemen stationed within view of the front door. The Henshaws had appeared unaware of their presence. As she was led to the second-floor guest room, Kathleen had gotten a pretty good idea of the upstairs layout. Of course, if Brett's instincts were right, Susan didn't need protection. But she would do her job nevertheless. Now, alone in the room she was to sleep in, she found herself wishing for a phone.

Of course the reason she wanted to talk to Brett was purely professional, she assured herself, thinking, at the same time, that the phrase "purely professional" sounded phony. It was just that the case was her major concern and with whom else was she to talk it over? Brett was a professional and would understand the way she thought. She just had more in common with him than with the suburbanites around here.

Susan had lent her a nightgown and she stopped in the midst of removing her clothes and looked at it. Pink, of course, and high-necked, and, naturally, not transparent. Suburbanites, she thought with disgust, wondering if they had sex for any other reason than to fill their schools and give the women a hobby running for PTA offices, and, in this case, murdering other people. She put on the virginal clothing and sat down on the bed to rummage in her large purse. She kept a small leather pouch of emergency supplies there; they usually came in handy for sitting in sleazy hotel rooms during all-night stakeouts, not in this type of luxury setting. She found the turquoise pouch and dumped it onto the white bedspread. Toothbrush, toothpaste, skin lotion, nail file, diaphragm . . .

There was a knock at the door. "Kathleen, may I come in?"

Kathleen was tired and had to resist answering "It's your house." She rushed over to the door and opened it for her hostess.

"I just wanted to see if there's anything you need. I didn't even think of a toothbrush or anything like that before . . ." She stopped, seeing the small pile in the center of the bed. "It looks like you have everything you might need."

Kathleen self-consciously picked up a small bottle of nail varnish and the diaphragm and put them back into the pouch and out of sight. "Yes, I've learned to be prepared in this business," she answered, looking at Susan's very silky, very expensive, very revealing negligee, then glancing at the Mother Hubbard that had been lent to her.

Now it was Susan's turn to feel self-conscious. She glanced at the peachy gown she was wearing, almost embarrassed. "I gave you that one because I thought it was more likely to fit you. You're . . . taller, and, well, more filled out than I am . . . and I thought everything I wear would be binding on you. My mother-in-law sent that for Christmas last year," she finished apologetically. "You know, it really is so very typical of what a mother-in-law would get you that it makes me laugh." And she did just that.

Kathleen found herself joining her. "Come to think of it, it looks a lot like one my mother-in-law sent me the first Christmas Peter and I were married. Only, that one was yellow and it made anyone anywhere near it look jaundiced." She laughed more.

"I didn't know you were married," Susan commented when she had her breath back.

"I'm not. Not anymore." Kathleen sobered up quickly. "My husband's dead." As usual, she was surprised how easy it was to say. My husband's dead, she repeated in her mind. Three, no, four words that anyone could repeat in polite conversation. And no one could or would guess the razor's edge of anguish that she felt each time she had to confront the truth: Peter was dead and she would never see him again.

There was an unusual silence; Susan had not rushed in to say the polite, soothing things. Kathleen was surprised. And because she was surprised, she explained more than usual. "He was a cop, too. In fact, I met him on my first assignment out of the Academy. We fell in love right away, and were married two months later. He died almost three years ago."

"How?"

Kathleen was surprised. Only the most insensitive people usually jumped right in with questions like that, and Susan hadn't struck her that way. She looked into the other woman's face and saw compassion and, she thought, understanding. She took a deep breath. "He was killed in an automobile accident on the way home from work one night."

Susan still didn't say anything, still waited for the rest of the story.

"He was drunk," Kathleen continued, surprising herself. "He was drunk and he hit a slippery patch of road and wrapped his car around a phone pole." She took a deep breath.

"He was an alcoholic. I knew that when I married him. I could say that I was young and thought that love would cure him, but I didn't think that far. I loved him. I loved his honesty, his integrity, his dedication to his work. He never drank on the job. He was a good cop. But when things got too much for him, when he saw the terrible things people do to each other—and cops are exposed to that part of the world more often than most people—then, when he couldn't take it anymore, he drank to forget. Usually he drank at home. This time he had been out on a case, a murder case involving a little girl. He had to forget, to escape the ugliness right away. So he went to a bar about halfway between the station and our house. Except that he never completed the second half of the trip."

Susan didn't say anything right away; instead, she reached out and covered the other woman's hand with her own.

Kathleen looked up and smiled at the gesture. "I feel you understand, but you couldn't," she said.

"Why not?" Susan said. "Your husband saw what was happening in the world and he tried to help and sometimes it got to be too much for him and he had to escape. At least he didn't turn his back on the people who needed help. He did what he could. I think that's wonderful. No wonder you loved him."

"But if only he had cared less about them and more about me. If only he had taken better care of himself for me," Kathleen cried out, starting to cry, horrified at her own words.

Susan tightened her grip on Kathleen's hand, but didn't say anything. She thought that Kathleen knew that an alcoholic wasn't in control of his own life, and she knew that Kathleen understood the terrible things that a policeman had to learn to live with. She let the other woman cry it out.

Kathleen did just that and then, with her customary determination, she pulled herself together. "I'm involved with another man now—engaged, in fact—but I still miss Peter," she said, not apologizing for her behavior.

"Of course you do. I would always miss Jed if anything happened to him. I know how you feel."

Kathleen, who had spent a lot of time in the past few days looking down on this woman, thought she did indeed know how she felt. "I think I'd better apologize," she said.

"For crying?"

"For thinking that you were a typical suburban housewife."

Susan laughed a bit bitterly. "There is no such thing as a typical suburban housewife anymore. I sometimes doubt if there ever was . . . say, do you want a nightcap?"

Kathleen, still sniffling, nodded yes.

"Let's go downstairs and get some brandy or Scotch or something."

Once settled on the couch with a drink in her hand,

Kathleen felt better. Susan got herself a drink and looked through the shutters out the window. "Your men are still there," she commented, going over to the fireplace.

"You knew they were there!" Kathleen was surprised again.

"While it's true that people do walk their dogs at night in Hancock, rarely do two men walk two ominous German shepherds in circles in front of a house for hours on end. Shelties, maybe, or huskies, or spaniels seem to be getting more popular I've noticed. But not German shepherds. The only person I know with a German shepherd is Carol Mann—come to think of it, one of those dogs out there is probably it. Adolph, I think it's called. I always thought it was rather a bad joke."

She stooped down and turned a switch near the andirons. Flames shot up through the logs which, Kathleen had just noticed, were artificial. Susan smiled at Kathleen's surprise. "Pretty tacky, I know. The people who lived in this house before us had it put in. We have a real fireplace in the den, but we've never gotten around to having this replaced. I guess we don't mind it. And it is convenient. It doesn't give off much heat, but it's nice to have on a night like this. Cheerful."

"I can see why you keep it," Kathleen said, sipping her drink and then setting down the half-empty glass. Without asking, Susan picked up the bottle of Courvoisier and refilled it.

"I think I have all the protection I need right outside that window," she said, when Kathleen started to protest. "And you've had a hard day."

"You don't seem very worried about your life," Kathleen commented, deciding not to make a fuss about the drink. Besides, it looked good.

"I think Lars Voos tried to kill me today—that is, if anyone tried. But I think that he is the person who hit me on the head. And he's probably decided that it's not a good idea," she finished.

"That's what Brett thinks," Kathleen blurted out, instantly regretting it.

"Then I'd better tell him about the aftershave or cologne or whatever. It's just like in a book or on TV, isn't it?"

"What is?"

"How I recognized Lars. His cologne. I smelled it when he hit me over the head tonight. In fact, that's all I remember thinking about the person who hit me. That he smelled good. He hit me before I could realize that there wasn't supposed to be anyone in the room but me."

"And you recognized the smell as Lars's?"

"Not until he came into the restaurant tonight. He really was wearing a lot and I thought to myself that it was too much. Jed doesn't like any scent with food and I rarely wear cologne when we eat. And then it occurred to me that it was the same scent that I had smelled before I was knocked out."

"Of course, it could be that the person who hit you on the head was wearing the same cologne or aftershave," Kathleen suggested.

"Of course," Susan agreed.

"You don't know that it's some little-known cologne sold only in a far-off eastern port that Lars's company imports just for his own use or anything like that?" Kathleen asked hopefully.

"Not that I know of," Susan answered. "It's just a hunch that it was Lars. But I'm pretty sure I'm right."

Kathleen knew of no way to argue against hunches. She didn't try. She sat and sipped her drink, thinking that if it had been Lars Voos, Susan may have been a lot luckier than she thought. Kathleen remembered the Voos child insisting her father owned a gun.

"You don't think much of Hancock, do you?"

"It's a very pretty town, at least what I've seen of it is," Kathleen responded, adding to the credibility of Susan's hunches.

"Oh, you don't have to see it all. It's all pretty. We have very strict ordinances to make sure it stays pretty, too."

"Well, then . . ." Kathleen didn't know what to say.

"But you don't think much of the people who live here—the women, I mean."

Kathleen looked at Susan and decided to answer. She'd been acting unprofessionally since entering the house, why stop now?

"I don't know them enough to not like them," she started, as tactfully as possible, "I just think that everyone here is a little too homogeneous and pretty—like your local ordinances that keep everything looking nice, I guess," she added.

She must have looked guilty, because Susan began her answer by excusing her. "I know how you feel. I felt the same way when we first moved here. Only I was going to live here. We had just spent every dime we had for the down payment and closing costs on this house. The first woman I met here told me that she had always known that she would have a mink coat before her fortieth birthday. The second, when asked in some context about her goals in life, said she wanted to get her oldest boy to eat vegetables. If we had had the money, I would have packed up and moved right back to the West Side of Manhattan. I thought if I stayed here I would become like them; I thought that because I was here I must be like them." She stopped talking and sipped her drink.

"And?" Kathleen prompted, interested in spite of herself.

"And I found out that the woman with the mink would go out of her way to help anybody. She was a materialist—dirty word, that—but when a friend of her son's slashed his arm sticking it through the glass on their porch door, she took care of that child immediately, including lying him down on her brand-new antique Oriental rug. Sure, she likes material things and maybe they aren't the things I like, but her priorities are in the right place."

"And the woman whose goal in life is to get her son to eat vegetables?"

209

"Oh, her. She's an asshole." Susan chuckled. "She really is. And they exist in the city too."

"Okay. Maybe I've been chauvinistic," Kathleen admitted.

"Hey, don't give up so easily," Susan suggested. "There's a lot wrong with living out here. And I can list those things."

"So let's hear the whole story."

"Well, a lot of people say that the worst thing about the suburbs is that the women spend too much time and effort over their children, but I don't agree. Oh, there are women who are giving up their own lives and trying to live out their dreams in the lives of their children, but I think that happens everyplace."

"So what's the worst thing then?"

"There's too much space between what the husband does and what the wife does, I think. The man of the house goes into the city and does his thing and the wife stays around Hancock and does her thing. Because of the commuting time, the husbands are away from home for long hours. A lot of the time, the couple starts living two separate lives. You know, if you get a group of women around the pool or wherever, they'll start talking about the marriages breaking up—there seem to be a lot of them right now in our group—and usually, the husband goes off with someone he works with. Of course, everyone thinks that it's a midlife crisis on the husband's part and that he's just out after more or different sex, but you know, I don't think so: I think it's because the wives shut their husbands out of their lives here."

"You mean. . . ?"

"I know, I'm not explaining very well. What I mean is that the wives build their own lives around their kids and school and their own social circle and the men pop in and out on weekends. I think the men begin to feel left out, whether they know it or not. And so they turn to someone who is more closely involved in their city life, their work life."

"That's interesting," Kathleen commented, trying not to yawn. "You know, though, the only couple around here that works and lives here is the Manns."

"And also the Ameses and the Vooses. Their main office is in Darien, although I understand they have a small office in the City. But they're usually in Connecticut, I think. And Charline and Julia seem more involved in their husbands' work than the rest of us—they're always talking about shipments coming in and things like that.

"But you're tired," Susan continued. "Let me turn off this fake fire so we don't wake up to a burned-down house and we'll get to bed. Unless you think that we should make some coffee and send it outside to the police first."

"They'll have brought their own," Kathleen murmured, too tired to remember all the stakeouts when she would have welcomed more than anything a cup of coffee that didn't come out of a machine at 7-Eleven. "Let's go to bed. I may be wrong, but I'll bet Brett is here at the crack of dawn tomorrow."

Susan, remembering the birth control, wondered for a moment about Kathleen's relationship with her partner. But it was too late to get into that—even if she had known how to bring up the subject.

Sixteen

—◆◆—

Brett and Kathleen were drinking coffee; Chrissy and Chad were off to tennis lessons; and Jed had left for the City. Susan sat on a stool near her stove, stirring eggs and trying to count the number of meals she had eaten with the police since Friday.

". . . I woke up this morning feeling that I know something that I don't know I know," Kathleen was saying.

"Maybe you need another cup of coffee," Brett suggested.

Kathleen, convinced that the key to all these events was now somewhere just at the corner of her mind, decided to say nothing. "You really think there's something to the idea that the Ames-Voos company is involved in bringing drugs into the country?"

"It's called Farnsworth Import/Export," Brett said.

"Farnsworth? Anyone we should know?"

"Evidently Farnsworth was the man who started the firm back in fifty-nine. It did a booming business during the Vietnam War. They got contracts for PX business and made a bundle, but after the war ended, either Farnsworth lost interest, or he had just been lucky to get those contracts in the sixties. The business was almost bankrupt when Miles Ames bought it in 1979. He'd been working for a big exporter in New York City, bringing in clothes from the Far East—sneakers from Korea, mainly—anyway, his father and mother died in a car crash and he used his inheritance to finance the deal. And—this is interesting—at the time, Farnsworth Import/Export was doing so badly that half-interest in the company was something like a hundred thousand."

"And now? Oh, thanks," she said, accepting the plate of scrambled eggs, sausage patties, and homemade scones that Susan had just put in front of her. Picking up her fork, she continued, "And now it's worth what?"

"Well, it's not a public company. Right now it is solely owned by the Ames and the Voos families, but I have a friend in the IRS and he went into their computers yesterday afternoon—what excuse he gave for voluntarily working on a Sunday in the summer might be interesting to know—and he says the company is reporting a profit of one hundred and fifty thousand dollars per year."

"Does that seem a little low to you?" Kathleen asked.

"Wait a minute. How can Julia and Charline live as well as they do on half of that?" Susan said, then realized that her comment was probably inappropriate. "I didn't mean to interrupt. I . . ." She was embarrassed. "I could eat in another room." She picked up her plate and coffee mug as if to make good her offer immediately.

"No, stay right here," Brett insisted. "In the first place, it is your kitchen, and in the second place, that is just the type of comment I want. My impression would be that the Ameses and the Vooses were living way beyond their income too, but you know better than I. So I'm inclined to suspect another source of money somewhere."

"Well"—Susan was thinking hard—"you know, maybe they get those expensive things wholesale?"

"What things?" Kathleen asked, putting a piece of sausage in her mouth.

"Furs. Jewelry."

"They have a lot?" Brett asked.

"Well, come to think of it, they probably have a new fur every two years or so. And they have marvelous jewelry—

both of them. Of course it could be fake. I'd never know the difference."

"Even if they get them wholesale, it's still a lot of wealth to pull out of a business doing that type of billing—"

"What if they're lying on their tax forms?" Kathleen interrupted. "Maybe they're making a lot more than they put down."

"They were audited two years in a row, according to my friend, and while, of course, you can hide things during an audit, I don't think they could hide that much—not enough to account for jewelry and furs and those houses. And they didn't get the houses wholesale. The money probably comes from an illegal source. The IRS thinks so too. They're very interested in Farnsworth Import/Export."

"You think drugs," Kathleen said.

"Yes. They probably just smuggle the drugs into the country. They would sell them to the dealers," Brett said. "I'm sure the Vooses and the Ameses aren't doing any street selling. Not that that makes it any better, of course."

The phone rang and Susan got up to answer it. "Hello . . . yes . . . he's here."

She handed the receiver to Brett, who had gotten up at the same time she had, obviously expecting a call.

"You think that this is all true? That it's drugs we're talking about?" she asked Kathleen, resuming her seat.

"It's hard to tell, but I think Brett has a good idea that it is. He's been talking to the various agencies involved in narcotics trafficking and the name Farnsworth Import/Export obviously wasn't unknown to them. But that isn't proof," she added, "Most companies are being checked out these days. The drug problem has gotten too big to ignore any possibilities. So the fact that they know of the company doesn't necessarily mean anything."

"In this case it does," Brett interjected, hanging up the phone.

"Our sources came through," Kathleen guessed.

"No. Kevin Dobbs has been found and he says that he was getting cocaine from the Ameses."

"What? I can't believe it." Susan was stunned.

"Maybe you'll believe it if you hear it from him directly," Brett said. "Come on."

"Where are we going?"

"The Field Club. It looks like he didn't run away at all. At least he didn't leave town. He spent the night in the boiler room in the basement."

"What?" Kathleen and Susan ran out the door after Brett, asking questions.

"Who found him?"

"Did he say the cocaine came from the Ameses directly?"

"Who is he talking to?"

"What—"

"Just wait till we get in the car and I'll tell you everything," Brett said.

"John Mann found Kevin in the boiler room this morning—about half an hour ago, in fact. He was checking up on some strange sounds he'd heard and went downstairs and there was the kid, asleep. The noises were Kevin snoring. Seems he had taken food from the kitchen and even had a shower last night after everyone left the Club. Evidently Kevin was confused and didn't know what to do when we started questioning him. He'd planned to take off and stay with a friend out west somewhere, but he couldn't bring himself to leave."

"So he stayed here and planned to do what?"

"He stayed here. I don't think he had any plans, at least I couldn't tell from what Sergeant Mann said," Brett said.

"But John said that Kevin has confessed to taking drugs? Drugs that he bought from the Ameses?" Kathleen asked, to be sure she had heard right the first time.

"Exactly . . . but here we are. We'll be able to ask him everything ourselves."

They found Kevin and John Mann in the bar, sharing a pot of coffee.

"Would any of you like some?" Mann offered.

They all refused and got right down to work. "I think you had better tell us the whole story from the beginning, Kevin," Brett said. "You might want to have a lawyer present, though."

"I've already told everything to Sergeant Mann," Kevin answered, obviously close to tears. "I don't think I need a lawyer now."

"Well, take your time. And don't worry. These things can be worked out," Mann said. "Let's just say this is all off the record, okay?"

Brett had never heard the term used in police work, but he was willing to go along with anything to get information. And if the locals were willing to bend the rules, he certainly was. "Just do as Sergeant Mann says and tell us everything."

Kevin got off to a slow start, but when he was finished with his story fifteen minutes later, they had a pretty good idea of what had been happening to Kevin Dobbs for the last year: how he had started using marijuana and cocaine on weekends and at parties, how he had found himself a part of a new crowd of friends, all of whom were involved in drugs to some extent, some more, some less; and how that world had broken up at the end of March.

There had been a drug bust at a party Kevin was planning to attend. Luckily, he was late, and as he drove up to the door, he saw the police take the kids away. It didn't take more than a glance for him to get the picture of what was going on and to turn his car around and get out of the vicinity. Kevin had already been picked up by the police that month and he knew that they were not going to hush up a repeat happening. He swore that he was going to lay off drugs and stay away from that group, period.

Well, he'd left that group all right. Summer was coming

216

and kids were going their different ways, and it was fairly easy for him to stop seeing them. And besides, he had started his summer job at the Field Club. It kept him busy, and for a few days, he thought that he wasn't even going to miss the drugs.

But he did. And with his friends gone, he didn't have access to dealers. Kevin had even thought about going into the City and seeing what he could find there when one day he had gone to the tennis shack for something. There he found Paula Porter doing a line of cocaine. It was the meeting of two minds. And what they had in common wasn't sex.

They met a few times the first week. Paula, it seemed, liked the company and was more than willing to treat him to the drugs. As Kevin explained it, she was hooked emotionally more than anything else: she was in need of the diversion that drugs gave her. And with Kevin around, she seemed to end the one worry left in her life: she felt more secure sneaking off to use the drugs. It was no accident that everyone thought that she and Kevin were having an affair. She had started the rumor herself, knowing that no one would break in on their trysts if they thought they stemmed from a romantic desire to be alone.

After a few weeks of meetings every afternoon, though, things changed. As Paula got to know Kevin, she became demanding. If she was willing to supply the drugs, she wanted more than an alibi for her time from him. She decided that he should be the one to run the risk of picking up the drugs.

"And that's when she told you that she got the coke from Miles Ames." Brett interrupted Kevin's story to get this straight.

"No, originally I was supposed to believe that the coke came from the Ameses' gardener. His name is Clancy. He's from the Dominican Republic—an illegal alien, I would guess. He doesn't know very much English and I was supposed to give him envelopes with money in them and he would pass over the drugs. But it didn't take any brains to guess that this guy probably couldn't add two and two in English and someone else was behind the sale. Then, about the third time I went to the Ames house, I saw Mrs. Ames and Mrs. Voos standing behind a hedge watching the whole transaction. Actually, I saw their reflection in the window of the garden shed. They were hiding and watching the whole thing. The next day, when I went back for more, I thought that Clancy would be gone and the police waiting for me. I was scared to death. I don't know why I went. I guess"—he hesitated—"I guess the drugs had gotten to me. I really couldn't stop going. Anyway, that day was the same as usual. And the day after and the days after that. I guessed then that the Ameses and the Vooses must know about everything. And I realized that they must be supplying the drugs. One day, when I got there a little early, I saw the gardener get a package out of the trunk of that big navy Mercedes that Lars Voos drives. He opened the package and took out the coke that he was going to sell to me, and then he took the rest of the box up to the house and gave it to Mrs. Ames." Kevin looked at the floor, not seeming to have anything to add.

"And this went on until the day Paula Porter died?" Brett asked.

"Yes, sir."

"Did you kill her?"

"My God, no."

Kathleen thought that the boy hadn't realized until this moment that he was a suspect in a murder case. Had he only been worried about getting caught using drugs? As Kevin went on, she thought that maybe that was the truth.

"I was going to meet Paula later that afternoon . . ."

"The day that she died," Brett clarified.

"Yes. I had picked up the coke early that morning and hidden it in the tennis shack when I came to work. She was going to meet me there around three in the afternoon. Anyway, I was busy that morning. I had lunch, and I was going to help with the kiddie class in the baby pool, but when I got to the poolside . . ." He hesitated, seeming to remember. ". . . she was lying there. Someone said she was dead and then I heard Dr. Hallard say the same thing. I . . ." He choked on some tears, but swallowed a few times and went on. ". . . I could only think about the coke that I had left in the tennis shack and how to get to it and get rid of it before the police got there. Paula and I were too connected to that shack for it to be found there. And then I heard someone say something about all the kids being around and a dead woman lying there and I got an idea. I rounded up all the kids. I've been working at the Club for a few years and know most of them and they'll do most anything I tell them to do. And I led them to the far tennis court. The excuse was to get them away from the horror of it all and no one questioned that. But, really, I had to get those drugs out of there."

"And you did?"

"Yes."

"What did you do with them?"

"I dumped them in the line marker that we use to re-mark the white chalk lines on the clay courts."

Brett smiled in spite of himself. "And . . ."

"And that's all," Kevin concluded. "I'm not using drugs anymore. I know it hasn't been that long since Paula's death, but I'm all through with that now. Honest." He looked around the group of adults, his eyes coming to rest on Susan.

"Nancy is worried about you, you know," she said gently. "Can he let her know that he's all right, John?" she asked the policeman, who had been taking notes during the story.

"I think you'd better, son."

"Are you going to arrest me?" Kevin looked more confused than pleased.

219

"Not right now, unless these people have a case against you," John Mann indicated Kathleen and Brett with a wave of his hand.

"No. I think that he's given us something to think about for a while," Brett said. "But I wouldn't plan on any more disappearing acts."

"No, sir."

Susan thought that he almost saluted.

"And you'd better tell your parents and have them get you a lawyer," John Mann added. "I'm not interested in prosecuting you for drug use, but I'd sure like to get my hands on the Ameses and Vooses. Parading themselves as big deals in the community and acting rich and all that and selling drugs to kids to keep themselves in minks and Jaguars. I sure wish I had known about this sooner." He shook his head and closed up the notebook he'd been writing in. "If these people don't want you, I'll drive you home," he added.

"No problem. But I'd like a few words with you before you leave," Brett said. "If you'll just wait in the police car, Kevin?"

"Of course."

Susan gave the boy a sympathetic smile as he almost sprinted from the room. She felt for him. To be so young and have your life in such a mess seemed terribly sad. And, she was pretty sure, his father wasn't going to be as understanding of his involvement with drugs as he had been in his supposed involvement with an older woman. She sat and thought over the story she had just heard, as Brett told John Mann about her recent assault and her conviction that Lars Voos had been the assailant. So Kathleen had told him about the cologne clue over breakfast! And he seemed to think that it was reasonable to assume that it was, in fact, a clue and not a coincidence. Maybe she was getting the hang of the investigative stuff.

But now that it looked as if the Vooses were getting into trouble, she began to feel sorry for them. She said as much to

220

Kathleen, who wasn't quite so sympathetic. "Don't waste your time feeling sorry for anyone who is selling drugs to kids. They don't deserve it."

And after thinking it over, Susan decided that she was right. She looked up at Kathleen and Brett. "But you still don't have your murderer," she said. "Unless you don't believe Kevin and think that he had something to do with the murders."

"No, actually I don't think he did. He admits to being at the Ames house in the afternoon after the first murder, but there isn't anything to connect him with that house the morning of the day Jan Ick died. And I believe him. I don't think that he had anything to do with these deaths. But, you know . . ."

"Yes?" Kathleen asked, wondering why he had paused.

"I keep thinking that there are things being said that would make sense if only I could put them all together. You know, a comment here and a comment there. If they could just be sorted out and put together, I think we would have the answer to our dilemma and the name of the murderer."

"So how do we do that? Pull out the comments and put them together?" Kathleen asked.

"I wish I knew," Brett sighed. "I wish I knew."

Seventeen

———•••———

"Let's go back to the place where Paula Porter died while we're here," Brett suggested.

"You think you'll find an answer there or just inspiration?" Kathleen asked.

"Who knows? I do know that we've just hit a dead end. Maybe going back to one of the places where it all started will help. So"—he held open the door for them, "if you don't mind?"

The Club patio was nearly deserted at this hour of the morning. Two men were cleaning last night's leaf drop from the pool. An elderly couple was over near the kiddie pool, sharing *The New York Times* and occasionally watching three toddlers jump around under the fountain in the middle of the water. Two blond girls in the navy suits of official pool guards were folding towels on a table next to the pool-equipment shed.

"She was sitting where?" Brett asked, trying to get his bearings.

"Over by the yellow-striped umbrella table," Susan answered, and led them there. "She always sat here."

"Any particular reason that you know of?" Kathleen asked.

"Well, a few. In the first place, it's only from this group of chairs"—she waved her arms to indicate three lounges and two tables with four chairs apiece that were in the immediate vicinity—"that a person can sit and see both the kiddie pool and the diving end of the big pool really well. Paula had a son, Eric, a friend of Chad's, who was nine years old and a terrific diver. He was one of the starters on the diving team, in fact. And she had the twins, who were five, Brad and Heather, and little Samantha, who was two. The twins and Samantha stayed in the kiddie pool and Eric was always going off the boards. This was really the only location she could be in and check on everybody."

"You said 'a few' reasons," Kathleen reminded her.

"Well, Paula had a great tan and she worked on it all the time. This is also about the only place around the pool with all-day sun. The trees block the sun most of the day in other areas. The other reason I'm guessing at . . ."

"What?"

Susan looked out toward the tennis courts and into the distance. "You can see the tennis shed from here."

Brett and Kathleen followed her stare, but neither said anything.

"Those little packets of sugar and sweetener aren't on the table," Brett said, suddenly realizing something was missing.

"They're not brought out until lunchtime," Susan told him. "They used to be put out in the morning, but parents started to complain that the kids were snitching them and licking out the sugar. So now they come out at eleven or twelve and they go in each evening. I don't know why. Maybe the nighttime dew would hurt them."

"So a person could put poison in one of the sweeteners on this table around noon and what would you guess would be the possibility of Paula picking it up and using it?"

"Well, I don't know for sure, but pretty good. In the first place, Paula spent most of the morning and early afternoon in the sun and was always ordering iced tea. We used to joke about how much of it she drank. And she put four packets of artificial sweetener in each glass. It must have tasted like sugar water."

"And everyone knew that?"

Susan shrugged. "I would think so. Anyone who had their eyes open and had been around for more than a day or two."

"Let's go back to the kitchen or wherever the sugar is kept overnight," Brett suggested.

"I don't know where that is," Susan said. "But we can find out. If we can't locate it on our own, the kitchen staff will be here soon. They start serving snacks around eleven."

They had no trouble finding what they were looking for. The small rectangular ceramic cups were on a counter in plain view when they went to check the bar for the pool area.

"Fourteen," Kathleen commented, picking up on what he was going to ask. "If you look closely, you can find little numbers painted on their sides. One through fourteen, just like the tables."

"And the cups would be put on the tables with the identical number? Could things really be so organized here?" Kathleen asked this question, remembering that this was the place where people casually left expensive jewels around because it was "just like home."

"Of course," Susan answered, taking the organization for granted, "And since people tend to sit in the same place time after time, they can get just what they want. See, some of the cups have only sugar and some only artificial sweetener . . ."

"And a person who wanted to get poison to the table where Paula Porter sat only had to check the table number and replace the sweetener in some of the blue packets with cyanide," Brett finished for her. "We could be doing that right now, in fact."

"Yes, I guess so," Susan agreed. "And, of course, she would use the sweetener almost right away."

"How so?"

"Well, Eric had diving practice at ten o'clock every morning, and Paula usually brought him for that, and by the time the bar opened at eleven, she was ready for her first iced tea of the day."

"You're saying that if her table was equipped with four

packets of sweetener the first thing in the morning, probably no one would get a chance to use them before her."

"I suppose so. She was here every day this summer. Of course, now we know why," she added, thinking of the drugs.

"So it was easy to kill Mrs. Porter," Kathleen commented.

"But if the same person killed Jan Ick . . ." Susan paused, trying to sort out what she was going to say.

"And we do think that it was the same person," Brett took advantage of the pause to interject.

"Then how could they be sure of killing Jan with the sandwich? I mean, how could they be sure the poisoned sandwich would be the last eaten? And that it was going to be Jan who got it?"

"Maybe," Kathleen repeated the suggestion she had made once before, "maybe the first murder was a mistake. Maybe the murderer was trying to kill Paula that time and accidentally killed Jan."

"Well, it's a possibility," Brett said, taking a stick of gum from his pocket and removing the wrapper.

"It seems like an awfully sloppy way to murder someone," Susan said.

"That's exactly what's wrong with it," Brett agreed. "It is a sloppy way to murder someone and this person isn't sloppy. Look around you: a person was killed here in full view of all of her friends and her children and we don't know who did it. There were no clues left, no one seems to have picked up anything out of the ordinary around the time of the murder. I don't think we're dealing with a sloppy person. And I think that Jan's and Paula's deaths were both planned and that their connection to the PTA—the only thing that they have in common that other people don't share—must have been the beginning of the motive."

"Unless Jan was involved in drugs, too," Kathleen said excitedly. She thought that she was getting something here. "And if Jan Ick was involved with cocaine, then not only is that a connection, but it involves her with the Vooses and the Ameses."

"You're right," Brett said. "Let's find out if that's true before anything else. You may just have found our answer, Kathleen.

"You know," he continued, "I have a feeling that we can find out a lot if we join John Mann and Kevin Dobbs, wherever they are. Let's spend some time with the car radio and see if we can dig them up."

Susan was impressed. It took one call to the police department to discover that Sergeant Mann was "with the suspect over at . . ." She recognized the address of the Ames house. "Do you want to drop me off at home on your way there?" she asked, thinking how furious the Ameses and Vooses would be that she knew that they were involved in drug dealings. She explained her concern to Brett.

"No, if you don't mind, I'd like to have you with us. Do you know how much time it has saved us having you along? We could have spent an hour or two figuring out where the sugar was kept in the evening and how it was distributed at the Club. For things like that, you've been a big help. And remember, the Ameses and the Vooses are just going to have to adjust to the fact that people know they were dealing in drugs. They're going to have to stand trial and probably be convicted, unless they find some way to overturn Kevin's evidence. And that's not going to be easy."

"Why are they at the Ames house?" Susan asked.

"Well, we'll find out soon," Brett answered, turning the police car out of the Club gates and back toward the main part of town.

"Who is that?" Kathleen asked, as the car entered Grant Road. There was a woman standing at the bottom of the driveway, and as she saw the police car turn toward her, she started waving at it.

"Isn't that interesting. I'd forgotten that," Brett muttered to himself.

"It's Ellen Cooper," Susan said, leaning over the front seats of the car. "I wonder what she wants. She seems to be trying to get us to stop."

"Are we going to stop?" Kathleen asked Brett. He appeared to be thinking of something else.

"Sure. I don't see why not." He smiled. Kathleen wondered what was behind that smile.

"I can't believe what is going on there" were Ellen's first words when the car stopped alongside of her.

"John Mann and Kevin Dobbs are here. I just can't imagine what is happening, but I had to come here to help. Is there anything I can do?" She saw Susan in the back seat. "Oh, Susan, you're here. I didn't see you. Are you involved in this?"

"Susan is helping our investigation, Mrs. Cooper," Brett answered for her. Susan wondered if her friend thought that she was a suspect. "And you've been a big help too, you know."

"Me?" Ellen almost blushed. "Well, I just want to do anything I can." She stopped talking, realizing that she didn't know how she had helped. Susan and Kathleen didn't know what Brett was talking about either, for that matter. "Well, I like to think that I can help. Is there anything else I can do for you?"

"I don't—" Brett began.

"What about the kids?" Susan interrupted him. She didn't like to think of children becoming involved in any talk of their parents and drugs. "Where are the kids?"

"Well, Peer and Kristen are at the Club for Peer's tennis lesson. Charline's housekeeper took them. I saw them when I dropped off Bethany. That's when I saw Carol Mann, and she told me about all of this. But I don't know where Julia's children are. Shall I find out? I could go around back and ask Gertrude," she offered.

"Gertrude?"

"Remember the Ameses' housekeeper?" Kathleen nudged Brett's memory.

"Wonderful. That would be a big help. And, if you would go back to the Club, and see if you can keep the Voos kids and their housekeeper as occupied as possible? They don't have to be involved in this," Brett said.

"Of course, anything I can do. You can depend on me."

"I know we can," Brett agreed, as Ellen jogged off around the back of the house.

"I hope she doesn't think I'm a suspect in this murder," Susan said, "but I'll bet she does."

"I'm sorry," Brett replied, pulling the car up in line with the police car in which John Mann and Kevin had arrived. "I know that's what the phrase 'helping the police with their investigation' sounds like, but don't worry. I think we may have this murder solved in the next hour or so. You don't mind if one or two people think you're a murderess for that short period of time, do you?"

"Well . . ." Why complain? She figured that she didn't have a choice anyway. "Anything you want from me particularly?" she asked as the three of them got out of the car.

"I don't know," Kathleen answered, looking at Brett to see what he wanted.

"Do you remember who brought the sandwiches that poisoned Mrs. Ick?" he asked.

"Of course. I did." Susan wondered if she was going to be a suspect again.

"Okay. Now tell me who else knew that you were going to bring those particular sandwiches and what they would look like."

"Let me think."

"All the kids are at the Club." Ellen arrived around the corner of the house. "The Ames kids are with the Vooses. I must have missed them when I was dropping off Bethany. Should I go there and stay with them, officer?" she volunteered.

"That would be very helpful. But, you know, you can give us some information right now, if you'll wait a minute. I hate for you to be late connecting with the kids at the Club, however."

"No problem. When the tennis classes are over the kids always go for a swim. They'll be busy for another hour at least, maybe more."

"Well, we won't keep you for as long as that." He glanced toward the large front windows of the house. "Let's walk down to the curb to talk, if you don't mind. I don't want to be overheard by anyone."

"Of course." Ellen was always eager.

Susan didn't expect to join them, but Brett insisted that they stay together. "Are you sure?" she asked.

"Of course; it's your canapés that we're going to talk about, remember?"

"Oh, Susan, they know that you made them," Ellen breathed.

"I wasn't trying to keep it a secret, Ellen."

"Well, of course, you couldn't, could you? After all, everyone saw the sign-up sheet for food that was passed around the PTA meeting the month before the luncheon. And your name was right at the top of it with what you were bringing. And, come to think of it, didn't Martha Hallard ask out loud at that meeting for you to bring the same sandwiches that you had made the year before? Yes, she did. I remember because you were mad that she had suggested it. You told me the next day—"

"Any reason why?" Brett interrupted.

"Because the damn things take forever to make, and when she asked out loud like that, I couldn't refuse. I mean, when someone says, 'Oh, will you make those wonderful little sandwiches you brought last year? We all loved them soooooo much,' you can't refuse, can you?" Susan asked, knowing damn well that, if she had any spine at all, she would have told Martha Hallard that she didn't have the

229

time, the energy, or the desire to repeat that particular performance, and that, if she had known how much work they were going to be, she wouldn't have made them that first time either.

"I thought we were going to talk down at the curb," she continued, noticing that they were returning to the house.

"No need. You've told me just what I wanted to know, Mrs. Cooper," Brett said. "And you've been a very big help."

"Well, I always try to be," Ellen said proudly. "I'll just go take care of the kids, shall I? Oh, my work is never done," she continued, obviously enjoying the fact.

Brett turned to Susan immediately. "So everyone who was at the meeting the month before the luncheon would have known that you were going to make those canapés?"

"Yes."

"And did anyone else have the recipe for them? Did anyone else try to make them?"

"I don't know. Anyone could have, I know that. The recipe comes from *Cheers*—it's a cookbook published by the Hancock Historical Society to raise money for a restoration of an old foundation that was found a few years ago out near the reservoirs. Everyone in town bought a copy when it was put out . . ."

"And that was?"

"Two years ago in the spring. About the time of the PTA lunch that year. A picture of the crab canapés was on the cover and I thought I would try the recipe for the lunch. Everyone raved about them and I would think that everyone knew just where they came from. It took a lot of time. But they did end up looking like the picture on the cover when I was finished."

"So anyone could have duplicated them. Is that right?" Brett asked, stopping before they arrived at the steps to the front door.

"That's right."

"Great."

Kathleen wondered just what was so great. That "anyone" knew about the canapés being present in advance and "anyone" was able to get a copy of the recipe and "anyone" was able to duplicate them didn't seem to be much progress to her. Weren't they ever going to eliminate anyone in this case? It seemed clearer than ever that every one of them could have murdered Mrs. Ick and Mrs. Porter, and that was where they had started.

"Let's see if John Mann minds us sitting in on his questioning of the Vooses and the Ameses," Brett suggested, ringing the bell.

"Do you think he might?" Susan asked. Kathleen was still thinking about "anyone."

"No, I suspect he'll be glad to see us."

"Glad?" Kathleen repeated, as the door opened. A uniformed policewoman whom she didn't recognize stood there.

"I'm afraid that there is confidential police business going on here," she began.

"We're here to see Sergeant Mann," Brett said, holding out his identification for the woman to see. "I think if you tell him that we are here—"

"I'll be more than happy for their help, Ann." John appeared in the doorway to the spacious living room. "Why don't you just go back there with everyone else while I bring these people up to date," he suggested. She followed his directions immediately.

"I didn't know we had a woman on the police force," Susan commented.

"She doesn't belong to us directly," John answered. "She's on loan from the Hartford Narcotics Unit. They sent her down here when they heard we were asking questions about Farnsworth Import/Export. They were very interested in what we've been able to find out."

"And just what is that?"

"Sorry, I should have told you about it sooner. Well, to start at the beginning, Kevin and I called the Vooses and found out that they were having a business meeting with the Ameses at their house. So we came over here and confronted both couples with Kevin's statement. We have a stenographer who is still trying to translate some of the profanity that resulted from that little confrontation."

"You mean Miles admitted to selling drugs out of his garden shed?" Kathleen asked, thinking that had been an easy catch.

"Miles Ames didn't know anything about it. Oh, he or his company have been bringing coke in from South America for some time now, but he thought it was going directly to his own dealers in New York City. He diverted a little once in a while for a private snort or two, and that's the problem . . ."

"I don't understand," Brett said.

"Sorry. My fault. Let me be more orderly. This is the biggest thing that I've ever run into, and I guess I'm a little excited." He was quiet for a moment before beginning again. "The drugs came in with other products and were distributed to one or two hoods in the City, who passed them along to dealers—the city police will have to do the work there. A small amount of the drugs came into Hancock for the Ameses' and the Vooses' personal amusement, as it were . . ."

"They used drugs too!" Susan breathed. "I didn't mean to interrupt. Please go on."

"Yes, that's true. And Julia Ames had the name of the man in the organization who would slip some of the coke out here to her house and then they would have a little party or something. It might have gone on like that forever except that Julia got greedy."

"You don't mean. . . ?" Brett began.

"Yeah, I do. She started having the city contact send out more and more drugs, without her husband knowing. And she started dealing in coke here all by herself."

Julia Ames is a drug dealer, Susan thought. She would have believed more easily that she was a murderess. Of course, she reminded herself, she might be both.

"She started dealing to the kids?" Kathleen asked, knowing now why she had disliked this woman so much at first sight. In her mind a murderess was almost preferable to a dealer, if the dealer was dealing to children.

"Yes, her baby-sitter first of all, if you can believe that," John said ruefully.

"That's right. Amanda Gordon used to sit for her," Susan cried. "I remember thinking of that when Kevin was talking about the kids who were arrested last spring. In fact, she had recommended her to me when I was having trouble getting any of my regulars." She stopped, thinking how close she had come to putting her own kids into the drug world. "Oh, God," she muttered, wondering if she would ever be able to trust anyone again. Kathleen reached over and put her arm around her shoulders, seeming to know how she felt. Susan was glad of the support.

"Anyway," John Mann continued, "she was selling the drugs through the gardener that Kevin told us about. She must have thought that the kids were pretty stupid not to realize that a guy who can hardly speak English isn't going to be dealing drugs all by himself. Or maybe she thought that everyone would think that someone else was his partner or something. I suppose that we're lucky that Kevin saw her and Charline watching the transaction that day. If the gardener had told us it was Julia or Charline and they had denied it, we might have had some trouble proving it."

"Have they admitted it then?" Kathleen asked.

"When Kevin told the story of seeing them, they both started blaming each other. Such screaming and hollering— you wouldn't believe they were good friends. Right now we don't know exactly what is true or when Charline became involved. Everything is rather a mess in there." He indicated the living room. "But they're all making sure that they don't take the fall for this one alone. Miles Ames was real surprised that his wife was taking in money on the side. Seems he had no idea this was going on and still doesn't know what the money was for. They'll have time to get it all straightened out, though. And they're going to need lawyers to defend them. Right now, everyone is accusing everyone else of everything . . ."

"Of murder?" Kathleen asked quickly.

"Well, not of murder. Not yet, but I'll bet that's coming. Lars Voos just confessed to trying to strangle you, Susan. Seems he thought you were getting a little too close to their drug activities. Said something about you seeing him and Mrs. Voos in the bushes at the Hallards' party Saturday night."

"They were . . ." Susan began.

"Snorting coke," he filled in for her.

Susan shook her head. Was she ever going to know what really went on?

"Do you want to come in now?" Sergeant Mann asked.

"I think we'll let you handle it, John," Brett said.

"I . . ." Kathleen began.

"Why don't you meet us at your office downtown later, after all this is sorted out," Brett suggested, interrupting Kathleen before she could protest. "We'll be at the Henshaws', if Susan doesn't mind." He looked for her agreement and got it. "You'll arrest everyone and keep them in jail overnight, won't you?"

"Yes, that's what we always do. Although we only have two cells. Well, I'll call you when we get there." He returned to the living room, presumably thinking about dividing two cells among two married couples and the gardener, if the gardener could be found.

Kathleen was professional enough to wait until they were in the car and out of range of the people in the house to blow up. Then she let Brett have it.

"Are you so damn sure that this murder has nothing to do with those people in there? With all this mess about drugs and drug dealing, you are willing to just turn your back on that house and go off without getting any more information?

234

Are you so sure that you don't need to know any more about the Vooses, the Ameses, Kevin . . ."

"No," Brett answered, quietly and firmly enough to stop Kathleen's ranting. "But, and I will repeat this—I think I know what happened at the PTA lunch that day and I think I know how the murder of Jan Ick was carried out and, yes, I do think I know who did it. Now I have some questions to ask Susan, if she doesn't mind, and I have some thinking to do. If you want to go back to the Ames house and sit in on that interview, I will be happy to turn this car around and take you back there. You certainly don't have to follow me around. If you think you know who the murderer is, and you think you know a better course for an investigation to follow, then please say so. I don't want to cramp your style or anything," he ended quietly.

Shit, Kathleen thought. She knew that he had her trapped. She didn't know where he was going. She didn't know enough to be sure whether he was right or wrong. But she did know that she wanted to be around when and if the last pieces of this puzzle fell into place.

"I'll stay with you." And dammit, you better know what you're doing, she thought.

"Is there any particular reason for going to my house?" Susan asked. "I mean, I know that you told John he could call you there, but what I'm asking is: Is there anything you're looking for there? I mean . . ." She knew that she wasn't explaining well.

"I need to think and I want to go over this with you again," Brett answered. "I just thought that your house would be convenient. I don't expect to find cyanide stashed away in the bathroom medicine chest, if that's what you're asking. You should have figured out by now that I don't think you're a murderess." He flashed a smile at her in the rearview mirror.

"Thanks." She wondered if there was anything left in the house to offer them for lunch. Was it possible that four days

235

had gone by without her being inside a grocery store? The last time she could say that, she had been in the hospital giving birth to Chad.

Susan half-expected to find someone from her family home when she got there, but there wasn't even a note on the kitchen table. It looked as if she was the first to arrive.

The phone rang as she entered the kitchen.

"Hello?"

"Susan, hi. It's Marty. Listen, I know that the police are there with you. I can see their car out my living room window. You probably can't talk as freely as you would like, but you have to tell me: Do they know who did it?"

"Did what?" Susan asked, mentally calling herself a bitch for doing it.

"Killed Jan and Paula, of course. Now I know that the police have Kevin Dobbs with them—not that I would tell anybody. Nancy called here and asked me if I know the name of a good criminal lawyer. She was so upset that she told Dan that it was Kevin they needed him for—the lawyer, I mean."

"Did you know one?" Susan asked, thinking of a friend of theirs who had a thriving criminal practice in the City.

"Yes. Dan's brother. Remember? I know you've met him at some of our parties. Anyway, Nancy was so upset that Dan thought that he should go over to her house and check on her. The first trimester is the most dangerous in terms of losing the baby, of course, and he wants her to calm down. She's really a little old to keep producing offspring so regularly. Anyway, I'm here all alone and I don't know what's going on, and when I saw the police car drive up to your house and then saw you get out, well, I just had to call."

"I can't say much at this point, Marty. The police aren't telling me anything," she lied. "You know, though, you could go over and help your husband with Nancy. You might learn something that way."

"Oh, I thought of that. Dan wouldn't let me. He's very big

236

on doctor-patient confidentiality, you know. Well, maybe I'll go over to Carol's. You know how she loves to snob us about her husband's inside information. Bye."

"Friend?" Kathleen asked, as Susan hung up.

"Martha Hallard. Her husband's gone over to check out Nancy Dobbs. Seems Nancy called there looking for a lawyer for Kevin, and Dan was worried about the coming baby. Marty's just looking for information. She saw your car."

"I wonder why she's so interested," Kathleen commented, considering Dan and Martha Hallard as possible murderers. Both of them had been at the Club when Paula died, and Martha, at least, had been at the PTA lunch. Were they in this together? She looked around and found herself alone by the phone. Susan had followed Brett through the house and into the backyard.

When she joined them, Susan was staring at a perennial bed that desperately needed weeding and Brett was gazing off into space. Kathleen sat down on a chair right between the two of them and, finding her own little patch of blue sky, focused her eyes and did some staring of her own.

Fifteen minutes passed this way. Brett did interrupt the time by getting up and making a thirty-second phone call. Everyone appeared content, except Susan, who was itching to get up and attack those weeds but thought that by doing so she might possibly disarrange the complex mental processes that were going on around her. Wasn't Brett going to ask her some questions?

As if he could read her mind, he asked, "Who was on the phone?"

Well, it might not be what she was expecting, but nothing had been so far. "It was Martha Hallard," Kathleen answered before Susan had a chance.

"Oh."

Well, that was about as noncommittal as a response could be, Susan thought. And then, when she could restrain herself no longer, she asked, "What are we waiting for?"

"The guys from Hartford. I asked for two officers because I thought we should have more help before anybody attempted to arrest anybody."

"Who are we arresting?" Kathleen was on her feet. "And why didn't you let the locals help us? Why do we have to wait for people an hour or so away?"

"In the first place, they aren't an hour away. It's more like fifteen minutes. They've been on another case a few towns over. Lucky for us, really. And as for why I called them: well, you don't expect a man to arrest his own wife, do you?"

Eighteen

———◆———

"Carol Mann?!"

"Of course, Carol Mann," Kathleen echoed Susan.

"'Of course'? What's so 'of course' about it?" Susan demanded.

Kathleen appeared to be talking to herself. "I guess I'd forgotten everything I've been taught. Here I was looking at two different events and trying to see the similarities between them and all the time I should have been studying the differences. How could I have been so stupid?"

"So stupid?" Susan echoed.

She was ignored.

"When did you realize what was going on?" Kathleen asked Brett.

"Not until recently," he confessed. "I'd been bothered by something all along—something I'd known and then forgotten—and when I saw Ellen Cooper standing near the street this morning, I remembered what it was. Then the last piece fell into place."

"Is someone going to explain this to me?" Susan raised her voice. "What differences?"

"The major difference between the two murders was the way the police handled them," Kathleen explained. "After Jan Ick died, they did some very credible investigative work. In fact, everything was according to the book, with the exception of allowing Julia Ames to take notes. And that wasn't significant: it was just a case of a small police department trying to make up for something that they lacked in an emergency situation."

"And it helped our investigation in the long run," Brett added. "It was obvious that Julia Ames was lying about something—that she had called her husband to come home before calling the police. Now a woman who's upset because someone dropped dead in her yard has every reason in the world to call her husband for help. But there was no need to try to hide that from us unless she needed him there for something besides support. In this case, to hide the drugs that she was selling . . ."

"But I thought he didn't know that his wife was selling drugs," Susan protested.

"True, but he had the drugs around for his own use and he sure didn't want a police investigation to turn them up," Brett replied. "Anyway, if Julia Ames had just admitted calling her husband, saying that she was upset over Jan Ick's death, we wouldn't have been suspicious. But when she insisted that he just arrived home early to help clean up after the party, we began to look closer.

"Also, Charline Voos's statement wasn't as truthful as it might have been. And Julia's presence helped us there, too. Charline was so worried that she was going to say something wrong that she kept deferring to Julia. So we knew that she had something to hide. We didn't know what it meant, but it was a valuable clue."

"And Paula's murder?" Susan asked, no closer to understanding than before.

"Well, after her death, your local police carried on no real investigation at all. They used the children present as an excuse and then broke every single rule of good police work. And I was so mad about that that I didn't stop to think about what it meant."

"You mean John Mann intentionally carried out a bad investigation to cover up Carol's guilt?" Susan asked. "Then Carol didn't kill both Jan and Paula?"

"She did, but her husband didn't know she was the murderess until after the second murder."

"And that accounts for the sloppy police work after Paula's death: this time John Mann wanted to be sure the killer wasn't discovered," Kathleen added. "But how do you think he found out that Carol was the murderer?"

"I'd guess it had something to do with the elaborate system of cameras he has at the Club. I'd bet he saw something that gave her away," Brett answered again.

"And then he had to protect her to keep everyone from knowing," Susan said quietly, beginning to understand the agony and horror of the situation that John Mann had found himself in: knowing he had to appear to be looking for the murderer and helping those who were doing the same, but all the while working to hide the truth. She shivered. "I feel so sorry for John. I . . ." She stopped, not knowing what else to say.

"It's probably killing him," Brett acknowledged, more accustomed to the sorrows of those who loved a criminal than she.

Susan took a deep breath. "When did you begin to think that it was Carol you were looking for?" she asked.

"Actually, I thought about her when we first heard the story of Jan's murder," Brett answered. "Remember how Julia Ames told us that Carol Mann had gone down to the curb to signal to the police and the ambulance so they would know which driveway to turn into?"

"Yes. I thought it was so smart of her at the time," Kathleen exclaimed.

"It also meant that she was the only person present to leave the scene of the murder. The only person who had a chance to dispose of something before the police searched the area and the suspects."

"Of what?" Susan asked. "What did she want to dispose of?"

"I'd guess some sort of covering: a piece of plastic wrap or aluminum foil or something similar. Whatever the poisoned canapé was carried in."

"I'm sorry, but I'm confused," Susan said. "I still don't understand how Carol could have known that Jan was going to eat that sandwich . . ."

"I couldn't figure that out myself," Brett said. "Although Charline's statement was a clue there too. I just didn't see it at the time. Of course," he added, returning to Susan's question, "I didn't see what reason Carol would have had for wanting Jan dead either."

"You mean it wasn't Jan that she wanted to kill?" Susan asked.

"Exactly," Brett responded.

"You mean . . ." Kathleen began.

"Yes. The murder of Jan Ick was a mistake. The wrong person died."

"Jan Ick instead of Paula Porter!" Kathleen exclaimed, thankful that she had been right all along.

"No, Jan Ick instead of Charline Voos." Brett saw the mystified looks on the women's faces and explained. "Charline Voos was the last person to get food. Remember Julia Ames explaining that they had arranged it that way? All the crab things were gone by then—they were very good and very popular. And then Carol must have put out that last one, the different one, the one containing poison that she had made at home. And she put it down on the tray just before Charline Voos chose her meal. Carol assumed Charline would pick it up. But Charline didn't and the first person to go up to the table for seconds did—Jan Ick."

"So the fact that Paula Porter and Jan Ick were on the fund-raising committee was a coincidence," Susan said.

"Yes, and that confused us for a while," Brett answered.

Kathleen was happy to be included. As for herself, she was still confused. "And Carol wanted to kill Charline because . . . because why?"

"Because she felt that Charline looked down on her."

"When she and Julia didn't want Carol to run for vice-president," Susan said.

"Yes, but that wasn't snobbery on their part," Brett said.

"Then what was it?"

"Common sense. They were protecting themselves. They didn't want the wife of a cop to get any closer to their drug dealing than she already was."

"That makes sense," Susan agreed. "There are a lot of meetings of various committees that take place in the homes of the PTA presidents and a lot of running in and out just to pick things up."

"Wait," Kathleen insisted. "That doesn't explain a lot. You just said that Charline's statement was a clue—a clue to what?"

"A clue to the fact that the wrong person had been killed. I don't think that Charline was just worried about the drugs being found in the house. I think that she believed something more significant was going on. You see, nothing was quite what it appeared to be—not just to us but to the people involved in the murders."

"You are going to explain?" Kathleen said a little sarcastically.

"Yes. You see, Charline was so worried about what she said because she thought that Julia had killed Jan Ick."

"For what reason?" Kathleen insisted on knowing.

"Oh, not intentionally. They knew immediately the wrong person had been killed and they both thought that the other had made the fatal error; they both thought that the other had been trying to kill Carol Mann."

"Because she was going to interfere with their drug-selling," Susan exclaimed.

"Exactly. When Jan Ick died, they were horrified not just because they thought a police search might turn up drugs in the Ames home but because each one believed the other had tried to kill Carol Mann and botched it. They had discussed the problem of Carol being vice-president and too near their homes and they must have believed that the other had tried to solve the problem by killing Carol. Of course, after the police left, they got together and straightened things out. So when we met them they were cool. They didn't know who had done it, but they knew they weren't involved. Which only left us with one question—something that Dr. Tyrrell had wondered about too: Just why did they want to be co-presidents? And Susan, of course, answered that one just now."

"I did?"

"Because the presidents have so much coming and going around their homes. It covered up the comings and goings of the people who were there for a different reason: to buy cocaine."

"And since Carol didn't know about the cocaine, she didn't understand the reason they didn't want her around. She thought it was snobbery . . ."

"Right. The tragedy here is that poor Carol's feelings of inferiority led her to misunderstand their motivation. It made a simple rejection for a reason she couldn't know into something she couldn't live with. That's what I meant when I said that nothing was what it appeared to be. Everyone—Carol Mann, Julia, and Charline—everyone was seeing things through their own eyes, with their own prejudices, instead of what was really going on."

"But what about Paula Porter?" Kathleen asked.

"That's a problem. I'm not sure I understand that now. Of course Paula was chairperson of the nominating committee and could have gotten an office for Carol, but I don't believe that was the reason she died. I think we'll have to check with John Mann about that one. He probably knows just what reason there was for Paula's murder."

"Carol thought that Paula knew the truth." It was John Mann who spoke. He was standing behind them, having walked up the driveway instead of coming through the house. "I overheard a conversation between the two of them in the ladies' locker room at the Club. Paula was asking Carol if she thought it was a coincidence that Jan got the poison sandwich. You see, Paula had taken what she thought was the last sandwich . . ."

"That's right. She was starting to tell me that at the Club the morning before she died," Susan cried, suddenly remembering the conversation.

"She probably told lots of people," John Mann said, "but only the murderer would realize that the information was dangerous. Carol knew it." He took a deep breath and continued. "But I didn't know that Carol was the killer when I heard the conversation in the locker room. Oh, I knew how much she hated the leaders of the PTA—except you, Susan. But I never thought it would cause her to kill. But, of course, it did."

He was silent and that silence was respected by the others.

"When Paula died I knew immediately that it was Carol. Not just because I had overheard that conversation in the locker room, but because I'd seen my wife fooling around with the sugar packets that morning. I didn't know what she was doing—didn't pay any attention to it at the time. But when Paula died, I knew what it meant. That's when everything began to make sense. Carol was a sick woman," he added. "Her sense of inferiority blinded her to what was really going on in this town—the drugs and everything—and all she could see was that these women looked down on her . . ."

Susan saw the tears in his eyes but couldn't think of anything to say.

"Has something happened to Mrs. Mann?" Brett asked gently.

Kathleen knew he had heard John speak of his wife in the past tense.

"She's dead. Took cyanide herself. I found her on the floor near our bed." He swallowed. "I should have known how hard it was for her, living in this town, never feeling like a part of things, no matter how hard she tried. I should have known. I could have stopped this . . ."

He started to sob just as the two uniformed police officers appeared around the corner of the house. "We were called . . ." one of them began.

"Come with me, gentlemen," Brett said, displaying his ID and showing them the way out of the yard. He motioned to Kathleen as he left.

"I think we're going to have to tell your children something before we go down to headquarters," Kathleen said gently, putting her arm around John Mann and leading him away.

"Mommy! Mommy! I won!" The gleeful voice of Susan's son preceded him into the yard.

"Mother! Chad borrowed my tennis racket without asking and he scratched it!" her daughter put in her two cents' worth.

"Susan? Are you back here? How about lunch and a swim at the Club? I saw Brett and he said it's all over, that you would tell me about it . . ."

"I will." Susan reached up and kissed her husband. "Later. And let's not go to the Club. Let's all four go someplace new, where we don't know anybody. Just for a change."